D0494893

LANCASHIRE COUNTY LIBRARY
3011813421902 5

GRAVEYARD SHIFT

Recent Titles by Casey Daniels

The Pepper Martin Mysteries

DON OF THE DEAD
THE CHICK AND THE DEAD
TOMBS OF ENDEARMENT
NIGHT OF THE LOVING DEAD
DEAD MAN TALKING
TOMB WITH A VIEW
A HARD DAY'S FRIGHT
WILD WILD DEATH
SUPERNATURAL BORN KILLERS
GRAVEYARD SHIFT*

**available from Severn House*

GRAVEYARD SHIFT

A Pepper Martin Mystery

Casey Daniels

This first world edition published 2016
in Great Britain and the USA by
SEVERN HOUSE PUBLISHERS LTD of
19 Cedar Road, Sutton, Surrey, England, SM2 5DA.
Trade paperback edition first published
in Great Britain and the USA 2017 by
SEVERN HOUSE PUBLISHERS LTD

British Library Cataloguing in Publication Data
A CIP catalogue record for this title is available from the British Library.

ISBN-13: 978-0-7278-8657-6 (cased)
ISBN-13: 978-1-84751-759-3 (trade paper)
ISBN-13: 978-1-78010-825-4 (e-book)

For you, the reader, and all the readers who couldn't wait to read Pepper's next adventure.

Thank you!

All Severn House titles are printed on acid-free paper.

Severn House Publishers support the Forest Stewardship Council™ [FSC™],
the leading international forest certification organisation.
All our titles that are printed on FSC certified paper carry the FSC logo.

FSC www.fsc.org MIX FSC C013056

Typeset by Palimpsest Book Production Ltd.,
Falkirk, Stirlingshire, Scotland.
Printed and bound in Great Britain by
TJ International, Padstow, Cornwall.

ONE

A chill like the touch of skeleton fingers reached under my ponytail and raked the back of my neck, sending an icy tingle all the way from the collar of my white polo shirt down my spine.

A block of ice filled my stomach.

My mouth went dry and I guess when it comes to life and death, lipstick just doesn't seem to matter so much because before I could remind myself that it would completely destroy the coating of Pretty in Pink I'd applied before I left my office, I caught my lower lip with my top teeth – right before I hauled in a breath that stuttered when it hit the tight knot in my throat and braced myself, arms locked against my sides, chin up and my jaw set so tight it felt as if it was about to snap.

Cemetery visitors who happened to be passing the chapel at Garden View at that moment would have seen the tall redhead standing on the shore of the picturesque little lake behind it and decided right then and there that she looked determined. Controlled. Invincible.

Little would they know that she was actually scared to death.

I'd left my phone on a nearby bench and it rang a couple more times, sending the same tremors of fear through me that had started up the moment the call came in. When it finally finished ringing, I let go of a breath.

That is, until the phone sounded the little chime that let me know I had a message.

I tromped over to the bench and snatched up the phone, all set to delete the message without even listening to it when it vibrated against my palm and rang again. On cue, my hands got clammy and my knees trembled inside the tall yellow rubber boots I was wearing. Yes, I know – so not a good look for me, but I was on the job as community relations manager at Garden View and about to venture into the newly drained and dredged lake to take pictures for the newsletter we sent out to cemetery patrons and visitors.

I didn't bother to check the caller ID on the phone. I didn't have to. I'd already gotten six calls that day. And it wasn't even noon.

I blew out a breath of frustration and told myself to get a grip.

I was the world's only private investigator to the dead, wasn't I? I'd faced down murderers and pissed off ghosts. I'd dealt with organized crime bosses, crazed scientists, and even a dead president.

I could handle this.

Before I convinced myself otherwise, I swiped the screen to answer the call.

'Hi, Mom.' I started talking even before I realized that my teeth were clenched. As if I didn't know, as if I didn't care, I made sure to keep my voice light when I asked, 'What's up?'

'You're busy at work. You must be. That's why you haven't returned my calls, right? Is it g-h-o-s-t-s?'

If Mom had been there, she would have seen me roll my eyes. 'No, Mom, no ghosts.'

'No case for us, either?'

There was no *us,* but I didn't point this out as I had pointed it out a couple dozen times since my mother announced that she thought it was a super idea for me, her, and my dad – the ex-con felon – to start a family private investigation business.

The words *when hell freezes over* came to mind.

Before I had a chance to mention this to her – again – she giggled. 'No matter! There will always be a chance for another investigation. But there won't be another chance like this. Pepper, the big bridal fair at the Renaissance Hotel is next Saturday.'

I knew it would come to this. Hence the feelings of dread each time my phone rang.

'Mom . . .' My voice was far more calm than even I expected, and I congratulated myself. Now if only I could talk some sense into my mother. 'No one said—'

'But you did say it, honey. You and Quinn. You said you were thinking about—'

'That we were thinking about it, yes. Not that we were going to do it. Not that we had to plan it. We're not there yet. We're talking about . . .' I hadn't mentioned this latest bit of news to my mother, mostly because I'd been dodging her calls for all I was worth. 'Quinn and I are talking about living together for a while. You know, before we decide to take the next step.'

'You can say it, Pepper.' Barb Martin is not given to fits of peevishness, but hey, it was Monday, so I cut her some slack. 'You can say the words *get married*. You can say *wedding*, too, and planning for an upcoming wedding is nothing to be ashamed of.'

'If I was planning for an upcoming wedding.'

'You missed your chance.' Monday might explain the irritability, but no way did it explain the little click of the tongue Mom added to the end of the sentence that told me she had just about had it with me. 'If you'd gone ahead with the wedding last summer when you had the dress and the minister was there and Quinn was willing and—'

This was something she should have known better than to mention. All bets were now officially off.

'Crazy man, Mom,' I reminded her. Maybe a little too forcefully. My voice pinged against the granite walls of the nearby chapel that looked like a Greek temple. It bounced around between the headstones across the road and echoed back at me, sharp and precise. 'You're forgetting the crazy man who kidnaped me and told me I had to marry him or he'd kill Quinn. That's why I was wearing the dress. That's why the minister was there. I'll tell you what, that sort of thing tends to sour a girl when it comes to weddings.'

'Well maybe, but—'

'But nothing.' Famous last words, because as everybody knows, the moment anybody says *but nothing* it means *but something*. The something in this case was the fact that at the time he proposed, Quinn was drugged and as drunk as a skunk. Sure, afterwards he said he really meant it, all that stuff about love and marriage and happily ever after, but the operative word in that sentence is *sure*.

'We need to be sure, Mom,' I told her and reminded myself.

'Of course you do. That's smart, and I know you're nobody's fool. It's the adult way to handle things. But that doesn't mean we couldn't just stop in at the bridal fair and—'

'And what?'

'And look around. You know, at bridal gowns. You hated your last gown. You told me so yourself and, let's face it, all that satin and beading and lace . . . well, it was a little over-the-top. The women in our family, we've always been a lot classier than that. You know, more understated. I understand that you didn't have a lot of choice when it came to picking out a gown,' she added quickly because she apparently knew I was about to remind her of the whole crazy man thing again. 'Which makes picking out this next one . . . this one . . . this real one, for your real wedding . . . all that much more important. Think of the fun we'll have looking at styles and trying on gowns! And while we're at it, I can try on a few mother-of-the-bride dresses, too. I'm picturing myself in emerald green. What do you think? With my coloring, it seems like a natural, doesn't it? We both look so good in green. And while we're at the bridal fair, we might as well check out flowers and caterers and invitations.' Her laugh drowned out the burr of the lawn mower working somewhere in section twenty-three behind me. Spring is a busy time at Garden View, what with three hundred acres to clean up, grass that's starting to sprout, and visitors who turn out in droves because they didn't want to fight the snows of a Cleveland winter to pay their respects to their loved ones and now they're making up for lost time. 'We'd have so much fun if we went together.'

'And we will. We'll do that. One of these days. Only not yet.'

It wasn't like I was waving the white flag or anything, but damn it, like it or not, I couldn't help but picture my mom back when she'd fled town after my dad was convicted of Medicare fraud and landed in the federal pen. All that time in Florida, dodging her friends and her past. All those days of missing Dad. So I'm a sucker. So what of it? I didn't think it would hurt to throw her a bone.

'When Quinn and I are ready, Mom,' I said and just in case there is such a thing as divine intervention or divine retribution, I crossed my fingers. 'When we're ready, we'll go to all the bridal fairs you want.'

It was as far as I was willing to go, concession-wise, and I did not cave further. Not even when disappointment colored her voice. 'Well, I hope it's soon.' Yes, she had the nerve to sigh. But then, it should come as no surprise that I had learned my awesome skills of ducking, feinting, and manipulation at the knee of an expert. 'You're not getting any younger, Pepper, and neither am I. And you are my only child. If I'm ever going to be a grandmother—'

I did not take the time to point out that I am not mother material. Or that Quinn, cop with an attitude, would never be anybody's idea of Father of the Year. But then, I was a little busy choking on my protest.

Mom laughed. 'I know, I know . . . you're not ready to talk about that, either. Not to worry, I've got everything covered. I'm taking knitting lessons! Did I tell you? I'm working on the most precious little booties. Wait until you see them.'

My stomach soured. So did my mood. 'Gotta go, Mom!' I held the phone at arm's length and yelled out a snappy 'Hello' to no one at all, just to give myself an excuse. 'The maintenance guys are here. Bye!'

I couldn't have ended the call any faster. I was only mad at myself for starting it in the first place, and I vowed I wouldn't get trapped again. Maybe like the very frisky Jack Russell my aunt once had owned, my mother needed to learn that bad behavior would not be rewarded. The next time she said the *W* word, the *M* word or, heck, even the *Q* word, the conversation was over.

I told myself not to forget it and, because I knew it would take my mind off my mother and the wedding that wasn't going to happen anytime soon, I clomped into the drained lake.

It had been a relatively dry spring, but this charming little lake (which if you ask me, is really more of a pond) was lined with three inches of muck. The ooey-gooey stuff sucked at my boots, and I inched cautiously toward the center, convinced that if I stepped too quickly or turned too fast or moved just the wrong way, my boots would stay put and I'd be ankle deep in mud.

The things I do for my job!

Finally, as near to the middle of the lake as I was willing to get, I snapped a few pictures and convinced myself that Ella Silverman, cemetery administrator and my boss, would be as thrilled as thrilled could be with them. But then, there's not much about the cemetery that doesn't thrill Ella.

Just to be sure she'd be happy, I turned ever so carefully and took a few more pictures in that direction. As much as I hated to admit it, Ella was right about one thing: the lake wouldn't need to be drained like this and dredged again for umpteen years. This was a once-in-our-lifetime project and the one and only chance either one of us was ever likely to have to get photos from this angle, thank goodness. Rather than have her tell me she wanted more pictures and I had to come back, I took another dozen.

Done.

I tucked my phone into the pocket of my black pants and maneuvered first one foot then the other through the mucky, yucky, clinging, sucking mud, glancing around as I did to be sure I was headed back in the direction I'd come from. That's the thing about a lake, see, no matter how tiny it happens to be. The lake bottom is lower than the land around it, and this lake was about six feet deep here at its center. I spotted the chapel roof and kept my eye on it, using it to guide me back.

Which, I suppose, is why I didn't realize anyone was anywhere around me until I heard a voice.

'Well, it's about time.'

I sucked in a breath and a squeal all at the same time and spun around. Or at least I would have if my body hadn't turned and my feet hadn't stayed cemented in the sludge. I toppled forward, screeched an appropriate word, and righted myself just in time.

'Who . . .?' I glanced over my shoulder. There was no one but me at the muddy lake bottom. 'Who's there? Who just talked to me?'

'Me, of course.'

The voice was a man's, calm, matter of fact, flat. It came from somewhere on my right, and I looked in that direction just in time to see a shimmer in the air, like the sparkle of snowflakes in sunshine.

'You, who?'

'This really isn't the time for foolishness. We need to get down to business. I've been waiting a long time.'

Careful not to lose my footing, I leaned forward as much as I dared and squinted at the eddy of sparkles.

'Are you a ghost?' I asked.

'I'm the essence of a life.'

'But I can usually see—'

'Not this time.' Though it was impossible to catch a breeze this far below sea level, I watched the sparkles twirl like a tornado and move closer. 'You can hear me.'

'I can, but just so you know . . .' Again, I glanced around, getting my bearings. The peak of the chapel was over to my right, and I clomped and swoshed in that direction, tossing a sort of *hasta la vista* wave toward the spooky sparkles as I went. 'Nice to meet you, but whatever you want, I don't have time for it. I've got this job, see. This real job. The one that gives me a paycheck every two weeks. The one that pays the bills. I can't go messing with—'

'It's important.'

I stopped myself just short of a sigh. 'That's what ghosts always say.'

'I can't speak for anyone else. Just for myself.'

'And you are?'

'Eliot Ness.'

All right, that got my attention. I carefully turned back toward the sparkles, planting my feet in the muck so I wouldn't go down. 'The Eliot Ness who—'

'Yes, that's right.' The way he said it, I pictured the spirit with his shoulders pulled back and his chin held high. 'There's a memorial in my memory just across the road.'

'Yeah.' I looked that way, or at least the way I thought was the way, over to where a dignified and unpretentious granite marker commemorated the life of the lawman who was most famous for being the head of the Untouchables but was once the Safety Director of Cleveland, too. 'What are you doing here in the lake? What do you want?'

Just for the record, there is nothing more brainless than asking a ghost what its intentions are. (Well, unless it's pairing navy and black together in the same outfit, but let's face it, I'm way too fashion savvy for that.) Ghosts, see, always want something. Something from me. And the something they want is always something that gets me kidnaped/shot at/waylaid/possessed by spirits/jumped . . .

And that's on an easy case.

'No! No! Pretend I didn't say that.' I waved my hands furiously, as if that would send my dumb question straight to oblivion. 'I don't want to know what you want. Whatever it is, I don't have the time for it. Or the patience. I'm already dealing with my mother, I don't need to add ghosts into the mix.' I clomped a few feet toward shore and stopped cold.

That's because that swirl of sparkles was suddenly right in front of me, blocking my path.

I pulled up short and remembered the lessons I'd learned in my years as PI to the dead. One of the most important ones was that touching a ghost can lead to disasters of the frozen Pepper sort. Did the same apply to ghostly sparkles? I wasn't sure, but I knew I didn't want to find out. The last time I'd touched a ghost (believe me, I'd had no choice), I was so chilled to the bone, I couldn't even grab a cup of coffee without instantly turning it into iced java.

'Fine. Good.' I pulled my feet out of the ooze and clomped in the other direction. 'If that's the way you're going to be—'

Now those sparkles swirled two feet in front of my nose.

My shoulders drooped and I grumbled a curse.

'Is that any way for a girl to talk?'

I hated when I had to give ghosts lessons in the history they'd been too dead to know about, the trends that had passed them by while they were busy being conked out, or social advances they'd never dreamed of, but hey, like it or not (and I mostly didn't when Ella started jabbering on and on about the famous people who were residents here at Garden View), I knew Ness had been dead for something like sixty years. He needed to get with the program.

'I'm not a girl, I'm a woman,' I told him. 'And these days, women aren't relegated to the outdated norms of a masculine-centric society.' Yes, I cringed. But then I was channeling Ella and the frequent lectures she gave me about how things were different for women in the old days, and how much things had changed since she was my age, and how far we still had to go when it came to job equality. I shook my shoulders. 'What I mean is, I can say anything I want.'

'Good.'

Not the response I expected, and I guess Ness knew it because a chuckle whooshed through the air.

'You're not afraid to speak your mind. And you stand up for what you think is right, even though, I must say, your enthusiasm for such progressive ideas is a bit misplaced. That doesn't matter. It seems I heard right. You're the perfect person for this job.'

Heard.

It should have come as no surprise to me that I was the talk of the Other Side. After all, there are plenty of ghosts over there – wherever over there is – and a whole lot of them need help to right wrongs, save their reputations, and solve their problems. Like their murders. But here's the thing about ghosts: they're incorporeal and nobody but me can see them, and nobody but me can hear them and talk to them, and they can't touch things. That means they need some human to do their dirty work for them. That human is me.

I eyed the sparkles. 'Who have you been talking to?'

It must have been a trick of the light or the way the musty breeze kicked up there at the bottom of the lake, but I swear I saw those sparkles rise and fall in what was almost a shrug. 'Oh, you know, a few people here and there. Including Gus Scarpetti.'

Gus was my first ghost, and yeah, he was a Mafia don and all, but I still remembered him fondly.

Which didn't mean I wasn't mighty suspicious of the recommendation.

'You and Gus?' I settled my weight back against one foot and crossed my arms over my chest. 'I can't believe a cop and a gangster would—'

'Sometimes you have to make a deal with the devil to accomplish good things. I needed someone to talk to. About you. And Gus said—'

'What?'

'That you can handle the job.'

It was high praise coming from a guy like Gus who'd been nothing but a big ol' pain in the tushy in the time we'd worked together. 'The cops had it all wrong,' I told Ness. 'About Gus's murder. I figured out who really killed him.'

'So I hear.' Those fuzzy bits swooshed and came back together on my right and now that he wasn't standing . . . er . . . hovering in front of me, I started for the shoreline with Ness at my side.

I hauled myself out of the lake and over to the bench where I'd left my shoes, and I sat down, took off those horrible rubber boots, and slipped into my snakeskin ballet flats (don't judge me, I got them for a song at a Nordstrom's sale).

'So . . .' I looked at the swirling bits that were once the celebrated cop who (according to what I'd read about him) had destroyed the bootlegging business in Chicago back in the days of Prohibition. 'You might as well get it over with. Tell me what you want.'

'I want you. For a job.'

'Like I said . . .' I got up from the bench, grabbed the yellow boots, and headed toward where I'd left my car. 'I've got a job and if I don't get back to the office and start doing it, Ella is going to wonder where I am.'

'Not this job. A real job. A detective's job.'

Before I had a chance to protest, a big, black car whooshed around the corner from the direction of the monument dedicated to President James A. Garfield and zipped past us. Believe me, when it comes to cars, I'm no expert, but I knew this one was old, and one look at the way the sun glinted off its gleaming surface and I knew it was well-loved, too. It had a long, sleek hood and headlights that were close together, lots of chrome, and wide whitewall tires.

Ness whistled low under his breath. '1938 Buick,' he said. 'And a real beauty. It's just like the car—'

'That brought your ashes to the cemetery.' I can't help it. Once in a while some of the stuff that Ella tells me sticks in my brain. And sometimes it just happens to pop out at the right moment. 'It's not like I worked here then or anything,' I told Ness just so he didn't get the idea that, like Ella, I was a lifer at Garden View. 'I mean, it was back in the nineties, right? But Ella, well, she loves to talk. You died in Pennsylvania in the fifties and your ashes were kept—'

'By a relative.'

I was glad he provided this part of the story because I didn't remember it at all. 'And eventually your ashes were brought here,' I said because I did remember that part. 'There was a big ceremony, bagpipes playing "Amazing Grace," the whole deal, and your ashes were scattered over the lake we were just in. I know, I read all about it.'

'Not all about it. See, those ashes . . .' There was no breeze, but the effervescent dust motes that were once Eliot Ness billowed, scattered, and clumped back together, thick and tight, like a thundercloud.

'Those ashes that were scattered,' he grumbled, 'they weren't mine.'

TWO

'So your ashes aren't here, so what?'

Not to worry, I wasn't talking to myself as I sat behind the wheel of my Mustang and drove toward the Garden View administration building. Ness was there. Or at least those sparkly, dusty bits of him were. 'Here I am, talking to you, so ashes or no ashes, it obviously hasn't made a whole lot of difference.'

'Do you think so?'

He gave me time to mull this over, but I guess he knew it would get me nowhere fast because Ness *harrumphed* his opinion long before I worked out what he was getting at. 'After my cremation, my ashes were kept by a relative and stored in her garage. Someone must have known they were there because, one night, someone broke in and stole—'

'Ashes? Really?' I slanted a look toward my passenger seat where the G-man didn't so much ride along as he hovered over the seat in a poofy little cloud. 'Why would anyone want to steal some old ashes?'

'There are people who collect—'

'Other peoples' ashes?' I'm pretty sure the twist in my voice reflected the ick factor that made my stomach jump. 'Who would want old ashes?'

'They weren't just old ashes. They were my ashes. And there are collectors—'

'Collectors of ashes.'

He breathed out a puff of annoyance. Or at least that's how it sounded. 'Collectors of everything! In this case, I'm sure the ashes were stolen by someone who collects Prohibition and gangster memorabilia. Someone who's read the stories written about me and seen the TV show and the movies and considers me something of a . . . well, something of a hero.'

It wasn't my imagination. He really did sound as if that last word actually made him blush.

'So that someone . . . that collector . . . he took your ashes.'

'Exactly. He emptied the box in which my ashes were stored and replaced them with ashes from an outdoor fire pit, and no one ever knew the real ashes were gone. But obviously . . . well, ashes are not easy to transfer from one box to another, not without some mess. A few of my ashes were mixed in with the others and, like those others, they were scattered over the lake in that formal ceremony here at the cemetery. No one ever suspected that the bulk of the ashes were nothing more than the remains of someone's weenie roast. No one but me, that is. Then, just recently, a man visited my memorial – that marker over there across the road from the lake. At the time, I had no idea who he was or what he was doing there, but it isn't unusual, is it? A lot of people stop by to pay their respects.'

He was right. So many Garden View visitors asked about the Ness grave, Ella had been urging me (in her fluffy middle-aged lady, kind and gentle but persistent way) to put together a tour that focused on the life and times of the famous Prohibition agent. As I usually did when she came up with ideas that involved research/work/effort, I'd been sidestepping the subject every chance I got.

'Maybe the person there at the memorial that day was feeling remorseful,' Ness said, drawing me out of my thoughts. 'Or maybe he had a guilty conscience. Whatever the reason, he brought a small packet of ashes – my ashes – with him, and he sprinkled them around the memorial stone when no one was around. So you see, it's simple detective work. That's how I know the real ashes exist. That's how I know who has them. I followed the man home. I know where he lives.'

It all made sense in the weird sort of way that my crazy, ghost-ridden life did. 'So is that why I can't see you?' I asked him. 'Because all your ashes—'

'Aren't in one place. Yes, exactly. That's why I'm not whole, why I never can be.'

I knew this was important, especially to Ness, but thinking about it, I couldn't help myself, I laughed. 'Hey, I guess you really are untouchable, huh? Untouchable, get it?'

I guess he did. That would explain the grumble.

When we rounded a corner and closed in on a section of

the cemetery studded with standing stones and grave sites topped with draped urns and angels, there was a funeral going on nearby and cars parked along the roadway, and I slowed down to get past them. I wondered how many funerals Eliot Ness had watched over the years.

Just like I wondered what he really wanted from me.

'So . . .' I turned into the administration building parking lot just as that big, black Buick pulled out, and I craned my neck for a better look at the classic car. Something told me Ness did the same, because we were both quiet until it wheeled out of the main entrance and disappeared down Euclid Avenue. 'Why are you telling me all this?' I asked Ness.

'I told you I had a detective's job for you. Maybe that wasn't exactly precise. It's more of a . . .' It wasn't like I knew a whole lot about the guy. After all, I had been pretty much tuning out Ella every time she talked about him. But let's face it, what I did know was pretty impressive in a *tough guy, knock the socks off the bad guys* way. He didn't strike me as the type who would be indecisive and yet he paused, searching for the right word. 'It's more of a recovery operation,' he finally said.

What had he called it? Simple detective work? It was simple, all right, so simple I didn't like the truth when it was finally staring me in the face.

'Oh, no!' I slapped the steering wheel to emphasize my point. 'You're telling me you want me to find this guy, this guy who sprinkled your ashes at the memorial? You want me to find him and, what, offer to buy the ashes from him? That's way creepy!'

'Buying and selling human remains. Yes, you're absolutely correct. That would be altogether and wholly wrong. It would be immoral and debase. I would never ask you to do anything like that. No. I simply want you to go to this man's home and steal the ashes.'

It took a few moments to come to my senses. While I was at it, I pushed open my car door and got out. 'I'm not in the burglary business,' I told him and slammed my door to emphasize my point.

'It isn't burglary, it's justice. The ashes belong to me. I simply want them back.'

'You simply want me to break into the house of some person I don't know, find the box of ashes, and grab it before I sneak back out again. Sounds like burglary to me.'

'Well, maybe yes. Technically. But you're the only one who can do it, Pepper.'

'But why do I need to do it at all?' I'd already raised my voice and thrown my hands in the air when I realized that anyone who happened to be looking out of one of the windows of the administration building might see me and wonder why I was talking to thin air, and with so much gusto, too. I muffled the words I was tempted to screech and stuffed my hands in my pockets.

'Why do I need to do it at all?' I said, and even though my lips were pressed together, I turned my back on the building just to be sure no one could see me and decide that I was acting strange. 'You seem to be doing all right for yourself. You're here, aren't you? Even if you're not all here. And it doesn't really matter if you were all here because I'd be the only one who could see you, anyway. And I can see you.' I squinted. 'At least I can see bits and pieces of you.'

'That's true.' It hardly ever happens, so I really appreciate it when ghosts admit I'm right. I guess that's why Ness saw some of the stiffness go out of my shoulders, read it as weakness, and pounced. 'But don't you see, without those ashes, without all of them together, all at the same time, I can never be whole. Not in this world, not in the next. And until I am, I can never rest in peace.'

It was an argument I'd heard before from murder victims, from a former prison warden who'd been wrongly convicted of a crime, even from a long-dead Native American who was doomed to prowl the world until his earthly remains were buried in the land of his people out in New Mexico. I was used to hearing the words *rest in peace* tossed around like some people say *have a nice day*.

I was not used to the sadness that touched Ness's words, the way his voice broke as if the grief was too much for him to bear. The emotion was real and solid, even if this particular ghost wasn't. It slammed into me and tugged at heartstrings most people who knew me would never guess I had.

'I'll think about it,' I said, and just so he didn't get the wrong idea, I quickly added, 'but that doesn't mean I'll do it.'

Fortunately, we were at the door of the administration building by this time, and I had to cut off my conversation with Ness.

'Oh, there you are!' Jennine was the lady who answered our phones and took care of a lot of the administrative work that goes along with keeping a place the size of Garden View running smoothly. She was older than me, and though Ella praised her work and her work ethic, she always seemed a little scattered. Dark haired, dark eyed, and wearing the maroon sweater she kept draped over the back of her desk chair for times when it was chilly, she glanced up from her computer keyboard. 'Someone just left a package for you. You might have seen him.' She craned her neck to look out of the window of the front door even though from where she was seated, there was no way she could see much of anything. 'I think he just pulled out of the parking lot.'

'The guy in the big old car?' I looked toward the window, too, even though I knew the Buick was long gone. 'Who was he?'

Jennine shrugged. 'Said the package was for you. I told him to leave it here, but he insisted on taking it to your office. I walked him back there and he left it on your desk. Cool car, huh? I caught a glimpse of it just as he was leaving. It's great how some buffs really work hard to restore those vintage cars.'

Curious, I mumbled some appropriate response and headed for my office, sidestepping our building maintenance guy, Wally Birch, as I did. Wally was a wiry guy in his sixties with big ears, bad teeth, and that leathery sort of skin that is the curse of smokers. He had half the hallway floor mopped in his usual half-hearted manner. There were dry patches here and there, places he'd completely missed, and puddles in other places where he'd no doubt stopped working so he could lean on his mop and check his phone messages.

'Hi, Wally!' I am not usually Mary Sunshine, but for Wally I made an exception. Wally is a known crabby-pants, see, and I got a perverse sort of pleasure in trying to coax a smile out of him. 'How are you today?'

Wally grumbled sounds that weren't quite words and, knowing a losing cause when I saw it, I kept walking.

Though Garden View is grand, our administration building is anything but. The floors are ancient linoleum, the walls are decorated with framed photographs that highlight Garden View history: Memorial Day programs, choral concerts, the grand funeral procession of a governor who is buried not too far away from the main entrance. I passed the three offices occupied by the folks who made recommendations to the bereaved about funeral arrangements and cemetery plots. Ella's office was next, and the door was closed – thank goodness. Before she could realize I was around and step out to chat the way she always did, I hurried into the office across from hers.

Now that I'd been officially promoted from Garden View's one and only tour guide to its community relations manager, I'd moved out of my tiny, windowless office at the far end of the hallway to the office that had once been Ella's before she was promoted and I took her job. It wasn't much bigger than my old office, but there was a window, a desk with two guest chairs in front of it, and bookshelves that lined the wall opposite the desk. There was a time, a time Ella never fails to remind me about, when my office was pristine, organized, and so much in order that I had every fact and file folder at my fingertips. What Ella didn't know – and what she probably wouldn't have believed if she did – was that all that organization was due to Jean Tanneman, a ghost I'd had the good fortune to meet very soon after she died.

See, according to the rules of how things work over there on the Other Side, ghosts can touch things until the first full moon after their deaths. Lucky for me, Jean died just after a full moon, and that meant she could touch things and move things to her non-beating heart's content for nearly thirty days. She was Little Miss Efficient, the former secretary to some bank president, and she had a mind like a steel trap and way too much energy for a dead person. Jean couldn't stand the thought of being bored for eternity, and she pitched right in to get my life – well, my work life, anyway – in order. For one full month, I had the benefit of Jean's organizational skills.

Unfortunately, that month had long passed, and these days,

there were files piled on my desk and more of them on the bookshelves. There was a stack of unanswered phone messages next to my computer along with a thicker pile of letters that needed to be read and responded to.

And there was Jean.

Like always, she was waiting just inside my office door, ready for anything and eager for orders. Jean was neat, petite, and as prim as any dead person could be in a gray business suit, a crisp white blouse, and sensible shoes. Every hair of her beehive 'do was exactly in place.

But then, ghosts have the advantage when it comes to things like that. It's not like they ever get mussed.

'Your files are deplorable,' Jean snapped. 'You'll never get them organized if you don't hop to it, young lady.'

I tossed my car keys and my phone on my desk next to a box wrapped in brown paper – the package delivered by the man in the Buick – and managed a tight smile. 'Hey, I might get lucky and another dead secretary will show up.'

She pursed her thin lips. 'No other secretary would be as efficient as me. I'm not bragging, just stating facts.'

'You got that right,' I conceded. 'But maybe she wouldn't be as annoying.'

Jean clutched her hands at her waist. 'I'm not trying to be difficult. You know I'd never do that. I'm only making suggestions. For the good of the organization. We are not employed so that we can run off, willy-nilly, and do as we like.'

'Speak for yourself, sister.' Just like that, Chet Houston popped into the chair behind my desk. Yeah, popped. But then, he was a ghost, too, just like Jean. Popping in and out is what they do. Chet puffed on a fat cigar and, when he tapped the end of it against the corner of my desk, the ash that flew off it fizzed and disappeared. It reminded me of Eliot Ness.

'As far as I'm concerned,' Chet said, 'going off and doing our own things, that's what it's all about. That's how you get the real good stories.'

Did I mention that Chet had once been a newspaper reporter? Lucky for me, the afterlife bored him to death, too (no pun intended, but it is actually a good one and I'd have to remember it). Always eager to chase the facts, Chet dictated my quarterly newsletter into a voice-activated tape recorder, and I entered his stories into my computer and took credit for writing them. It wasn't a bad gig.

'Who's the new stiff?'

Chet peered to my left, and when I looked that way, I realized that bits and pieces of my newest ghostly acquaintance whirlpooled in the air next to me. I motioned that way. 'Chet Houston, Eliot Ness.'

'Ness, huh?' Houston leaped out of my desk chair, his teeth clenched so tight around his cigar I thought it would snap in half. 'Never had a chance to interview you back in the day. How's about you give me a few minutes? You know, to talk about the old days? I'd love to get the scoop on what you did here in Cleveland. You know, how you tackled corruption in the police department and instituted all them reforms. Oh, and the Torso Murders. If you could give me the dope on the Torso Murders—'

The sound that came out of the Ness cloud reminded me of thunder, and I thought I knew why. According to Ella, the Torso Murders (a string of killings that rivaled Jack the Ripper's) was the one case Ness had never been able to solve.

'We can talk about Prohibition,' Ness said. 'We can talk about Capone. We can talk about anything you want except the Torso Murders.'

I guess Chet knew it was as good an offer as he was likely to get because he checked to make sure he had a pencil behind his ear and quicker than anybody can say 'deader than a doornail,' he was around to the other side of the desk, a notebook in one hand. The last I saw of him and that swirl that was Ness, they were headed out of the office together, talking up a storm.

But then, according to Ella, Ness had always been a sucker for headlines.

'Well, now that the distractions are over . . .' Jean gave me a tight smile. 'Perhaps we can get down to business. We can start with the file cabinet.' She floated that way. 'And then there are the magazines.' She clicked her tongue by way of telling me what she thought of the latest issues of *Vogue* and *Elle* and *Marie Claire* that I'd had no choice but to buy. Hey,

I worked at a place where dead people were our main concern. How else was I going to find out what the living considered hip and cool?

Lucky for me, a knock on my open office door interrupted Jean's crusade. Even luckier, my visitor was none other than Quinn Harrison.

What can I say about Quinn? He's dark-haired, tall, gorgeous, and as pig-headed as any man I'd ever met. It was a good thing he had wide shoulders, because he carried around a chip that just about filled them. He was a great cop and an even better lover. He has fabulous taste in clothes and always looks like a million bucks, and that day was no exception: dark suit, white shirt, a tie with dashes of green in it that perfectly matched his incredible eyes. Quinn and I had known each other for a few years, and I'll be the first to admit that for some of that time, our relationship had been more than a little rocky. These days we were lucky enough to enjoy each other's company, and most of the time we did it without arguing.

We watched a lot of movies and loved discussing the ones I loved and he hated (or he loved and I hated). He liked to cook, I liked to eat, and it never took us long to decide on which bottle of wine would make the perfect pairing. He put up with my parents, and believe me, that was not always an easy thing to do. Sometimes he was so annoying, I couldn't stand being in the same room with him, but most of the time, I couldn't imagine my world if it didn't include Quinn.

Yeah, I was nuts about him and, as always, thrilled that he'd made time in his busy schedule to drop by.

He leaned into the office, then carefully stepped around the puddle Wally had left on the floor outside my door. 'You free for lunch?'

'Are you?' Quinn was working a big case, and it had been a few days since I'd seen him. That gave me extra incentive to give him a kiss when he finally came over to where I was standing.

He didn't argue. In fact, Quinn made a noise from deep in his throat and kissed me back.

'Maybe not lunch.' His words brushed my lips. 'Maybe we

should head over to your apartment for a while.' He hooked his arms around my waist and inched me back so that I was perched on my desk and, when he kissed me again, I leaned back, savoring the taste of his mouth and the heady scent of his aftershave. I wrapped my arms around his neck and—

'Ouch!' The corner of the box that had been left on my desk poked me, and I sat up and glanced over my shoulder. 'Forgot that was there,' I grumbled, rubbing a hand to my back.

Quinn looked where I was looking. 'And what exactly is it?'

I slid off the desk and turned around to take stock of the package. It was about a foot long and maybe four inches wide, the size of a shoebox. It was wrapped in brown paper and my name and the address of the cemetery were written on it in black Sharpie.

'Came for me a little while ago,' I told Quinn. 'I have no idea what it is.' I thought about the Buick, the one Eliot Ness told me reminded him of the car that had brought his ashes (well, his supposed ashes) to Garden View. 'Jennine said the guy who brought it insisted on leaving it here in the office for me.'

'And you haven't opened it yet?'

'I haven't had a chance. I've been dealing with . . .' Quinn knew about the ghosts. I mean, how could he not? We'd known each other long enough for him to realize my life was not normal, that I got pulled into cases that were colder than most for clients who were as cold as cold could get. And if that wasn't enough, Quinn had been dead himself once. Just thinking about it made my heart start thumping a crazy beat. He'd been dead for a few minutes following a shooting, and while he was, he'd visited me and given me a vital clue that led to finding the man who'd tried to kill him.

It should have been enough to prove to him once and for all that I was not as crazy as I was gifted, and I think sometimes – most times – he really did believe it was true. But there were those other times when logic crept in and reasoning overshadowed even the irrefutable evidence I always presented as proof that the Other Side and I were on talking terms.

'Eliot Ness showed up this morning,' I told him.

His dark eyebrows did a slow rise up his forehead. 'Eliot Ness, the Untouchables Eliot Ness?'

'One and the same.'

Quinn had the nerve to grin. 'Does he look like Kevin Costner?'

My smile was tighter than his, but then my jaw was clenched. 'He doesn't look like anything. I can't see him. Not exactly. I can only hear his voice.'

'Hearing voices.' He nodded and barely controlled a smile. 'That's not a good thing.'

I boffed him on the arm to let him know what I thought of his diagnosis.

'I'm not kidding,' I said, picking up the package and giving it a shake. 'He's worried about his ashes. He wants—' I weighed the wisdom of letting a member of Cleveland's Finest know that Ness wanted me to engage in a little breaking and entering. 'Well, you know ghosts.' I added an elaborate shrug. 'They always want something.'

'As long as the something this one wants doesn't involve you putting yourself in any danger.' He gave me a quick smooch. 'Now let's see what this mysterious package is all about.'

Fine by me. Not talking about Ness meant I wouldn't have to take the chance of lying to Quinn. I mean about the burglary and all. Not that I'd decided to give in to Ness's request, but in case I did, I thought it best if Mr Tall, Dark, and By-the-Book didn't know the details.

I gave the package another little shake.

'It would be easier just to open it,' Quinn said.

The look I slid him told him I knew that.

I ripped the brown paper off the package and saw that I was right; inside was a Nike box, and inside the box . . .

I lifted the lid.

Inside the box was a whole lot of bubble wrap.

I slowly dug through it, but let's face it, shoeboxes aren't all that big, and it didn't take very long.

I leaned closer and peered at what I had uncovered.

'It's a bottle,' I said. There was nothing else. No note,

nothing to say where the bottle had come from or why it had been delivered.

Quinn lifted the brown glass bottle from its wrappings and looked at the label. 'It's a beer bottle. Sieben's Beer. I've never heard of them. Why would anybody—'

Exactly what I was asking myself, but before either of us could come up with an answer, my phone rang. I had a bad feeling I knew who it was, but Quinn is nothing if not quick. Before I had a chance to warn him, he grabbed the phone. 'It's your mom,' he said, checking the caller ID, and while I was still cringing, he answered the call.

'Hey, Barb!' Quinn switched the phone to speaker. 'I'm at the office with Pepper. She's right here.'

'Hi, Quinn. Hi, honey.' The perkiness of my mother's voice did not bode well. 'I've been doing some poking around online. I know you said earlier that you weren't interested, but—'

But nothing.

I made a grab for the phone, but again, Quinn was too quick for me. Obviously, the look of horror on my face was enough to tell him that something was up between me and Mom. The gleam in his eyes told me he couldn't wait to find out what it was.

'You were saying, Barb,' he said.

'Well, I just want Penelope to know, about what we were talking about this morning. I can get discount tickets, honey, but I've got to act fast. The deal is online and it's only good for the next couple of hours. I'm thinking it's an opportunity that's too good to pass up. So I just wanted you to know, keep the date open. I'm going to pick up a couple tickets to that bridal fair.'

I swear, after that everything happened in slow motion. I saw Quinn wince, and I saw that old beer bottle jump in his hand. The sunlight streaming through my office window glinted on the brown glass when the bottle slipped from his hand. The bottle arced through the air and long before I made a move to try and catch it, hit the floor and smashed to smithereens.

THREE

While Quinn and I were still staring at the shards of glass that glittered like stars on the green linoleum, Wally Birch stuck his head into my office, mumbled something about careless people and big messes and how hard it was to be him, and shuffled out of sight. Big surprise, he was back in a moment, and he had a broom and a dustpan in his hands.

'Everything OK?' My mom must have heard the commotion, too, because from the other end of the phone, she sounded concerned. 'Pepper? Are you all right?'

'Fine, Mom.' I scooped up the phone and turned it off speaker. It was anybody's guess what other embarrassing things my mother might say before we ended our conversation, and I wasn't taking any chances. 'Something broke in the office. No big deal.'

'I hope it wasn't a valuable something,' Mom said.

I glanced at Quinn, but of course by this time, he couldn't hear Barb, so he didn't offer an opinion. 'I'm pretty sure it wasn't valuable,' I told her and reminded him, though truth be told, he didn't look as upset about dropping the bottle as he looked a little green around the gills. Then again, he'd heard Mom loud and clear.

Mom talking about a bridal fair.

I would have groaned if I thought it would do any good.

'Gotta go, Mom,' I told her. Before she could object, I ended the call and tossed my phone back on the desk.

'Sure is a mess.' I guess Wally was much more of a thinker and a planner than I'd ever given him credit for, because instead of just sweeping up the glass and getting it over with, he leaned on the broom and took stock of the situation, staring at the broken glass for so long, I wondered if he was counting the pieces. 'I don't hardly get paid enough to clean up other peoples' messes. Supposed to be my lunch hour in just a couple minutes.'

'Sorry.' I wasn't sure I'd ever heard Quinn say the word

before so I had to be excused for turning to him with my eyes wide. Turns out he wasn't even talking to Wally, but to me. 'Somebody sent that bottle to you,' he said. 'There must have been a reason they wanted you to have it. It just sort of slipped out of my hand. I guess I wasn't paying attention. You know, because your mother . . .' As if it were a snake, reared up and ready to bite, he looked over at my phone.

I glanced that way, too. 'No, I'm the one who's sorry. My mother . . .' I swallowed down my mortification. 'Sometimes she gets a little carried away. Just so you know, that wasn't my idea. That stuff about the bridal—'

'This is all very touching.' When Wally interrupted us, I looked over just in time to see him shiver and clap a hand over his heart, a smile as wide as Lake Erie on his face. 'But if you two lovebirds would just move out of the way, I could get this glass cleaned up. What do you say?'

I would have said I'd never heard Wally speak so many words in one week much less at one time, but I was too amazed. Quinn and I moved out of the way and Wally stepped over, broom in hand. While he swept, he whistled a song called 'Ain't Misbehavin'.' Don't get the wrong idea, I'm not some kind of oddball who enjoys things like old music; it was one of the things Mom told me she used to sing to Dad on Saturdays when she called him in prison.

As it turned out, Wally was right about the size of the mess; when the bottle hit, it pretty much exploded and the glass shards were everywhere. He had to sweep under my desk and over by the file cabinets, too. He whistled the whole time, and when he was done and all the pieces of that bottle were swept onto the dustpan, he kept right on whistling and sauntered out of the office.

'Thanks, Wally,' I called after him.

He turned in the doorway and gave me a wink. 'No problem. No problem at all, my sweet.'

'Sorry.'

Another apology from Quinn snapped me out of my Wally-induced astonishment. I pointed toward my open office door and the hallway. I couldn't see Wally, but I heard him change from whistling to crooning.

'. . . savin' my love for you.'

'Did you see that?' I asked Quinn. 'Did you hear that? He's whistling. He's singing. He called me—'

'My sweet!' A wicked grin on his face, Quinn laughed. 'You cheating on me with Wally?' He was kidding and I knew it and I was glad, I had enough weird stuff going on in my life, I didn't need to add Wally and Quinn and jealousy into the mix.

I picked up the box that old bottle had come in and the brown paper it was wrapped in and dumped it all in my trash can. 'It was just an old bottle,' I told Quinn. 'If it was important, whoever sent it would have written a note, or called to let me know it was coming. Or told me what it was for. Maybe somebody thought we put stuff on display. You know, old stuff that might relate to the lives of our residents.'

'It's actually not a bad idea.' Quinn perched on the edge of my desk. 'And speaking of your residents . . .' He wiggled his fingers in the air. I guess it was supposed to be a sign that he'd changed the subject from old beer bottles to the woo-woo. 'Eliot Ness. Tell me about him.'

'You're curious.' He usually wasn't, so like Wally's sudden walk on the wild side of actually carrying on a conversation, I was intrigued. 'Why?'

Quinn lifted those broad shoulders of his. 'He's famous. And a legend in the Department. You know, he came to Cleveland—'

'After he was done working in Chicago and put Al Capone in jail.' I remembered this from what Ella had told me.

'He didn't exactly put Capone in jail,' Quinn corrected me. 'Because Capone went to jail for tax evasion, not for Prohibition violations. But Ness sure helped. By taking out a lot of Capone's bootlegging operations and the supply chain he used to bring booze in from Canada, he destroyed Capone's financial base.'

I crossed my arms over my chest. 'And you're suddenly an expert on Eliot Ness because . . .'

'Hey, you remember the time I got on the bad side of my lieutenant and she made me put in some volunteer hours at the Police Museum? There's an exhibit there about Ness. He's

Cleveland's most famous lawman. Well . . .' He had the chutzpah to give me a grin that was as hot as sin. 'The most famous after me, that is.'

I had absolutely no choice but to lean over and gave him a peck on the cheek because hey, as far as I was concerned, it was absolutely true.

'He was a great safety director,' Quinn said at the same time he hooked an arm around my waist. 'He was the first person in the country to use two-way radios in cop cars. Did you know that?' He nipped a kiss against my ear. 'And he took those cars . . . you know, most cars back then were black . . . and had them painted blue and white so that people could see them more easily and know when there were cops around.' He glided a kiss along my neck.

I made a little noise deep in my throat that told Quinn he could go right on doing that all day if he wanted to and he obliged. At least until I pulled away long enough to tell him, 'If you're going to keep that up, one of us better go over there and close the door or Wally's going to get an eyeful!'

Quinn chuckled and sat back. 'How about we save it for later? Dinner tonight? My place? Even if I have to go back to work after, I can manage a couple hours. We can grill some steaks, catch up on what's going on, maybe take a little time to—'

I knew exactly what he wanted to take the time to do, and I kissed him to let him know I thought it was an excellent idea.

'Then I'm going to get back to work to see what I can get done before six o'clock. If I could wrap up the case I'm working on and not have to go in later, we could add a bottle of wine to tonight's menu and you could stay over.' He slid off the desk and before he got to the door, I already had a plan: I'd leave the cemetery a little early so I could stop home and change into something a little more appealing than black pants and a white polo shirt with *Garden View Staff* embroidered over the heart. While I was at it, I'd take a quick shower, refresh my make-up, pack an overnight bag, and make sure I added a spritz of Viva La Juicy behind my ears and between my breasts because Quinn always said the smell of wild berries and mandarin made his head spin.

I was already debating between wearing the black sheath dress I'd bought for last New Year's Eve or the black cherry-colored front-slit pencil skirt I'd picked up just a couple days earlier because it looked fabulous with ankle-strap heels. Pencil skirt had just about come out the winner when Quinn spoke up.

'So what did Ness want?' he asked. 'I mean, no offense or anything, but, well, I'd think that Eliot Ness would have better things to do in the afterlife.'

'Better things than talking to me, you mean.'

Quinn had already taken his car keys out of his pocket, and he tossed them up and caught them in one hand. 'You know that's not what I meant. I just thought . . .' He tossed the keys again. 'Well, I just think a famous guy like that—'

'He's dead, Quinn. That pretty much takes care of his social calendar.'

'But he's hanging around with you.'

'Don't they all?' I added a long-suffering sigh that wasn't entirely put on and yes, watching the way my white polo shirt rose and fell . . . well, I was hoping that would be enough to distract Quinn. I should have known it wouldn't work. He can be as bullheaded as any man I'd ever met. It was a great asset in his job, a not-so-great thing to have to deal with when I would rather have been dodging his questions than answering them.

'It's that tour!' Another sigh and this time, I made sure I added some oomph to it at the same time I congratulated myself for being quick on my feet. 'The tour about Ness that Ella wants me to put together.'

'I told you it was a good idea the first time she mentioned it.'

'Yeah, I admit it. You're right. You and Ella are right.' I ambled over to where Quinn stood. With any luck, he'd be so busy checking out the sway of my hips, he'd completely miss the fact that I was lying to beat the band. 'Ness got wind of it. I mean, you know how it is with ghosts, Quinn. They have this sort of spooky grapevine and they keep track of what's going on, and Ness, he knows Ella's talking about a tour. And he just wants to know how the planning is going, and he offered to help, too. You know, if I need any interesting facts or stories.'

'Cool.'

There was a time I would have given anything for him to be so enthusiastic about any of my own personal ghost adventures. There was also a time I would have left well enough alone and changed the subject and been done with it.

But then I remembered that there was also a time – and not all that long before – when Quinn wouldn't have believed a word I said when I talked about ghosts, a time he would have been convinced I was just another nutcase.

Just knowing that he bought into the whole Gift thing now made my insides get all mushy. I guess my brain did, too, because I blurted out, 'He wants me to find his ashes.'

Quinn had just caught his keys again, and he closed his fingers around them. 'Ness? But his ashes, they were—'

'Scattered over the lagoon. Yeah, that's what everybody thought. But Ness says those ashes weren't his, and he told me he knows where his are, and he wants me to get them.'

'So you're going to . . .' Quinn is a good and honest man. It's an essential part of his nature, and it's big percentage of his job description, too. I guess that's why he couldn't fill in the blanks.

I was glad.

'Ness, he knows where his real ashes are?' Quinn asked.

'He does.'

'And he wants you to go get them?'

'Right. So he can finally rest in peace.'

'OK. If you say so.' Quinn gave me the kind of look I imagined that over the years, had intimidated bad guys from one end of Cleveland to another. 'You're not going to do anything illegal, are you?'

There is only so far a mushy brain and a mushy heart can carry a girl. I mean, before common sense kicks in. Like I was an old pro at lying (and actually now that I think about it, I was, but that came with my job description, too), I whisked one of those pink phone messages off the pile on my desk. 'Don't be silly. It's all arranged.' I waved around the pink slip of paper, grateful that Quinn was standing far enough away so that he couldn't see that it was in Jennine's handwriting and said, *Your dentist called, time for your bi-annual cleaning.*

'He's a Ness fan,' I said. 'A groupie. You know, the guy who has the ashes. He wasn't sure what to do with them that would honor Ness properly and when I called him and said I was interested, well, you can imagine how grateful he was! I'm going to go pick them up and—'

'Excellent!'

The voice wasn't Quinn's, but then, I wasn't surprised. There were suddenly swirling sparkles in the air between me and Quinn.

'I'm glad you've decided to cooperate,' Ness said. 'We'll have this whole thing taken care of in a jiffy, then I can finally get some rest.'

'He'll finally be able to get some rest,' I told Quinn, without bothering to mention that his idol was there, even if he wasn't all there. There was no use drawing out Quinn's visit. Not when I might slip up and tell him the guy who had Ness's ashes had no idea I was about to pay him a visit. 'I'm going to take care of it today,' I said. 'And Eliot Ness, he's finally going to be able to rest in peace.'

'The guy worked hard and he did a lot of good.' Quinn stepped out into the hallway. 'I'm glad to hear it. I'll see you at six.'

I raised my hand to wave goodbye. 'Six,' I told him and pictured myself in that front-slit pencil skirt.

'I'm glad to hear it, too.' Ness whirled closer. 'You changed your mind.'

'I guess I did.' I didn't exactly grumble. It was more like a loud mumble. 'I changed my mind about Eliot Ness.'

'Oh, I'm so glad to hear it!' My boss, Ella Silverman, must have been out in the hallway at exactly the wrong moment, because she was talking even as she swooped into my office.

That'll teach me for being so busy talking to ghosts; I wasn't paying attention to what was going on around me.

Ella is a believer in go big or go home and that day's outfit was no exception: grassy green skirt, yellow top, gauzy scarf in blocks of turquoise, purple, and orange. She'd added a variety of bracelets to spark her getup and when she stepped into the sunlight that streamed through my office window, she twinkled in green and gold and blue. Her hair was short and shaggy and when she'd last had it dyed, she'd had her stylist add streaks of Crayola red to her usually plain old mahogany locks.

'I knew you'd decide to do the tour,' she said, bouncing on the toes of her low-heeled Clarks. Ella is a full head shorter than me and at least fifty pounds heavier and as I watched her spring up and down encased in those bright colors, I will admit I thought of a beach ball. I'd never mention it. Not for all the world. Sure, Ella is a cemetery geek, but she's also big-hearted and kind and as sincere as any person I'd ever met. When my mom and dad were gone, she stepped in and stepped up and, whether I liked it or not, she made me a part of her family. Don't ever let her know because if she does, she'll think she can get away with pushing me to do more and more around Garden View, but the truth is, I adore Ella.

'I'm so glad, Pepper!' Her smile was even more dazzling than the glimmer off all those beads. 'Our visitors are going to go nuts for an Eliot Ness tour.'

'But I didn't say—' I bit off my words. Because, of course I had. Or at least Ella thought I had.

'I'm going to get started right this minute,' I told her instead, grabbing my phone and my car keys and heading out of the office. 'I'm going to go over to the Ness monument and do some thinking. You know, about what to tell people and how long the tour should be and what else we could include in it.' I remembered Quinn's comment earlier. 'You know, we could get some artifacts in, things from the twenties and thirties. We could have a display here in the administration building. Visitors could stop here first, and it would give them a better idea of what it was like to live in those times.'

Like I'd seen her beam at her own three daughters, Ella smiled at me. 'I knew it! I knew one day you'd embrace the excitement of this job the way I have, Pepper! Just think . . .' Twinkling for all she was worth, she walked out of the office ahead of me. 'By the time I retire, you'll be ready to step into my shoes and take my place as cemetery administrator!'

I did my best to try not to think about those frightening last words from Ella.

Still working at Garden View when she retired?

Taking her job as administrator?

I shivered more at the thought than I ever had when there were ghosts around.

And speaking of ghosts . . .

I parked my car near the granite monument erected to honor Eliot Ness and his family and glanced around. It was lunchtime, and here and there, joggers zipped by, students from the university, maybe, or staff from the nearby hospital, making the most of the good weather. I waited until three young and energetic guys trotted out of sight before I raised my voice.

'Are you here?' I asked and looked around for the telltale flurry of ashes.

Nothing.

'Well, you'll be happy to know I got roped into doing a tour about you,' I added just in case Ness was playing hard to get. 'I'll need interesting details about your life. You know, stuff nobody else knows. It will make me look like a genius.'

Still nothing.

Apparently Ness didn't know how these things worked, or at least how they should work.

'It's the least you can do for me,' I told him. 'You know, since I'm going to go get your ashes.'

More silence, and with a sigh, I leaned against the granite marker and decided that ghosts can sometimes be real jerks.

No matter, I told myself, now that Ella thought I was out here communing with history and coming up with ideas, I could zip home for a few minutes and pack the overnight bag I'd take to Quinn's. With any luck, he wouldn't have to go back to the office that evening, and I'd have him all to myself until the next morning.

Smiling at the thought of what we'd do to fill the hours, I strolled back to my car, cursing my bad luck before I was halfway there when I saw Ella's car coming down the road that intersected the one I was on, headed in my direction.

'Oh great.' Yeah, I was mumbling. Like anyone could blame me? 'She wants to talk about the tour.'

Knowing I was trapped like the proverbial rat, I turned back around and went to stand next to Ness's stone.

I fully expected Ella to slow down and park right in back of where I'd left my Mustang so when she sped up and took the curve from one cemetery road to another on two wheels, of course I was surprised.

But no more surprised than I was when she revved the engine, stepped on the gas, and aimed the car right at me.

FOUR

I didn't scream.

But then, I didn't have a whole lot of time.

In the one split second I had to decide what to do and hope I made the right choice, I ducked behind the Ness monument, then realized that wasn't going to do me much good. If the car hit it square on, the monument would get flattened.

And so would I.

I sucked in a breath for courage and darted out from behind the granite marker long enough to watch the front end of Ella's three-year old Camry get closer and closer and, with a whispered prayer that my timing was just right and my legs were strong enough, I jumped to my left just as the car careened off the road and onto the grass. It veered to my right. I hit the ground, rolled, caught my breath and—

I could now officially take the time to scream.

But not because I was in more danger; just behind the Ness monument was a small pond similar to the one behind the chapel.

And when Ella veered around the marker, she headed right for it.

I scrambled to my feet, shouting her name, and took off running, my lungs filled with fire and my heart slamming my ribs. The turf had slowed the car down, thank goodness, and I came up behind it and somehow managed to get to the driver's side door just feet from where the grass met the pond.

'Ella! Ella!' I pounded on her window and, for a couple frantic seconds, I knew in my heart that it wasn't going to do any good. Ella never even looked my way. In fact she stared at the murky green pond water, glassy-eyed and with a blank expression, both her hands wrapped so tight around the steering wheel, her fingers looked like they belonged to a skeleton.

'Ella!'

When she twitched, I let go a shaky breath and pounded

for all I was worth, scrambling to keep up with the car. 'Step on the brake. The brake.' I poked my finger against the window, pointing down at her right foot. 'Step on the brake!'

The car slammed to a stop. I, however, kept going. I skidded and windmilled my arms, fighting to stop myself, but before I knew it, I was knee-deep in water, mud, and pond scum.

We were both safe.

For a few minutes, all I could do was stand there with water soaking into my pants and mud oozing into my shoes, considering what had nearly happened and how amazing it all was now that it was over. I did my best to breathe, but dang it hurt, and I pressed a hand to my chest and bent at the waist, fighting to regain control. When my heartbeat finally slowed from speed of light to faster-than-a-speeding-bullet, I wrenched first one foot then the other out of the muck and mud and dragged myself onto shore. My lungs burned and my legs ached, but then, exercise is not my thing. Luck, apparently, is, because I knew beyond a doubt that it was luck and luck alone that had kept me – and Ella – from sleeping with the fishes that day.

My hands shaking, I braced myself against the car, dragged myself to Ella's door, and wrenched it open.

'Ella, are you all right?'

Both her hands were still glued to the steering wheel, and there was not a speck of color in her face except for the spots of flaming red in her cheeks.

'Ella!' I put a hand on her shoulder and felt her shiver at my touch. She still didn't look at me, though, and I gave her a shake. 'Ella, here, sit back, relax.' I turned off the car, then, one finger at a time, I pried her hands off the steering wheel and spun her around so that her legs were out the door and her feet touched the ground, and I leaned over so I could look her in the eye.

She was in shock.

That would explain the emptiness in her eyes, the icy feel of her hands.

I rubbed them in mine. 'You just sit here,' I told her. 'I'm going to call 911 and—'

'No!' Her hand closed around mine. 'I'm fine. I'll . . . be . . . fine.'

'You don't look fine.'

Ella blinked as if she'd just woken up from a long sleep and a bad dream. 'I'm . . .' She blinked again and studied my face as if she'd never seen me before. 'What are you doing here, Pepper? Why am I . . .' Ever so slowly, as if she wasn't sure what she'd see, she glanced around at our surroundings. 'Section six. What are we doing in section six?'

Once a cemetery geek, always a cemetery geek.

Just realizing she had that much of her act together made me more grateful than I could have thought possible. I sunk to my knees in one of the ruts that sliced through the grass, created by her tires when she'd slammed on the brakes.

Trembling, Ella scraped a hand through her hair. 'I must have . . .' She squinched up her nose and narrowed her eyes. 'I left the office to run out and pick up something for lunch. Salad. I was going to get a salad for lunch. I told Jennine I'd see her in a little while and then—' When Ella looked at me, there were tears in her eyes. 'I don't remember another thing,' she said. 'Not until right now. But Pepper . . .' Again, she glanced all around, confirming that she was where she thought she was. 'The office isn't all that far from here. It can't be more than a couple minutes since I left there. How could I . . . I mean, how is it possible that I . . .' She sniffled. 'What happened, Pepper? What's wrong with me?'

I was hardly the person to ask. 'You must have blacked out or something.'

'Maybe I did. But it's never happened before. Do you think . . .' She folded her hand over mine. 'Do you think something's wrong . . . with my brain?'

What I thought was that maybe a woman of Ella's age – who had to be sixty if she was a day – shouldn't work as hard as she did, shouldn't worry as much about her daughters as she did, shouldn't think that every little thing that happened at Garden View was her responsibility.

'You're probably just stressed out and tired,' I said. 'Maybe you nodded off. Or you were so busy thinking about something else you weren't concentrating on the road. Maybe you were thinking about the Eliot Ness tour. Could that have been it?' Yes, this was a blatant attempt to get her mind on something other than the near-death experience we'd both had and, while I was at it, I was hoping to stop the flow of tears that trickled down Ella's cheeks. 'You know how excited you are about the Ness tour. I bet that's exactly what you were thinking about.'

'The Ness tour.' She nodded. 'That might have been it. Yes, I remember! I remember now that I was thinking about Eliot Ness. When I left the office, I was thinking about the tour. About how proud I was of you for stepping forward and agreeing to do the extra work. Only Pepper . . .' When she looked at me, her eyes were pleading. 'You're sure that's all you're going to do, right?'

'You mean about—'

'About Eliot Ness. You're planning a tour that focuses on his life, I know that. But you have to promise me, Pepper . . .' She put a hand on my arm, and her fingers closed around it hard and tight. 'You have to promise me that's all you're going to do. Promise me, Pepper, promise me you won't have anything else to do with Eliot Ness.'

What else could I do? Of course I promised. Then, my shoes squishing out little splurts of mud with every step and my pants dripping a trail of pond water behind me, I helped Ella into my car and I drove her home, all the while assuring her that she'd feel a lot better once she had a cup of the Indian gooseberry tea she loved so much. Once we were at her house and my muddy shoes were left at the door, I called Jennine and told her Ella wasn't feeling well and wouldn't be back in that day, then I called Chuck in the landscaping department so he could take care of Ella's car as well as all that turf that had been chewed up when she'd plowed off the road and nearly smooshed me. Chuck was a good guy and he adored Ella, as most of our employees did, so I made up some half-assed story about how Ella had been driving along minding her own business when one of the cemetery's resident foxes had darted out onto the road. 'She lost control of her car, Chuck,' I said, my voice appropriately serious. 'But Ella, she saved that fox's life.'

Chuck was a sucker for the wildlife in the cemetery; Ella rose a couple points on his admiration meter.

All that taken care of, I sat Ella down in her living room, threw a knitted blanket over her, and left her there, that cup of stinky herbal tea in her hands and classical music playing softly on the radio. Back in the kitchen, I rummaged through the cupboards and found a can of chicken noodle soup and, while it was heating up, I ducked into the girls' rooms. I found green and red flannel sleep pants that fit (even if they were a couple inches too short) in Rachel's room and a T-shirt with a picture of Bugs Bunny on it in Sarah's. Ariel is Ella's youngest and she wants to be a librarian when she's finished with school. Go figure. Still, I knew she wore the same size shoes that I did, and a search of her closet uncovered a pair of tennis shoes that fit. They weren't exactly fashionable, but they weren't filled with mud, either, and I scooped up a pair of socks from Ariel's dresser drawer, then took a quick shower. Once I was dry and un-muddied, I called Quinn and left him a message, telling him that Ella wasn't feeling well and cancelling our date for the evening.

'Thank you.' When I delivered the soup on a tray I found in the kitchen, Ella's smile was weak, but I knew it was sincere.

I sat down in a chair across from hers. 'I'll stick around until Rachel gets home.'

'Oh, no!' She had the spoon halfway to her mouth, and soup dripped back into the bowl when she shook her head. 'You can't sit here with me all afternoon, that's—'

'I'll stick around until Rachel gets home,' I repeated, louder this time so she didn't fail to get the message.

Ella looked at me through her shaggy fringe of bangs. 'She's got a late class tonight.'

'And I've got nothing better to do.' I was a crackerjack liar and satisfied she actually believed me, I watched Ella polish off her soup, then tip her head back and close her eyes. She fell asleep almost instantly.

I let go a long, slow breath and sank back in my chair, too, reminding myself that the crisis was over and, for now, all was well. It was good. It was all good.

Well, except for the part about how I wouldn't be seeing Quinn that evening. And the part about Eliot Ness. Because no matter how hard I tried to make sense of it, I couldn't help but wonder why Ella was so dead set on me making that promise to her.

The tour was OK.

But don't have anything else to do with Eliot Ness.

Thinking about it, I watched Ella stir in her sleep. Her lips moved, and she exhaled a long, soft breath and mumbled something. Curious, I leaned forward.

Ella spoke again. Just two little words. And for some crazy reason, I was suddenly chilled to the bone.

She moaned and twitched, and Ella's words, even though her voice was drunk with sleep were unmistakable.

'My sweet.'

As it turned out, Rachel's biomedical engineering class was cancelled that night and she showed up at home just a little after six. Ella was still snoozing and I gave Rachel the same song and dance I'd given Chuck: car, fox, Ella nobly sacrificing herself for the sake of the critter, nobody hurt. I also told her to call me if she needed anything.

By the time I got back out to my car, I wondered if there just might be enough time to get home, get out of my borrowed clothes and into something slinkier, and make it to Quinn's for dinner. I was just about to call him when a voice from my passenger seat interrupted me.

'You'll probably want to wait until the sun goes down.'

It's not that I'd forgotten about Eliot Ness, I just wasn't expecting him to start yapping as I pulled out of Ella's driveway. I clapped a hand to my heart. 'Do you suppose you could let me know when you're around? I mean, in some way other than just talking and scaring the bejabbers out of me?' I thought about what he said. 'And what does the sun going down have to do with me going to Quinn's, anyway?'

'Who's Quinn?' I could tell Ness was irritated; his voice was sharp. 'I'm talking about going to Dean McClure's.'

It was my turn to ask, 'Who's Dean McClure?'

Ness clicked his tongue. Or at least that's how it sounded. 'Dean McClure, the collector. The man who has—'

'Your ashes.' By now I was out on the road and headed in

the direction of my apartment. I slid Ness a look. 'You want me to get them? Tonight?'

'Why not tonight? I've waited long enough. There doesn't seem to be any point in waiting any longer. Tonight's as good a time as any.'

'Maybe in your book, but I had something of a busy day. I met you, and that weird bottle showed up at the office, and I had to cancel a date I was really looking forward to, and oh yes, Ella almost killed me. Seems to me that's enough for one Monday.'

'I've had endless Mondays.' A sigh rippled the little cloud of ashes. 'Dozens and dozens of endless Mondays.'

'So another day wouldn't exactly make a big difference.'

'Darnation!' Ness grumbled. 'I should have believed Gus Scarpetti. He told me you can be difficult.'

For reasons I couldn't explain, this cheered me right up. 'Then you know there's really no use arguing about it. I'm going to get my own way.'

'And you know there's no use arguing with a ghost!' With a whoosh like a winter wind, Ness cannonballed from the passenger seat over to my side of the car. Those dusty bits of ash gritted in my eyes and fogged the windshield. I waved a hand to scatter them, and bits and pieces of them clung to my skin, freezing every spot where they landed.

'Not fair!' I yelled and I waved and I rubbed my eyes. It didn't do any good. I had no choice but to pull over by the side of the road because there was no way I could see. 'That's cheating!'

'I'm making a point and doing what I have to do. You're avoiding what you said you would do.'

My shoulders drooped. 'I'm not avoiding it, I'm just putting it off. You know, until I feel a little less tired and a lot more capable of breaking into some stranger's home.'

'There's no time like the present.' Ness sounded so perky, I gritted my teeth and, cold be damned, I slapped away another blast of the dust motes. 'The sun will be down soon,' he said. 'And that will provide us with the perfect cover. You do the driving, I'll give you directions. We'll get there and get the ashes and you'll be home in two shakes of a lamb's tail.'

* * *

I wasn't at all sure about that whole lamb's tail thing, but I did know that we arrived at our destination in less than thirty minutes. Dean McClure, the man Eliot Ness said had his ashes, lived in a trying-hard-to-be-trendy part of town known as Gordon Square. It was just a bit west of Cleveland's downtown, and there were a few nice restaurants around, some hopping bars, a really good ice cream parlor, and an old movie theater that had been restored and was now the center of a lot of the neighborhood's activity. From what I'd been told by those in the know about these things (people like Ella who care about all things oldy and moldy), Gordon Square had once been a vibrant commercial district that served its working class neighborhood. When we turned off Detroit, the main street that cut through the area, and on to a side street, we passed small, weathered houses that stood close together on the other side of minuscule front lawns and slate sidewalks.

'This is the place,' Ness said when we rolled by a skinny two-story house with a tiny front porch and zero curb appeal. By this time it was dark, and the house looked to be tan with dark shutters that were maybe red, maybe green. There was a waist-high chain-link fence around the yard and a couple straggly bushes on the other side of it that, in a few weeks, might bloom into lilacs.

I slowed the car.

'Not here! Don't you know anything about an operation like this? Up the street! Drive farther up the street!' Ness snapped out the command and I obeyed, not because I'm especially compliant (or compliant at all, as anyone who knows me will gladly testify), but because I was honestly just too tired to care. I parked the car along the curb five houses up from Dean McClure's.

'That's better,' Ness purred. 'You can't afford to make any mistakes, and parking right in front of the house . . .' I had a feeling he shivered. Or at least his words did. 'Someone could easily see you and write down your license plate number.'

'Thanks for the tip. I'll remember it if I ever decide to rob another house.'

'It's not a robbery, it's a burglary. Burglary is when you enter a building illegally with intent to commit a crime, especially theft. Robbery, on the other hand, is the action of robbing a person.'

This was something I hadn't thought of, and my blood ran cold. 'You mean this McClure guy might actually be home, and I'd have to like yell, "stick 'em up," and rob him? Oh, no!' By this time it was dark and the streetlight next to where we were parked was out; I couldn't see Ness at all, but that didn't keep me from turning slightly in my seat and pressing my back against the door of the car in an effort to put some distance between myself and what he said. 'What, you expect me to conk him on the head so I can get in and out of there with your ashes? There's no way I'm going in there if McClure's home.'

'He's not home.' Ness had been in my passenger seat, but now the voice came from right outside my door. I looked out the window and saw a quick flurry of sparks. 'He's gone tonight. He's gone every Monday evening. That's when his collectors' group meets.'

'You're sure?'

'Come on, let's get going.'

The sparkle of ashes moved far enough away to allow me to get out of the car without making contact, and when I did, I scampered onto the sidewalk, the better to keep out of the glow of the light that spilled out of the window of the house across the street.

'Now here's what you're going to do,' Ness said from beside me. 'Walk along the street and keep on walking, all the way to the corner there. When you pass McClure's house, don't look at it, just keep going. You'll walk all the way around the block, turn around, and come back from the other direction.'

'Is there some part of "it's been a long day" you don't understand?' I asked him, but honestly, I didn't expect an answer. Apparently though he was dead, Eliot Ness had more energy than a cemetery community relations manager who'd had one heck of a nasty Monday.

Following his directions, I dragged myself around the block, and if I hadn't been so darned worried about what he wanted me to do and how I was going to do it without ending up in the hoosegow, I might have actually enjoyed the stroll. The evening was crisp, but not cold, and from somewhere over on the next block, the strains of a jazz combo floated through the air.

The sound of a police siren came from the other direction and, hearing it, I froze.

'Relax.' His voice purred in my ear. 'They're not looking for you. You haven't done anything illegal. Not yet, anyway.'

Oh yeah, that cheered me right up.

I shot a look toward where I figured he was standing. 'If you're a cop, how do you know so much about doing things that are illegal?'

'That's exactly how I know about them!' He chuckled. 'Now, let's get down to business. There's McClure's.' We were back in front of the tan house with the indeterminate-colored shutters, and I pictured him pointing. 'Go on up to the front door and ring the bell.'

'I thought I was being sneaky.'

'You are being sneaky, but you have to be sure no one is home.'

'You said he couldn't possibly be home. You told me—'

'I told you tonight is his collectors' club meeting. McClure isn't home. He'd never miss a meeting. But we have to make sure his wife isn't home.'

'Wife?' My voice rose a couple octaves. 'You didn't tell me he had a wife.'

'Don't worry about it.'

Oh yeah, I knew these were famous last words. I also knew I didn't have much of a choice. I opened the chain-link gate, went up to the front porch, and rang the bell. 'And what am I supposed to say if she answers?' I asked Ness.

'You'll think of something. Tell her your car broke down and you need to use her phone.'

'Maybe back in the thirties I'd need to use her phone. I have a phone with me now. She'd never believe me.'

'Ring the bell again.'

I did. There was no answer.

'All right. So far so good.' In an anemic stream of light from a streetlamp, I saw Ness's ashes move off the porch. 'Nobody's here. We know that now. Let's get inside.'

I tried the door handle.

'Don't do that. You don't want to leave any fingerprints!'

This, I should have known. I'd watched enough cop shows on TV in my day. I used the hem of the Bugs Bunny t-shirt to wipe down the doorknob and while I was at it, I wiped down the doorbell, too. 'So how am I supposed to get in?' I whispered.

'Come on.' The dusty cloud crossed the front yard. 'We'll go around to the back.'

In total darkness, I maneuvered along the side of McClure's house. The perimeter of his neighbor's yard was planted with tall bushes with thin, pointy branches and, like I said, the properties were small. Those branches caught my clothing and scratched my arms and tangled in my hair. By the time we rounded the house and stepped onto a tiny back porch, I was not a happy camper.

'Now what?' I asked Ness.

I had a feeling he was looking around. 'You could probably get in that window,' he said, and I guessed he was looking over on our left. The window there was at least four feet up from a flowerbed.

'I don't think so,' I told him and I figured, what the heck, I tugged the T-shirt over my hand and tried the back door.

It opened right up.

'Well, I might be entering,' I mumbled when I stepped into Dean McClure's house, 'but at least I'm not breaking. Come on, Ness, let's get this done so we can get out of here.'

I didn't dare turn on a light, so I hit the flashlight app on my phone and tried not to notice the way the light shimmied in my trembling hand. That bouncing light guided me through a small kitchen and into a dining room that was lined with glass-fronted bookcases that contained an assortment of things. I saw a man's fedora, a pocket watch, a few books.

'So where are they?' I whispered. 'Where are your ashes?'

'I have no idea.'

'What?' The single word came out too loud, and I clapped a hand over my mouth. 'What do you mean you don't know where they are?' I demanded in a harsh whisper. 'You told me you knew exactly where your ashes were.'

'I do know where they are. They're here in McClure's house. Somewhere in McClure's house.'

'Great.' The way I bit through the word should have told him that sarcasm was in play. 'How am I supposed to find them?'

'I'll look around here in the kitchen. You start in there. In the living room.' I had a feeling he would have given me a little nudge if he didn't have the whole incorporeal thing going on. 'That's where McClure displays the best pieces in his collection. No doubt that's exactly where he'd have the ashes.'

I was in no mood to dispute this. I snaked my light into the living room and stopped cold when it glanced against something lying on the worn beige carpet. It was one of those old-fashioned pen holders people used to keep on their desks, a thick marble base with a little cup on top of it where the pen – now missing – was meant to go. There was a statue of a brass elephant next to that empty cup, its trunk raised as if in greeting.

And it's not like I'm into pen holders. Or elephants, either, for that matter. Still, I couldn't help but stare. But then, there was something dark and wet and sticky looking smeared all over one side of the marble base.

Dean McClure wasn't far away, on his back in the middle of the floor, with his arms thrown out at his sides, his eyes wide open, and his head resting in a big ol' pool of blood.

FIVE

'You want to explain?'

This wasn't the first time I'd seen Quinn at a crime scene. I knew he had his small, leather-covered notebook out to jot down anything a witness – in this case, me – could tell him. He wasn't looking at the blank notebook page, though. He was giving me the same once-over he'd already given me as soon as he was inside Dean McClure's door.

As if it would somehow help him make sense of what he was seeing, he shook his head, and a strand of inky hair curled across his forehead like a question mark. 'Why are you dressed like that?' he asked.

'Dressed?' I glanced down at myself and cringed. I'd forgotten the flannel pants that were inches too short, the Bugs Bunny T-shirt, the tennis shoes. Ariel's socks had pink flamingoes on them. My current oh-so-unfashionable state was pretty traumatic so I could be forgiven for blocking out the memory, still, I reminded myself that in the great scheme of things, it was a good thing Quinn and the two uniformed cops who'd showed up with him weren't there because of my felonious plans at McClure's. I'd hate to go to jail looking like this. 'It's kind of a long story,' I told him.

'And I kind of need to know.' He tapped the tip of his pen against the notebook. 'What are you doing here, Pepper? And where . . .' The reality of my appearance did not exactly jibe with Quinn's expectations of me, thank goodness. I guess that's why he had a hard time getting over it. 'Where did you get those awful clothes?'

'Ella's. I told you I was at Ella's. When I left you that voicemail. She was sick, see, and I was muddy. Because I was at the Ness monument, and she was driving, and there was this fox and—'

'Got it.' He held up a hand to stop the flow of my words. 'So let's get back to what's really important.' He glanced at the body on the floor and the crime scene technicians who'd arrived just a little while after he had showed up in response to my call. 'How do you know the victim? And what are you doing here?'

'I told you, Quinn. Back at the cemetery, I told you all about it. I didn't know Dean McClure at all. I never met him.' I couldn't help myself. As much as I didn't want to see it or to relive those heart-stopping moments when the light of my flashlight first raked over Dean McClure's smashed skull, I looked at the victim and the pool of blood that had soaked into the carpet and turned it from plain old ordinary beige to sickening red. I took a couple steps back from it all and lowered my voice. 'Dean McClure is the guy who has Eliot Ness's ashes,' I said. 'You know, the guy I told you I was coming to see.'

'To get the ashes back.'

I nodded, but since Quinn was writing something in his little notebook, I don't think he saw me. At least not until he gave me an eagle-eye look. 'And the ashes are . . .'

I shrugged and, as soon as I did, realized it was a mistake. I should have told Quinn I knew exactly where the ashes were. I should have told him McClure had left them somewhere for me like on the back porch, and that I only found the body because I wanted to thank him in person and he didn't answer the door when I knocked.

Now I'd have to come up with some other half-assed story to explain myself when I finally did find the ashes and whisked them out of the house.

'What time were you supposed to meet him?'

Quinn's question snapped me to. 'Time?' I had no idea what time it was so I had no idea how to cover for my lies. 'He told me to stop by anytime,' I said. 'I was over at Ella's. You know, on account of the mud and the fox and all, and I had to wait until Rachel got home. You know, Rachel—'

'Ella's daughter. Yes, I know. What does that have to do with our victim?'

'Well, I'm just trying to answer your question. About the time. McClure . . . when he called and left me that message this morning . . . he said to stop by anytime, and I guess I got here sometime around seven.'

Quinn made note of this.

'How did you get inside?'

This time, the truth seemed the easiest course of action. 'The back door.' I poked a thumb over my shoulder in that direction. 'It was open. And when he didn't answer when I knocked . . .' I hoped my shrug said it all. 'That's when I came in here and that's when I saw . . .' Again, I looked at the gash on the back of McClure's head. Thanks to the ghosts in my life, I might know more than most about death, but I knew next to nothing about dying. Still, even I could see that the marble paperweight had been used to bash in McClure's head. It was a hefty piece, and I'd bet anything, he'd died pretty quickly.

'And the ashes?'

When Quinn spoke, I flinched and turned back to him. 'The ashes . . . I can just go get them right now.' As if I actually knew where I was headed, I backed a few more steps away from Quinn. 'I'll get those ashes and I'll be out of your way in a two shakes of a lamb's tail.'

I winced at my choice of words, but luckily, Quinn had no way of knowing that I was suddenly talking like a certain cop from the thirties.

'Oh, no!' I knew it would come to this so I wasn't surprised even if I was disappointed when he cut me off at the knees. 'What you're going to do is wait until I'm done here so I can get some more details from you.' Quinn pointed to the dining room. 'In the meantime, in there. Sit down, and don't touch anything, and don't make any phone calls and don't do anything except wait until I'm done here. Got that?'

'Right.' I gave him a crisp salute. 'Dining room. That's where I'll be.'

I sashayed that way, making sure I took as much of a look around the living room as I could. Now that the lights were on, I saw what I hadn't had a chance to see when I'd snuck in with the light of my flashlight app leading the way. Two walls of the room were lined with bookcases and there were clear plastic display boxes on each shelf, lined up like soldiers. Ink pen, a typewriter, a man's hat, an old black telephone. Each display case had a single object in it and a little engraved brass plaque in front of it.

Ness was right, McClure was a collector, all right, and I could tell he cherished his collection. There wasn't a speck of dust on any of the display cases, and those brass plaques shined.

Once I was in the dining room, I saw that there were even more items on display in there, including the framed photograph of a man with a big smile and a round face who was standing in front of a car that reminded me of the Buick I'd seen at the cemetery earlier that day. There were more display cases, too, and I glanced over a heavy gold cigarette lighter, a wristwatch with a worn face, an ashtray, a black leather wallet.

There were other framed pictures on the wall, and though Quinn had told me I couldn't touch anything, he hadn't said anything about looking. One gold frame with elaborate curlicues on it was home to the birth certificate of someone named Joseph Anthony Triccorio, and it wasn't hung, it was set on top of a buffet, leaning against the wall. So was another frame that had nothing in it but a scrap of paper and whatever was scribbled on it in faded pencil, I sure couldn't read it.

Yeah, there were lots of things displayed in Dean McClure's home, all right.

None of them looked like Eliot Ness's ashes.

On cue, there was a swirl of sparkles near the table, and I sat down right next to it. 'So . . .' I made sure I kept my voice down; Quinn might suspect what I was up to, but there was no way I wanted anyone else to notice. 'What's going on here, Ness? What do you make of it?'

'It's not good.'

'Thanks, I needed someone to tell me that. Walking into a murder scene is nobody's idea of good.'

'Not what I'm talking about. I had a quick look around while you were busy talking to the detective.' As if to prove he could, that swirl swished over to the other side of the room and was back again in a flash. 'Like I told you, McClure kept his most valuable items in the living room. Did you notice them when you were in there?'

'I saw a couple things. The phone, the pen.'

'And the empty case?'

I leaned back to look into the living room, but from here, I couldn't see anything but the backs of the two uniformed officers who were standing between me and Dean McClure, and the crime scene people who were on their knees next to the body, searching for evidence.

'There's an empty case?' I asked Ness.

As if he was nodding, the swirl moved up and down.

I was almost afraid to ask, 'Your ashes?'

'Gone.'

It didn't take long for his words to sink in or for the reality of the situation to come crashing down. 'So you're telling me you had me break into the house when—'

'Shhh!' Maybe he forgot that nobody could hear him but me, because Ness whispered. 'You don't want anyone to know you weren't supposed to be here. You actually . . .' He cleared his throat. 'You did very well talking to that detective. You're quick on your feet, and you covered your tracks.'

'No thanks to you who had me break into a house to steal something that isn't even here.'

'But they were here!' Ness insisted. 'I know they were. Someone must have—'

'Killed McClure to get your ashes?' This was a new thought, and I sat up like a shot. 'You think someone knew the ashes were here? That they broke in just like I . . .' I stopped myself just short of saying it. 'That they came for the ashes just like I came for the ashes, only McClure was still here, he hadn't gone to his collectors' meeting yet? You think that someone killed him, then walked off with your ashes?'

'It's possible,' Ness conceded, 'though we don't have enough evidence yet to prove it. Why don't you . . .' I don't know why, but I had the feeling he looked over his shoulder to see what the cops were up to. 'Take a look around,' he said. 'Maybe you'll find something useful.'

What I'd find was big time trouble from Quinn.

If he caught me.

Since he was busy and those two cops were still standing between us, I took the moment to slip out of my chair and into the kitchen.

'All right.' I rubbed my hands together and looked around.

Dean McClure's kitchen was as bare bones basic as the rest of the house. There was a stove and fridge on one wall, a sink on the other and, above it, a window that looked out over the backyard. Someone had turned on the back porch light – no doubt to look for evidence back there – and the light glowed against a sink where dishes and pots and pans were piled in a mound that looked none too balanced. In contrast to the mess in the sink, every inch of wall space in the room was crammed with framed photographs lovingly arranged: black-and-white pictures of guys in old-fashioned clothes standing in front of big houses and tacky looking restaurants, a gigantic poster from *The Godfather*, another picture of the same man I'd seen in that photo that included the old car. This picture was taken closer up, and I could see that the guy had three jagged scars on his left jaw.

Behind me, I heard Ness mumble. 'Al Capone,' he said.

'The gangster?' I studied the photograph with new interest. 'I thought this McClure guy thought you were the main man when it came to old time stuff.'

'He collected all sorts of memorabilia from the thirties. Things that once belonged to me, like that wallet you saw. And things that belonged to gangsters. That cigarette lighter in the other room, that was Capone's. So was that telephone and, if I'm not mistaken, that fountain pen holder, the one that was used as the murder weapon.'

'I don't get it,' I admitted. 'Why?'

'I assume because it was on hand and it fit the bill. That marble base must weigh at least—'

'Not what I'm talking about,' I interrupted him. 'Why this stuff? Why would McClure or anybody else collect it?'

'Why do some people collect stamps? And some collect coins? It starts out as an interest, and in some people it turns into an obsession.'

I thought about the living room and the dining room. I glanced around at the photos that filled the walls. 'McClure was obsessed.'

'Obviously. No one but a person with a fixation about his collection would have stolen my ashes from that garage in Pennsylvania.'

'Then if whoever killed McClure did take the ashes, he must be even more obsessed than McClure was. It's one thing to break into a garage to take ashes. It's another to kill a person to get your hands on those ashes. We're dealing with one sick individual.'

'Or one who's very clever.'

Thinking this over, I turned my back on the picture of Capone and glanced around the kitchen. There was a pile of mail on the green Formica countertop and, with a quick look into the living room to make sure Quinn was still busy, I checked it out. 'Bills and advertising flyers,' I grumbled. 'And this. Look!' I held up a newsletter so Ness could see it. 'The latest issue of something called *The Hit List*.' I read the line underneath the name of the publication. 'A newsletter for collectors of gangster memorabilia.' This I decided might come in handy, so I folded the newsletter in half and tucked it into the waistband of my flannel pants.

'Hey, Harrison!' Another cop stuck his head in the front door. 'A basement window is broken. Come on out here and have a look.' Quinn left, those two uniformed cops went with him, and since there might be evidence to be found, the crime scene folks tagged along. I saw a chance I might not get again. Before they could return, I scampered into the living room and acted like I had every right to be there.

One eye on the door to watch for the return of Quinn and his buddies, I scanned the display cases and found the one Ness had talked about.

The one that was empty.

I moved in close and checked out the brass plaque. It didn't say a thing about ashes, and I guess that's understandable. If McClure stole the ashes all those years before, he'd hardly want to advertise that he had them. No, in fact, the engraving on the plaque was simple and to the point: *Eliot Ness, 1903–1957.*

Satisfied that I'd seen all there was to see, I scampered back into the dining room just as Quinn came back in through the front door. This time, there were paramedics with him who got ready to remove the body.

I settled myself in a chair with my back to all that activity in the living room. 'What were they in?' I asked Ness out of the corner of my mouth.

'You mean the ashes? They were in a wooden box about yea long . . .' I wrinkled my nose and screwed up my mouth to remind him that though he might be holding his ghostly hands apart to show me the dimensions of the box, I couldn't see him.

Ness cleared his throat. 'When McClure found the ashes originally, they were in a cardboard box. Just an old cardboard box. He apparently didn't think that was fitting, and he had a box specially made for the ashes. It's mahogany, about a foot long, maybe three inches high.'

'Like a mini coffin.'

'I suppose so.' Ness sniffed. 'I've had a look around and I don't see the box anywhere.'

'Because the killer took it with him.'

'You talking to . . .' Quinn walked into the dining room, and I looked over my shoulder at him just in time to see him glance around uncertainly. 'Is Ness here?' he asked.

I nodded.

'What can he tell us?' Quinn wanted to know.

There was a time I would have jumped on the table and done the happy dance at hearing this. The fact that Quinn accepted my crazy Gift – and all the weirdness that went with it – made my heart squeeze.

But it did not make me stupid.

'You sure you want to talk about this here?' I asked Quinn.

He called over his shoulder. 'Hey, Rodriguez, I'm going to have a look around. I'm taking the witness with me.'

'Got it,' one of the cops called back, and Quinn and I went through the living room and up the stairs.

There was a time – a time when I lived in a grand suburban McMansion with parents who indulged my every whim – when I would have said McClure's house was tiny. These days when I was living in a third-floor apartment about the size of the closet I'd once had at home, I was not one to judge. Quinn and I walked down a short, narrow hallway and into a bedroom that contained a double bed, a dresser – and barely enough room to move. Never one to take chances, Quinn closed the door behind us.

'So?' OK so he bought into the whole Gift thing, that didn't mean Quinn was exactly comfortable with it. As if he couldn't believe what he was saying, he shifted from foot to foot against carpeting that was the same boring beige as the stuff downstairs, at least the stuff without the blood soaked into it. 'Is Ness here? Can he help us?'

I glanced around, but there was no sign of the little cloud I'd come to associate with the country's most famous Prohibition agent. 'He was here,' I told him. 'He came with me when I came to . . . er . . . pick up the ashes. Makes sense, right? They are his ashes.'

'And you said you didn't have them yet. That you could just get them and get out of here.'

I couldn't help but sigh. 'There's an empty display case downstairs, Quinn, and a plaque with Eliot Ness's name on it in front of the case. Ness says that's where the ashes were. They're gone now.'

'Gone before tonight? Or taken by the same person who murdered Dean McClure?'

'I don't know. And Ness doesn't, either. He swears McClure had them.'

'So in addition to a murder, we might be talking about a robbery.'

Without my name associated with it, thank goodness.

'Why would anybody want ashes? Anybody's ashes?' I asked Quinn.

'I don't know.' He shivered, and I wondered if looking at dead bodies was finally getting to him. It was as warm as blazes in the tiny bedroom. 'But we're going to find out. You saw McClure's face, right?'

I admitted that I hadn't taken a good look.

'Bloody nose,' Quinn told me. 'Somebody took a poke at him. So we know there was a struggle, and it could have been because someone other than you wanted those ashes.'

'Makes sense.'

He made a note of the robbery and, when someone called out his name from downstairs, he opened the bedroom door.

'You're going to have to work late tonight, aren't you?' I am not the emotionally needy type, but after all I'd been through that day, it would have been nice to sleep with Quinn's arms around me. 'I could wait for you at your place.'

When he turned around, there was a smile on his face. He brushed a finger against his left cheek 'I'll tell you what, I'll stop by your place if I can.'

'I'll wait up.'

'Don't.' He stepped out into the hallway. 'It might be pretty late, and I don't want you to miss your beauty sleep, my sweet.'

'My sweet!' Good thing we were upstairs where nobody could see us when I bopped him on the shoulder. Echoing what he'd heard from Wally that morning was Quinn's idea of a joke. Only I wasn't laughing. I couldn't help but remember that it was the same thing Ella had said when she'd drifted off to sleep that afternoon.

While I thought about this, Quinn headed back downstairs and I trailed along. By the time I got into the living room, the paramedics had Dean McClure's body on a gurney and the crime scene techs must have been busy, too, because that pen holder with the bloodied base was nowhere in sight. Neither were Quinn and his cohorts, so I took another minute to look around and, satisfied there was nothing else for me to see, I headed out the way I'd come in.

Outside on the back porch, I took a second to take stock of the yard. Not that there was much to see: a couple rose bushes that were still bare, a spindly looking tree, a garage with the door closed.

And no one around.

I checked over my shoulder just to be sure and scrambled over to the garage. There were windows in the door that was rolled down, but it was dark in there, and I couldn't see a thing. I checked along the side of the garage, found a door, and slipped inside.

Don't ask me what I thought I might find, but I guess I was hoping that McClure, obsessed Ness fan that he was, might have decided to return his hero's ashes to a garage, the place he'd originally found them.

Then again, that would have been too easy.

I inched into the garage in the dark, just barely able to make out the hulking shape of a car that looked mighty familiar. Caution be damned, I needed a better look. I felt along the wall, found a switch, and flicked on the light.

That's when I saw exactly what my gut had told me I'd see.

A shiny black 1938 Buick.

The exact car that had brought that mysterious package to the cemetery.

SIX

I would have been in a considerably better mood the next morning if Quinn had showed up at my place the night before like he said he would. He'd texted somewhere around midnight and said he was still at the office and would be there all night and probably wouldn't be going anywhere the next day, either, except to follow up on any leads he might uncover in Dean McClure's murder. Instead of enjoying some quality time (and a whole lot more) with my main squeeze, I'd slept alone that Monday night. That is, when I wasn't lying wide awake thinking.

About the way Dean McClure's skull looked, all bashed in and bloodied.

About the car in McClure's garage.

About that old bottle that had been brought to the cemetery by a man I didn't know.

A man whose house I'd visited with the intent of breaking and entering.

A man who'd been murdered.

That much thinking wasn't good for anybody. Was it any wonder that I was crabby and out of sorts that Tuesday morning?

As it turned out, not even throwing on my leopard-print raincoat before I left the apartment helped cheer me. When I dragged into my office (almost on time for a change, but then, I hadn't slept, so I couldn't oversleep), rain pounded my window, and the scene outside it was appropriately gloomy. Clouds the color of gunmetal perched on top of the trees, and fog snaked around tombstones and drifted past mausoleums in wisps that looked the way most people who aren't in the know about these things – lucky them – think ghosts do.

'It's a perfect day to file. You won't be out in the cemetery today. Not in this terrible weather.' In spite of her own personal perkiness, in her gray suit, Jean Tanneman fit right in with the whole gloomy mojo. She met me just inside my office door. 'If we get started right now, we'll be done before you know it.'

'Forget it.' I slipped out of my raincoat and draped it across the back of my guest chair, then tossed my purse in the bottom drawer of my desk and plunked down in my chair. In honor of the weather, my mood, and the grim thoughts that pounded through my head, I'd worn black pants, a creamy colored shirt and a black blazer to the office that day. It was chilly in there; I hugged my arms around myself.

'No filing,' I told Jean. 'Not today. I've got other things to think about.'

'Never put off until tomorrow what you can get done today.' Hands clutched at her waist, she gave me the kind of smile mothers reserve for very naughty children. She was at the end of her rope, her expression told me, but she could easily be jollied along. If only I'd do what she said. 'Yes, it's an old saying, but a wise one. In fact—'

'Put a sock in it, Jean!' I leaned forward and tried for a growl that came out sounding more like a whimper. Blame it on my lack of sleep. Just so Jean knew I meant business, I gave her a narrow-eyed glare. 'I'm not filing today. You got that? I'm not working on the speakers' bureau today.' To prove this, I scooped up all the files pertaining to the bureau that Jean had insisted I keep on my desk so that I could snap to and get working on requests, and I shoved those files in my top desk drawer. 'And I'm not returning any phone calls, either,' I told her and as long as that desk drawer was open, I dropped all those pink message slips inside, too, then slammed the drawer shut.

'I've got other things to worry about, so you can take a hike.'

'Well, really, Miss Martin!' She sniffed like her ghostly little nose smelled something nobody on this side of the Other Side could possible detect. 'If that's the way you feel—'

'It is. And I'm the boss, right?'

Jean's pointy chin rose an inch or two. 'I have never been comfortable with all this newfangled equal rights for women nonsense. Men have always been in charge. Yes, women often do the important administrative work that supports them. But a woman as boss—'

'But I am the boss, right?' My hands flat against my desktop, I rose to my feet. I was way taller than Jean, and I looked down at the top of her hair-sprayed-within-an-inch-of-its-life beehive. 'That means I get to tell you what to do. And I'm telling you . . .' Oh, what I wanted to tell her! I somehow controlled myself. 'Jean Tanneman,' I said instead, 'I'm the boss, and I hereby order you to take the rest of the day off.'

'Off? On a Tuesday?' If she wasn't already dead, she would have gone as white as a snowcap. 'I don't know . . . I mean . . . what would I possibly do?'

'I don't care what you do.' I made a shooing motion toward my door. 'Just go do it somewhere that isn't here. Go on. It's your day off. What do you do . . . what did you used to do on Saturdays?'

'I always spent a few hours at the office early in the morning, then went to the grocery store.'

'And Sundays?'

'Church,' she answered instantly. 'Then the paperwork I brought home from the office.'

I groaned. Back when I'd first met Jean, she'd agreed to help me out around the office if I made sure there were pink flowers on her grave once in a while. Turns out the woman craved the romance of roses because, when she was alive, she'd had zero when it came to a love life.

Now I saw why.

'There are plenty of ghosts around here,' I told her. 'Can't you go . . .' I wasn't exactly sure what I was advising her to do when I wiggled my fingers and waved my hands. 'Can't you incorporeal types get together and talk? Or have a few ghostly drinks or something?' I thought about the day before when Eliot Ness and Chet Houston had walked off chatting like old friends. 'Hey, Eliot Ness is around. I bet he was an organized kind of guy. Maybe you two could discuss filing systems or alphabetizing stuff or—'

'Eliot Ness? You mean like Robert Stack? In the Untouchables TV show?'

I had no idea who this Robert Stack guy was, but the way

Jean suddenly twinkled like a schoolgirl told me I was onto something. 'Yeah, that Ness. Check over by his monument. He could be over there. Go on.' I waved again, this time toward my door. 'Get lost.'

She did. In a poof like a raincloud that dissipated and disappeared in the gust of air that resulted when Ella opened my office door.

She glanced around. 'I thought you had someone in here with you. I heard you talking.'

I patted the phone on my desk. 'Telemarketer. Imagine them having the nerve to call me here at work when I have more important things to do.'

That day, Ella had obviously decided to defy the weather gods. She was wearing a pink pantsuit and white beads and, had she stepped a little more lively, she would have reminded me of the Easter Bunny.

Instead, she took a couple hesitant paces into my office, looking all around as she did. 'Well?' she said.

'Well?' I looked where she was looking, at my desk and the bookcases and the file cabinets. There was nothing different about them, nothing that hadn't been piled and stacked and tossed on them just like it had all been piled and stacked and tossed the day before. 'Are you looking for something?' I asked her.

'No, no.' She shook herself and hurried the rest of the way into the office, still glancing around as she did. 'I just thought . . . well, he did say it was a surprise. Have you looked in all your desk drawers?'

'Looked for what?'

'Well, I don't know. Like I said, it was supposed to be a surprise. I thought of flowers, of course, or candy, though you young girls, you aren't all that impressed with candy, not the way we were when we were young and a boy would come around with a box of chocolates. That was always the height of romance!'

'And calories,' I reminded her.

Ella laughed. 'Well, yes, I suppose that's why no one does it anymore. Everyone is so weight conscious. So . . .' She bent at the waist, the better to look around at the other side of my desk.

'If there are no flowers and there is no candy, maybe there's something else? Like a little box? You know, the kind from a jewelry store? The kind that might have a diamond ring in it?'

I flopped back down in my chair. 'What are you talking about?'

Ella sat down in my guest chair. The one that didn't have my raincoat chucked over it.

'I just thought . . .' When she sighed, those white beads winked in the light of the overhead fluorescents. 'Maybe he changed his mind.'

'He being . . .?'

She laughed. 'Quinn, of course! Who else would leave a small box from a jewelry store for you?'

A little background here: when my mother was hiding out in Florida from the humiliation of my dad's arrest, Barb and Ella had somehow hooked up and become fast friends. Their favorite topic of discussion was me.

It looked like nothing had changed since Mom had come back to town.

'Quinn and I are not getting married,' I told Ella.

As if I'd started talking another language, her nose wrinkled and her top lip curled. 'Not ever?'

'No, *not* not ever. But not soon. And besides, I wouldn't want to marry anyone who left an engagement ring in my desk drawer. That's a totally lame way to propose!'

She smiled that soft, understanding smile of hers. 'I suppose you're right. It's not exactly romantic. But he did say he wanted to surprise you and . . . well, I don't see any surprise.'

'Quinn said he wanted to surprise me? When?'

'This morning!' Ella settled back in the chair. 'He came into the office just as I arrived. In fact, he got here so quickly, I wondered if he'd been sitting outside somewhere waiting for me to show up. And he said—'

'This morning?' I thought back to that text message from Quinn, the one in which he said he was stuck at the office and would be for who knew how long. 'Are you sure?'

'Well, of course I'm sure, Pepper. I got here around seven. I needed to look over some budget projections, and I thought if I had some quiet time to myself before anyone else arrived,

I could get more done. And like I said, no sooner was my key in the door of the building than Quinn showed up.'

'And he came inside with you?'

'I couldn't leave the love of your life out in the rain!' Ella laughed. 'Of course he came in with me, and I told him I had to get busy and get working and he said not to worry, that he was just going to pop into your office and leave a surprise for you. Of course I imagined it would be something terribly romantic, but . . .' Her shoulders rose and fell. 'Maybe I heard him wrong. I had a headache last night and I didn't get much sleep and it was pretty early, and I hadn't had a cup of Yerba Mate yet.'

Ella's choice of herbal tea aside, what she said didn't make much sense. 'Well, he sure didn't leave anything for me,' I pointed out. 'You're sure he came in here?'

She thought about it for a second. 'That's what he said he was going to do, but of course, I can't say for certain. I went into my office . . .' This time, that rise and fall of her shoulders turned into a full-blown shrug. 'I just assumed he'd do what he said he was going to do.'

'But he didn't. And then he left.' I mumbled these words to myself and grabbed my phone.

'I'm going to find out what's going on,' I told Ella.

'Well, don't tell him I told you. I mean about the surprise. Maybe part of the surprise is that he wants you to be surprised about not getting a surprise. You know, so he can surprise you when you're not expecting the surprise. That would be just like him, wouldn't it?' I guess this all made sense to her because she was smiling when she left my office.

I was not smiling when I called Quinn.

Or when he didn't answer the phone.

Or when I left the message that asked what was going on because he said he couldn't leave his office and I'd heard that he had.

Done with that, and not feeling one bit better about my love life or about the murder of Dean McClure and the theft (again) of Eliot Ness's ashes, I pulled out a legal pad and hoped that if I made a list of some sort, the pieces of the puzzle that was the last twenty-four hours would start to fall into place.

It actually might have.

If I could have thought of anything to write on the list.

I drummed my pen against the yellow paper. I checked for text messages on my phone and found one from my mother that said, 'Got the tickets!' and did not cheer me one bit. I spun around in my chair, hoping that spinning might jar loose a thought in my brain that actually might help.

It didn't, but when I turned back around, there was a flurry of ashes in the air in front of my desk.

'You disappeared last night,' I grumbled. 'What was the deal? If you hung around, you would have seen the—'

'Thirty-eight Buick in the garage. Yes.' The fuzzy cloud of ashes moved over, as if Ness had taken a seat in my guest chair. 'I wondered how long it would take you to find it.'

'You knew about it? And didn't mention it?'

'I saw it right before you did. There wasn't time to mention it. What do you make of it?' he asked.

'You're the detective.' I tossed my pen down on the desk and sat back. 'You tell me. The guy shows up here at the cemetery in that big-ass car of his, he leaves me a package—'

'Did he?'

I realized that though Ness had come into the administration building with me the day before, he hadn't been around when Jennine had told me about my visitor and the package. And he was long gone with Chet Houston by the time I opened the package and found the old bottle.

'He brought . . .' I looked into the garbage can near my desk, thinking that I'd show Ness the wrappings the package had come in, but the can had been emptied. 'He brought me a package,' I explained instead. 'And there was nothing inside it except an old bottle.'

Like he was thinking this through, Ness was quiet for a few moments. 'If we could examine the wrappings, we might be able to determine where the package came from.'

'Apparently it came from Dean McClure.'

'Yes, of course.' Ness chewed this over. 'Can I see it?' he finally asked.

'The bottle? Well . . .' I remembered that mortifying call from my mother and Quinn's reaction to it, and I cringed.

'The bottle got dropped. It broke into about a million little pieces.'

'What kind of bottle was it?'

I shrugged. 'A bottle. Just an old bottle.'

'Color?'

'Brown,' I said.

'Label?'

'Yeah, it had one, but really . . .' I thought back to the whole incident. 'It all happened really fast, and I wasn't paying a whole lot of attention. There was no letter, though, nothing from Dean McClure that said why he wanted me to have the bottle.'

'If he was the one who sent it.'

'You mean he might have been—'

'Just the messenger, yes. Now you're thinking like a detective!'

'It doesn't help much.' I had a feeling he knew this, but I figured it didn't hurt to point it out. 'No matter who sent that package, it doesn't make sense. Why would anyone want me to have an old bottle?'

'Maybe it depends on what kind of old bottle it was,' Ness suggested.

Maybe I was finally thinking like the detective he thought I was, because I thought I knew what he was getting at. Our maintenance staff carries walkie-talkies, and I had one, too, so that I could communicate with them when necessary. I dug mine out of the desk drawer and turned it on.

'Wally. Wally Birch, it's Pepper Martin. Are you around?'

I didn't get an answer.

'Wally, I saw your car out in the parking lot. I know you're here somewhere. Could you answer me?'

'You're supposed to say "Come in."' Wally's voice snapped and crackled at me from the other end of the walkie-talkie. 'That's how you talk when you're on a walkie. You're supposed to say, "Come in, Wally."'

I swallowed my annoyance and hit the talk button. 'Wally Birch, come in, Wally Birch.'

'Now you say "Over,"' Wally grumbled.

I grumbled right back. 'Wally Birch, come in, Wally Birch.

Over. And it's going to be over for you, Wally, if you don't stop messing around.'

'What'ya want?' Wally drawled.

'I wondered about that stuff you swept up here in my office yesterday afternoon. You know, that bottle that got broken. I wondered if the pieces of that bottle are still around. And the box it came in. It was in my trash. I wondered if you wouldn't mind bringing it all to my office as soon as you can.'

Wally grumbled what might have been a yes.

Or it might have been a far ruder response.

No matter, within fifteen minutes, he was at my office door.

'You look lousy,' I told him. Believe me, I do not usually critique Wally's appearance, but that morning, the shadows under his eyes were the same color as the gray pants and shirt he was wearing. 'Are you feeling all right?'

Wally pressed a hand to his forehead. 'Headache,' he said. 'And I didn't sleep last night. Which means people really shouldn't be bothering me.'

'What, I'm not your sweet anymore?'

'What's wrong with everybody around here? Acting all crazy.' He shivered and rubbed a hand over his eyes. 'Asking for crazy things, too. Like that package. And that broken bottle.'

His hands were empty so I raised my eyebrows, then looked from Wally out into the hallway where he'd left the metal cart with wheels where he kept his broom and his dustpan and such. 'So where is the bottle?'

He grumbled something I was probably glad I didn't hear clearly and shuffled out into the hallway and, when he came back, he shoved a piece of cardboard into my hands. It was maybe four inches square, and there was nothing on it except a few scraps of torn paper and some shards of glass so tiny, they looked like needles.

'What's this?' I asked Wally.

'Your bottle.' He poked his chin in the direction of the cardboard in my hands. 'That's it. That's all that's left.'

'But there was . . .' I turned away from Wally so I could tell Ness this news, and honestly, I don't think Wally even noticed that I was talking to thin air. His eyes squeezed shut, he massaged his temples with his fingers. 'There was a lot of glass. And an entire label.' I turned back Wally's way. 'What happened to the rest of it?'

Like he'd forgotten I was there, Wally jumped and his eyes popped open. 'After I swept it all up yesterday, I dumped it down in the boiler room trash can where I always put broken stuff. Figured I'd get rid of it all on Friday when the city garbage truck picks up. But that . . .' Another poke for emphasis. 'When you asked me to get the bottle, I looked in that trash can. That's all that was there.'

'But . . .' I looked down at all that remained of the mysterious bottle. I looked up at Wally. 'But what happened to it?'

'Got me.' Wally shuffled out of the office. 'Alls I know is that it was there yesterday and it ain't there today.'

When he walked out of my office, he didn't bother to call me *my sweet.*

I sat down in my chair and examined the bits and pieces on the cardboard. 'Well, that's weird,' I said.

'Someone else emptied the trash.' Ever the logical lawman, Ness sounded sure of himself. 'Someone wanted to do Wally a favor.'

'Wally? Favors? I think not. That would mean he has friends, and he doesn't. Or that he sometimes does nice things for other people and they wanted to show their appreciation. That's never going to happen.' Careful to stay as far away as I could from those tiny slivers of glass, I turned over one of the pieces of torn paper. 'This is all that's left of the label,' I told Ness and I pointed. 'Look, this little piece is a dark, golden color, and there's green around the edges. And this piece . . .' The second bit of paper I turned over was a little larger than the first and I scrambled to remember what the label said. 'Black, with white lettering. S-I—'

'Sieben's?' The little flurry that was Ness was around on my side of the desk in an instant, hovering over my right shoulder. 'Sieben's beer? Could it possibly be?'

'That might have been what the label said,' I told him and, to prove it, I got on the Internet and searched and found a picture of the beer Ness was talking about. It came in a brown bottle, just like the bottle that had been delivered to me by

Dean McClure the day before. It had a dark gold label with green around the edges with a black band across the middle and white lettering SIEBEN'S.

'I didn't just get an old bottle, I got an old beer bottle.' I sat back and studied the bits and pieces of what was left of the bottle. 'And even though it was broken into a million pieces, somebody took the rest of the bottle. It doesn't make any sense.'

'It doesn't,' Ness conceded. 'Or it does and . . .'

There was something about the way he said it that made me sit up and take notice. 'What? What is it? What do you know about Sieben's beer?'

'Not much about the beer itself,' Ness admitted. 'I was always a Cutty Sark man myself.'

'Then about the bottle. What do you know—'

'Not about the bottle, either, I'm afraid. Or about why Dean McClure might have brought it to you. But I do know something about the brewery. It was in Chicago and, you see, back in the days when Prohibition was in force, Al Capone himself owned that brewery.'

SEVEN

As Eliot Ness kept reminding me, I was a detective. Sure, all my clients were dead, but in the great scheme of things, what difference does that make? Thinking like a detective, I did a little research and a lot of thinking, and here's what I came up with:

I had one murder victim, Dean McClure, and he was a collector of gangster and Prohibition memorabilia, including those ashes that were once the body of Eliot Ness, the ashes that were now missing.

At this point, I also knew that Dean McClure was the one who'd delivered an old bottle to me at the cemetery and that the old bottle had come from a brewery once owned by Al Capone.

Pardon the pun, but my next move was elementary.

Remembering that newsletter I'd scooped up at Dean McClure's – *The Hit List* – I pulled it out and read it over, and I found out two very interesting things:

1. If I'd arrived at McClure's that Monday night before he was murdered and attempted a break-in, I probably would have gotten caught. See, in spite of what Eliot Ness had told me about Dean being gone for sure, Dean wasn't gone. (Well, obviously since I found his body in the house.) But the reason Dean wasn't gone was that Bill Dennison, president of the gangster collectors' club and his lovely (or so the newsletter said) wife Vivian were celebrating their fiftieth wedding anniversary that night. In honor of the special occasion, the Monday night meeting had been cancelled and rescheduled for
2. The next evening.

This was good news. I mean, other than for Bill and Vivian who I hoped were very happy. It meant that after work that

Tuesday, I headed to the meeting of History's Ill-Gotten Treasures Society.

Yes, it was a lame name for the group and as corny as hell, but I had no doubt someone had worked long and hard to come up with it just so they could call themselves the HITmen.

The HITmen met on the other side of town in an area called Westpark, one of those comfy neighborhoods where the sturdy older homes are neat and well-maintained and there's a bar on every corner. It would have made perfect sense to me if the HITmen met in one of those bars, and I pictured it as dark and smoky, the sort of place where they're still debating the pros and cons of Prohibition and where there are secret rooms in the basement, perfect spots for bootleggers to hide their wares. Alas, there was to be no bar in my Tuesday evening plans. I followed the directions on the back of the newsletter and found myself in the parking lot of a church that had been closed a few years earlier. The building now served as a community center, and I found the HITmen down in the basement in a room with bright overhead lighting, cheery floral pictures on the walls, and a table in the corner that had a coffee carafe on it and was stacked with homemade pastries.

A little background here: in the course of my very first ghostly investigation which involved Gus Scarpetti, a notorious mob boss who'd died back in the seventies, I'd actually once dealt with hit men. I mean, as opposed to HITmen. The guys I had to interview back then were made men. Wise guys. They might have been coffee drinkers, but as far I could remember, there were never homemade cookies involved.

'Hey, we got a visitor!' With the cookie in his hand – it looked like oatmeal – one of the men pointed to the doorway where I stood. He was eighty if he was a day and wearing old-man pants cinched around his scrawny waist with a belt along with a black T-shirt with the words *Leave the Gun, Take the . . .* well, I guess the last word was *Cannoli* but his pants were pulled up so high, I couldn't see the rest. When he called out, the other people in the room, all of them men, looked my way.

I waved and smiled the smile that never failed to charm. But then, not a one of these guys could have been younger than fifty, and I suspect they hadn't been smiled at any time in the recent past by a tall redhead in skinny black pants. 'Is this the HITmen meeting?'

'You got it, sweetheart.' I couldn't tell if the man who rose to greet me was playing a sort of tough-guy part or if he always talked that way. 'Come on in! You want we should get you some coffee?'

I told him I'd get my own and, while I was at it, I got a couple cookies, too, since I hadn't had dinner, and I took my time so I could look over the lay of the land.

That part was pretty easy because there wasn't a whole bunch to see. A dozen men were seated on either side of a long table in the center of the room, and most of them had coffee and pastry in front of them. They were a motley crew: the old guy who'd first noticed me, a couple younger (relatively speaking) fellows in plaid flannel shirts who checked me out as I poured coffee, a few retirees who looked harmless enough. There were various objects in the center of the table, and I had no doubt they'd been brought in for a HITmen show and tell. I looked over the collection before I took a seat, calling up anything I could remember from what I'd seen at McClure's the night before along with anything Ness had told me.

'Ah, Al Capone!' I set my plate of cookies down near a photograph of the man I'd seen in two pictures over at McClure's, but before I could take a better look at it, the lights in the room flickered.

'Darn old fuse box,' one of the men grumbled, but as it turned out, the darned old fuse box kicked right back in, the lights came on and stayed on, and I had a chance to check out the picture of the most famous gangster of all time.

In this particular shot, Capone was wearing a dark suit and a straw hat, the old-fashioned barbershop quartet kind with a flat top and a round brim. 'Nice picture,' I said.

'Autographed.' The guy closest to me was one of the guys in the flannel shirts. His was red, and he inched back his shoulders. 'Bought it for a song at a flea market. Guy didn't know what a treasure he had.'

The old guy who pointed me out when I walked in leaned over and studied the picture. 'And you don't know what a sucker you are, Stan,' he said. He flicked the picture with thumb and forefinger. 'It's a fake.'

Stan's cheeks turned an ugly maroon color. 'What do you mean fake, Louis? I checked it out when I was at the flea market. I looked online and—'

'And look at the signature.' Louis dragged the picture closer to where he was sitting, and oatmeal cookie crumbs landed on Capone's nose. 'This *C* is nice and round and even, see. Capone's real signature . . . well, tell him, Bill . . .' Louis looked down the table at another older man. 'You've got a couple authentic Capone autographs. Tell him, Bill, the way Capone signed his name, the bottom loop of the *C* always curled around and went under the *a* in his name.'

'You got that right,' Bill said and when Stan's picture got passed to him, he shook his head. 'Hope you didn't pay too much for this one, Stan.'

Stan crossed his arms over his chest and plunked back in his chair.

I figured it was my job to change the subject and, while I was at it, to get the conversation headed in the direction I wanted it to go.

'So . . .' The picture of wide-eyed innocence, I looked up and down the table. 'Will Dean McClure be here tonight?'

Ol' Bill nearly choked on his coffee, Louis dropped his cookie, and everyone else started talking. All at once. At least until I wrapped my knuckles against the table.

'It was a simple question,' I said, loud enough to drown out the couple voices that still droned on. 'Anyone want to tell me why your knickers are in a twist?'

Bill had a shock of thick white hair and Coke bottle glasses. He peered through them down to where I sat. 'How do you know Dean?' he asked.

Don't worry, I was prepared for the question. 'We've been talking,' I said. 'Well, not exactly talking. We've been emailing each other. I'm just getting into collecting, see, and I'm interested in buying one of the items in his collection.'

Louis waved a hand in my direction, and cookie crumbs spilled from his fingers and rained down on the white plastic tablecloth. 'That doesn't sound possible. Dean never sells anything. He's the ultimate pack rat. He has a lot, but he wants more.'

'He wants it all,' one of the other men said.

'That's for sure,' Stan grumbled. 'Like that arrest record. The one from Capone—'

The fuse box took that particular moment to act up again, but just as quickly as the lights went off, they were back on, and Stan continued. 'That arrest record that included his fingerprints. Nathan, he had that arrest record and—'

And once again, the place erupted. Voices overlapped, and I didn't have a clue what anyone was arguing about, I only knew that Stan's mouth was flapping, Louis's eyes were wide, and when he tried to raise his voice and call for order, there was spit in the corner of Bill's mouth.

He finally pounded the table with his fist and that worked.

'All right then.' Bill was breathing hard. But then, he was no spring chicken and there was no telling what he and Vivian had gotten up to at their fiftieth anniversary celebration the night before. He looked like he needed a strong drink and a long nap. He scraped a hand through his hair. 'You know the rules, Stan, that's the one thing we said we weren't going to talk about. Not ever again.'

'We said we weren't going to talk about it when Dean was around,' Stan pointed out. 'And you know as well as I do, Bill, Dean ain't around.'

'You mean he's not going to be here tonight?' Big points for me, I wasn't a blonde, but I could play dumb with the best of them. I tilted my head and stuck out my lower lip. 'He promised he'd be here. Last time we emailed, he said he'd be here and he was bringing the leather wallet that once belonged to Eliot Ness.'

Bill scratched a hand behind his ear. 'Well, if that isn't the darnedest thing. Dean just bought that wallet from a collector in Fresno. You sure he said he was gonna sell it to you?'

'That's what he told me.' Just to make sure they all knew I was miffed, I tossed my head. 'If he says he's going to do something and he doesn't do it . . . well, then this Dean guy isn't very ethical, is he? It's a good thing he didn't show up tonight. I guess I don't want to do business with him, anyway.'

As loud as the HITmen had been before, they were suddenly quiet. Louis chewed his cookie. Stan and his clad-in-flannel buddy looked at the ceiling. A man down toward the end of the table grabbed that Capone picture and studied it like he'd never seen the face before, or for that matter, a photograph.

Bill cleared his throat. 'Well, it's like this, Miss . . .'

'Martin.' I supplied the last name, but not the first. Who knew how far my detective reputation had gotten me! I didn't want to take a chance that some of these wise guy wannabes might have gotten wind of what I did.

'Well, Miss Martin, if you saw the news this morning—'

'No time for that.' I waved away the thought.

'Then if you read the newspaper—'

'Who wastes time on that rag!' I added a little laugh. 'When I'm not working, I spend most of my time reading. You know, about Eliot Ness and Prohibition and Al Capone and—'

For the third time in as many minutes, the lights flickered.

Bill waited to be sure they'd stay on and, when they did, he said, 'Well, then I hate to be the one to tell you . . .' I could tell he had a good heart. Uneasy and probably worried about me fainting dead away once he broke the news, he ran a finger around the inside of his collar. 'Dean McClure . . . well, Dean is dead.'

Yeah, I had anticipated this little scenario, too. I leaned forward, my mouth open in a tiny 'O' of surprise.

'Does that mean I won't be able to buy Eliot Ness's wallet?' I asked.

That was it. Just as I anticipated, that was all it took. My priorities clearly in line with their obsession, I was instantly a member of the club.

Just call me a HITman.

'You didn't hear?' Louis had piled cookies on his plate and he reached for another one, chocolate chip this time. 'From what I read . . .' He looked up and down the table. 'Nothing was taken from the house. That's a blessing, huh? Nothing taken. Dean's collection is intact.'

Not completely, but then no one who wasn't actually looking for Eliot Ness's ashes would have known they were missing.

'So this Dean guy . . .' I nibbled on a sugar cookie. 'What happened to him? He didn't say anything to me about being sick when he emailed me on Saturday.'

Bill shook his head. 'Murdered.'

I pretended to be surprised, and I did it pretty well, too. It took me a full minute before I could stutter out, 'That's terrible! Did the police arrest anyone? Do they know who did it?'

'I read somewhere that it was some druggie from the neighborhood,' a man down toward the end of the table said. 'Hey, I warned Dean. We all did. We warned him not to move into that neighborhood.'

'The neighborhood is fine!' Bill waved away this bit of information. 'The whole thing's a crying shame. Dean, he was so excited when I talked to him last week. Said he was going to Chicago for the weekend.'

'He mentioned something about Chicago in his last email,' I said. 'Does he have family there?'

Louis shook his head. 'No, Dean didn't have no family. No one but Cindy.'

Bill snorted and since no one explained why, I kept digging. 'So why Chicago?' I asked.

Stan's top lip curled. 'Bet he was buying something. That's the only time Dean got really excited about anything, when he had a seller on the hook and was all set to pounce on some new find. He called me last week, too, told me he was headed to Chicago. You know what Dean was like. It would have killed him to pick up the phone and just call and ask how the hell anybody was. He never called. Not unless he knew he was going out buying and he was going to come back with something that was sure to make us all jealous.'

There were mumbles of assent up and down the table.

'So he went to Chicago to buy something, and it must have been something special.' For all the HITmen knew, I was simply trying to get the facts straight rather than working out this bit of the mystery in my head. 'Do you think it might have been a bottle from Sieben's Brewery?'

'Capone's place?' When the lights flickered, Bill grumbled, but they came right back on again, just as they had the first three times. 'We're going to have to talk to the people from the city. They got to do something about the wiring in this place.' He shook his head and looked my way. 'What's that you say? Could he have been going to Chicago to get a Sieben's bottle?'

'I don't think so.' Louis sounded pretty sure of himself. 'A Sieben's bottle, yeah, that's fine. But Dean, he even called me to tell me he was going to Chicago. Stan's right. Dean, he would only call everybody when he was excited, really excited, about something he was going to buy.'

'And the beer bottle wasn't worth getting all that excited about.' This was an interesting bit of info, and I tucked it away in my brain for further review and asked no one in particular, 'So what could Dean have been going to Chicago to buy?'

'I haven't seen anything go up for sale on any of the chat boards,' one man commented.

'Last thing I saw on eBay wasn't worth the powder to blow it up,' another man said.

'But Dean was excited, really excited,' I reminded them.

'Yup.' Like he couldn't understand it, Bill shook his head. 'Dean, he must have had the inside track on something. Something none of the rest of us heard about.'

'Dean, he was a son-of-a-bitch like that,' Stan grumbled and, all around the table, there were mumbles of consent.

I took a bite of cookie and decided to get into it with them. Hey, they were HITmen, but not hit men, and I'd gone toe-to-toe with real hit men and come out on top. 'So what you're telling me . . .' I looked up and down the table. 'Is that none of you liked Dean and any of you could have killed him.'

I expected outrage. Or at least a little bit of sugar-induced anger.

I got laughter instead.

'Of course none of us liked him.' Bill chuckled and bit into a donut covered with powdered sugar. 'I'm pretty sure no one who ever met Dean liked him. But that doesn't mean any of us killed him.'

'If this was a TV show, the cops would want to know if you have alibis.' Oh yes, I sounded as innocent as a lamb when I said this. 'You know, so they could eliminate all of you as suspects.'

Louis scrubbed a finger under his nose. 'Not one of us liked Dean. He was greedy.'

'And he bragged a lot,' another man offered. 'And he liked to rub it in our faces when he bought something fabulous for his collection.'

'Or when he outbid us at an auction,' a third man said.

'But none of us . . .' Bill was so sure of this, his chin rose. It would have been an impressive show of force if there wasn't powdered sugar on the end of this nose. 'None of us would kill the guy. Heck, Dean McClure, he wasn't worth going to prison for.'

'Nathan might not agree,' Stan said.

He was seated over on my right on the same side of the table where I was sitting, and I needed to spin in my seat so I could look Stan's way. 'That's the second time you mentioned this Nathan guy. Anyone want to tell me what it's all about?'

As it turned out, they all did. All at once.

I waited for most of the hubbub to settle down and tried my best to make some sense of the bits and pieces of the words that flew around me. 'So this Nathan guy had an arrest record from Al Capone.' The lights flickered and, this time, I didn't even react. I knew they'd come back on again. 'And you say that Dean, he went to see that arrest record and—'

'Not just Dean. We were all there that night,' Bill said. 'It was the HITmen Christmas party, and Nathan volunteered to host.'

'And when we got there,' Louis informed me, 'that arrest record was right where it was supposed to be. In a display case in Nathan's den. He just bought it a couple months before and he was anxious to show it off.'

'And the next day,' Stan said, 'Nathan calls each and every one of us and tells us it's gone.'

'Did this Nathan make a police report?' I asked.

'I know he made an insurance claim,' Bill said. 'And he said that Dean was the last person in the den.'

'And what did Dean say about that?' I wanted to know.

'Well, if you listened to Dean, Nathan was scamming the system,' Louis told me. 'But then, Nathan and Dean, they never did get along. Dean said that Nathan got the insurance payout for that arrest record, but that he made up the whole thing about how it was stolen. Some of us . . .' He looked around and I did, too, and saw that a few of the men nodded. 'Some of us agree. We think that arrest record is right in Nathan's house where it's always been.'

'That don't explain how much Nathan hated Dean,' Stan insisted. 'Hated him with a fiery passion.'

'Enough to kill him?' I asked.

Stan nodded. Louis wasn't so sure. Bill shuffled some papers on the table in front of him.

'You want to find somebody who hated Dean,' Louis said, 'maybe you should talk to Cindy.'

'And that's Dean's—'

'His wife,' Bill told me. 'But I don't know. A woman like Cindy—'

'That Cindy's as mean as a snake,' Stan put in. 'Don't you remember, Bill? Last meeting, Dean, he told us how Cindy was giving him a hard time about every little thing he bought. She even wanted him to sell some of his stuff.'

'Which is maybe why Dean contacted you,' Bill told me, and since it fit in with the cock-and-bull story I'd given them, I pretended it was true.

'So now we better get down to business,' Bill added, clearly uncomfortable speculating about the murder. He rapped the table with a wooden gavel. 'I hereby call to order this meeting of History's Ill-Gotten Treasures. Louis, you start us out with the secretary's report.'

Louis did, though truth be told, I didn't pay a whole bunch of attention. Secretary's report, treasurer's report, ways and means (these guys actually held car washes to raise money for the group). I zoned out through it all and only paid a little more attention when the guys who'd brought things in to show explained what they were and how they'd gotten him: A cigarette lighter that had once belonged to a cousin of a friend of Bugsy Siegel. An old FBI badge. A license plate from the thirties. None of it was especially interesting, and aside from that picture of Capone, none of it had anything to do with the things I wanted to find out more about: Dean McClure's murder and Eliot Ness's ashes.

By the time the HITmen wrapped up and told me they hoped they'd see me at the next meeting, I might have been in a gangster-induced coma, but I hadn't completely fallen down on the job. I paid my ten dollars to join the group for a year and, in exchange, I got the club roster. Yes, it included Nathan's full name, his address, and his phone number.

I am not a detective for nothing.

'You did well.' The flurry that was Eliot Ness met me just as I got out to my car.

'Yeah, you want to reimburse me the ten bucks I just spent?'

He actually laughed. 'That's a small price to pay for information.'

'Maybe.' I slid into the car and started the engine. 'But being bored all night is going above and beyond.'

'Well, then it's a good thing the rest of the night isn't going to be boring.'

I had already pulled out of the parking lot, and I slanted Ness a look.

'The rest of my night is going to consist of going home and falling into bed.'

'Yes. Later. After.'

Good thing I was stopped at a red light when I closed my eyes and groaned. 'After . . .?'

'After we stop back at Dean McClure's, of course,' he told me. 'My ashes are still missing, and whoever stole them might have left a clue as to where they went.'

'Should I even ask?'

I guess Ness was a pretty good detective himself; he knew exactly what I was talking about. 'Well, you never had a chance last night,' he said. 'So tonight you'll make up for it. Tonight, you'll finally have your chance to break into Dean McClure's house.'

EIGHT

'Don't touch the doorknob.'

Really, if I knew exactly where Eliot Ness was standing, I would have tossed him a withering look. The way it was, I knew only that he was somewhere to my left, so I sent a glare in that direction and tugged my jacket sleeve over my right hand.

'What, you think I don't watch *CSI*?' I asked him.

And I guess I wasn't surprised when he asked, 'What's *CSI?*'

Unfortunately, I was not as lucky that Tuesday night as I had been the night before. The door that led into the kitchen of Dean McClure's house was locked up tight, and I was left standing on the back porch with a cloud of ashes that used to be a famous lawman wondering what to do next.

'You're the big brain,' I said. 'So now what?'

'Now we break in.'

'Isn't there just a way for you to . . .' I wasn't exactly sure how to explain what I had in mind, so I pointed toward the back door and made a face. Neither conveyed my meaning with success and I screeched. Quietly, of course, so the neighbors wouldn't know anything was up. 'How about if you just slide or fly or poof under the door. Then you could open it and . . .'

But of course, he couldn't. He might have had the chops, but he didn't have the body that would allow him to open the door.

I sighed my surrender. 'Break in how?'

'Now you're talking!' I actually might have felt better about this if Ness didn't sound so darned pleased. He fluttered down the steps and over to the back of the house, and I followed.

'Up there,' he said, and since we were standing under a window, I guess that's where he was looking. 'If it's locked, you can break the glass, stick your hand inside and—'

'Get blood on a perfectly good black jacket? I don't think so.'

'There won't be any blood. Not much, anyway. Not if you're

careful. And if you're lucky . . .' Apparently, he was studying the window because he was quiet for a while. 'The house is old and the windows are, too. You might just be able to jimmy it. Go on. Get to work. The sooner we figure out what happened to my ashes, the better.'

All this talk of blood had done little for my mood, but I had to admit that he was right. The sooner we got this over with – and the sooner I got Eliot Ness out of my life – the sooner things could get back to normal. Or at least as normal as my life could be. With that in mind, I glanced around the yard and spotted one of those molded plastic chairs over near a tree. I dragged it over and tested it, one foot on the seat.

'I'm going to fall and kill myself,' I said, 'and don't tell me you're going to help me if I do.'

'I'm not going to help you if you do. I can't.'

At least he was an honest ghost.

I climbed onto the seat of the chair, balancing myself as carefully as I could, and it's a good thing I'm tall and the window wasn't all that high up. The bottom of the window was at my waist level, and I was easily able to see inside and into a dark room. Sleeves still over hands, I tried to slide the window open and found it locked, but Ness was right. I wiggled that window and jiggled it, too, and before I knew it, it slid free of the lock enough so that I was able to slide the window up a couple inches, reach inside, and flip the lock.

Crawling inside the house was another story.

I got in, and not gracefully, and found myself in a back room that was obviously used as a sort of den. My flashlight app revealed a flat-screen TV in one corner, a couch across from it, and movie posters on the walls: *Road to Perdition*, *Goodfellas*, *Donnie Brasco*.

I pictured Dean in there watching hour after hour of endless gangster movies, feeding his obsession day and night.

And I wondered what Cindy was up to when he was doing that.

'Cindy!' The name escaped on a whisper that was half surprise, half terror. 'What if Cindy's home?' I asked Ness.

'She's not. I had a quick look around while you were

climbing in the window. Come on.' I saw the cloud head toward the door and, from there, out into the kitchen. 'Get moving!'

I did, but I didn't follow Ness into the kitchen. Instead, I passed a tinier than tiny bathroom and checked out the room next to it. If the room I'd come in through was a den, this was an office of sorts. Desk, chair, computer. It didn't take Ness's big brain or any real experience as a detective to know there might be evidence around.

I closed the mini blinds, turned on the desk lamp, and got to work.

It should come as no surprise that the computer was password protected, and I knew there was no use wasting my time there. Techie stuff is not my forte. The desktop had the usual assortment of bills and grocery store flyers, the desk drawers—

I pulled open the top drawer and stopped cold.

There was a sheet of paper there, handwritten, as if whoever had composed it was just jotting down notes, getting the facts straight, and though they were written in the same blue ink as the rest of the note, I scanned the page and saw three words that stood out as if they were written in red.

In all upper case letters.

And on fire.

Detective Quinn Harrison.

I sucked in a breath and – fingerprints be damned – I grabbed the paper for a better look.

'It's a . . .' I glanced over the words quickly and tipped the page so Ness could see it, but honestly, my hands were suddenly shaking so I'm pretty sure he couldn't read it, anyway. 'It looks like Dean was writing a sort of report. Look, he even signed his name, and it's about . . .'

Because I couldn't believe my eyes, I looked over the note again.

'It happened a couple weeks ago,' I told Ness. 'McClure says he was in a bar downtown and he had a confrontation with Quinn and things got physical. He says Quinn threw a punch.' This did not jibe with the cool-as-an-iceberg, calm-as-a glassy lake, collected-as-a Tibetan monk Quinn I knew, but really, that wasn't the point. 'McClure says it wasn't the first time he had a run-in with Quinn. He says there was an incident a couple years ago and—'

I swallowed hard and remembered that back when I first met Quinn, he was on administrative leave. He never told me what he'd done to end up in the boys in blue doghouse, and I'd never asked. Now I wondered if McClure was the reason.

Just like I wondered why when he arrived at the scene and saw who the victim was, he'd never mentioned that the two of them had a history that included punching.

'This is crazy.' I was talking more to myself than to Ness, but leave it to a lawman not to keep quiet.

'He was the detective who was here last night?' Ness asked and I nodded. 'Interesting. He knew the victim.'

'And the victim . . .' I pointed to a line at the end of the page. 'Dean McClure has Margaret Roadhouse's phone number written down. Margaret, she's Quinn's lieutenant.'

'McClure was going to report the incident at the bar, and then—'

'And then?' It was a legitimate question that only a cop could answer. The paper clutched in my clammy fingers, I looked over to where the little cloud hovered in the air in front of a closet. 'What would happen to Quinn if this got back to his boss?'

'I can't say for sure,' Ness admitted. 'It would depend on if there have been other complaints. According to that note—'

'McClure claimed it had happened before.'

'Then that detective might be suspended. Or fired. Maybe even brought up on charges depending on the severity of the attack. But now that the complainant is dead—'

I sucked in a breath that barely made it past the painful knot in my throat. 'Now that he's dead . . .?'

'If a complaint was ever filed, the department could follow up and keep investigating,' Ness told me. 'You'd think this Detective Harrison wouldn't want to take any chances. I'm surprised he didn't take the note with him. Unless he never saw it. Maybe he didn't search in here well enough. Maybe he's just not thorough.'

I knew Ness was wrong. When it came to his work (and other things, too, but that was a thought for another time),

Quinn was plenty thorough. He wouldn't have missed the note from McClure, and he would have known exactly what it meant if Roadhouse got hold of the information.

'There's obviously nothing to it,' I decided right then and there. 'If there was, if Quinn was somehow involved in covering up the incident by' – I couldn't make myself say it – 'by doing something to McClure to make sure he never filed the complaint, if he was trying to cover up the incident, he wouldn't have left the letter right here where anybody could find it. That proves it.' I thrust the note back in the desk and slammed the drawer shut. 'Quinn wasn't worried. That means he knew he had nothing to worry about.'

'You know,' Ness said, 'I originally came to Cleveland back in 1935 and I was given the job of Safety Director because, at the time, the police department here was one of the most corrupt in the country. I've seen plenty of cover-ups in my day.'

'This isn't a cover-up!' Could I be any clearer? 'If Quinn was trying to hide something, he wouldn't have left the note here. Are you listening to me?' Since I couldn't see Ness, it was hard to tell, so just to be sure, I raised my voice. 'Quinn is an honest cop. He's not trying to hide anything.'

'Maybe not,' Ness conceded. 'But we can't turn a blind eye. There may be more going on here than you want to admit.'

'Really?' Fists on hips, I glared at the lawman, or at least at what was left of him. 'You want to explain?'

'We'd be foolish not to consider the fact that McClure was murdered and that Detective Harrison had a very good reason to want to see him dead.'

Sure, the thought had crossed my mind for a nanosecond, but I never would have had the guts to actually say the words and, for a moment, I was too shocked to speak. But then, it's hard to get words past outrage that was so overpowering, it nearly knocked me off my feet. When I was finally able to sputter, my voice would have been as cold as Ness's grave. If he had one. 'What you're thinking, it's crazy and it's wrong. Dead wrong.'

'Maybe that's how you see it, but—'

'But nothing.' I stomped toward the door, but just as I was about to go out into the hallway, I spun around and went back to the desk. I yanked open the drawer, grabbed that paper, and folded it in half.

'You can't tamper with a crime scene,' Ness warned me.

'And you can't stop me, you're a ghost.' I put the paper into my pocket. 'Quinn is as honest as the day is long, and he's a good man. I mean, a really good man. If he was trying to cover up something that happened with McClure, he wouldn't have left that note there. Which means he's not trying to cover it up. Which means that nothing happened. Which means this piece of paper doesn't mean anything. Nobody needs to see it. Ever. End of story.'

I didn't even check to see if Ness came along with me; I turned off the desk lamp, switched on my flashlight app, and followed its light through the kitchen and into the living room. Ness or no Ness, I didn't much care. All I wanted to do was to get this over with.

I tried to keep the thought in mind. No easy thing considering that my blood boiled and my pulse pounded like a jackhammer. Through it all, I managed to check out the display case I'd seen briefly the night before, the one with Eliot Ness's name on the front of it.

'Nothing,' I grumbled, settling my weight back against one foot at the same time I looked over the display case again, just to be one hundred percent sure. 'It doesn't look like there was a lock on the case, which means whoever took that little wooden box where the ashes were stored just lifted the lid on the case and made off with the ashes. And he also,' I reminded myself, 'killed Dean McClure.'

Where this left me was at the end of my rope, investigation-wise, and I was in no mood to hear it from Ness. I'd just decided to leave and leave the what-next thinking for another day, when a couple things happened all at once:

Car headlights skimmed the wall, and I watched that car turn into the driveway.

I heard a car door slam and, the next second, I heard something even more disturbing, the sound of a key turning in the front door lock.

Before I could tell myself to move and move fast, the front door opened.

'Oh!'

Both the woman at the front door and I let out our startled cries at the same time.

'Who are you?' I blurted out at the same time she said the same thing and added, 'What are you doing in my house?'

I didn't need an old and dead Prohibition agent to tell me I was in big trouble if I didn't think fast, and think fast I did. My phone was still in my hands and I tucked it away in my pocket and turned on the nearest light.

'Mrs McClure, I'm so glad you're finally home.'

Whatever she had expected this stranger standing in her living room to say, it was apparently not this. Cindy was a short, heavyset woman with dark eyebrows and a double chin. Her eyes squinched, she curled her top lip until it met her nose, and kept a death grip on the front door handle.

'Who . . . are you . . . what are you . . .?'

I had a feeling we'd stand there all night asking useless questions if I didn't make a move.

I stepped forward and extended my hand. 'I tried to call you earlier to let you know I was going to stop by.' Sure it was a lie, but it helped put her at ease; some of the stiffness went out of her shoulders. 'I was here last night. With the police.' This, of course, was not a lie, and though it was not the full truth, either, it worked wonders.

Cindy pressed a hand to her heart. 'Oh, thank goodness! I was so afraid someone else had broken in. What on earth are you doing here in the dark?'

Of course she was bound to ask. 'I was just checking to see . . . you know, what the scene might have looked like last night when your husband was . . .' Even thinking I might have to say the word made me wince, but Cindy didn't hold this against me. 'There were no lights on when your husband's body was found,' I said without bothering to point out that I was the one who had found it. 'I just wondered what the killer was and wasn't able to see in the dark.'

'That's really smart.' Cindy ventured farther into the room and tossed her purse down on the brown-and-orange-plaid couch that faced the display cases where Ness's ashes had once been displayed, and I couldn't help but wonder how many hours Dean had sat on that couch admiring his collection.

'There's something missing,' I told Cindy.

'Is there?' She came to stand at my side – she smelled like peppermint – so she could look at the empty case on the shelf. 'What was it?' she asked.

'You don't know? It was your husband's collection.'

'My husband's collection.' There was acid in her voice and in the look she shot around the room at that old telephone, the cigarette lighter, the pictures and the autographs. 'My husband's collection was nothing but a whole crapload of junk.'

I remembered what I'd heard from the HITmen. 'You aren't into gangster collecting, not like your husband was.'

'You think?' Cindy's laugh said it all. 'I'm telling you, I should have seen it from the start. But what's that old saying? Love is blind? In my case, love was deaf, dumb, and blind. Even back when I first met him, Dean was obsessed with all this gangster crapolah. It was his great-uncle's fault, you know. You know about his great-uncle?'

I admitted that I did not.

'Back in the day,' Cindy explained, 'Dean's Uncle Lindy lived in Chicago. He was a chauffeur. He used to drive for that What's-His-Name once in a while, that Al Capone. He used to drive for Capone, and back when Dean was a little kid, Uncle Lindy gave him a button and said he'd found it in the back seat of the car right after he gave Capone a ride. Told Dean that button came off Capone's coat and after that . . .' When Cindy sighed, her broad chest rose and fell. 'What's that they say about stupid people? That they don't need much encouragement? Dean sure didn't. From that day on, he ate and slept and breathed this stuff. It was all he thought about. What he could buy, what he could trade, how he could get more.'

'And I hear he was very good at it,' I ventured.

'Those other crazies thought he was. You know, the other collectors. I can't tell you how many times they showed up over here, sometimes just one of them alone to see Dean, sometimes the whole lot of them all at once. And they always expected me to feed them!' The way she harrumphed at the end of the sentence told me what she thought of that. 'They'd sit here for hours and look at all Dean's gangster shit, and they'd talk and they'd talk and they'd talk.' She pressed a hand to her forehead. 'It was enough to give me migraines.'

'And I bet Dean loved it all,' I said. 'Not the migraines,' I added quickly. 'His collection.'

'Yeah, well truth be told, I don't think he minded the migraines, either. If I had a headache, I'd be upstairs in bed and him and his HITmen buddies, they could stay down here until the wee hours watching gangster movies and talking about gangster stuff.'

Cindy rolled her eyes. 'Dean, he loved all this garbage, loved the idea of gangsters and what he called the excitement of the Prohibition years. Excitement! I never understood. Why, those stupid gangsters he loved so much are even the reason we live in this lousy little house. We used to have a nice split-level. In the suburbs. Then this house came up for sale, and Dean, he found out that some guy named Johnny Vitale grew up here.'

'Johnny?' Just like you never forget your first kiss, you never forget your first ghost, and Gus Scarpetti was mine. In the course of investigating his murder, I'd met Johnny at a home for retired mobsters. 'He was a known associate of Gus Scarpetti.'

'You into this gangster stuff, too?' Cindy asked and, even if I was, I would have denied it because it was obvious what Cindy thought of Dean's obsession and I couldn't afford to alienate her.

Cindy threw her hands in the air. 'He had to have the house. Dean had to live here. He said he wanted to soak up the atmosphere.'

'And you said . . .' I asked her.

'What do you think? I told him he was crazy. I said he was a jerk. I said he shouldn't spend all his money on this gangster garbage, but Dean, he never listened. This piece of junk?' She strode forward and slapped a hand against the display case that held what I think is called a candlestick telephone. It had a base where there was a dial for the numbers, a tall, thin stem with a round thingie the caller could talk into at the top, and a sort of arm where the thing the caller listened on was hung.

'Used to belong to Al Capone,' Cindy said with a sneer. 'Big, hairy deal! Dean paid as much for that stupid phone as some people pay for a car. It was our money. Our money!' Something told me that if she knew she wasn't the one who'd have to clean it up, she would have spit on the display case. 'He shouldn't have bought all this stupid stuff with our money!'

'I heard he was going to buy something else for his collection. That's why Dean went to Chicago last weekend, wasn't it?'

'You know what . . .' She pursed her lips and puffed out a breath of annoyance. 'I stopped asking because I didn't want to know. I got home from work on Friday and there he was packing the car.'

'The car out in the garage? That old car?'

'Yeah, that car. The car of his heart, Dean called it. Like anybody could actually care about some old pile of rust and bolts.'

'So he left on Friday and he came home . . .?'

'Sunday night. And he was so darned excited, I'll tell you what, Dean couldn't stand still.'

'Did he bring a beer bottle with him?'

'What, it isn't enough that Dean got murdered? Now you're thinking that he drove back from Chicago while he was drinking?'

'No, no. Not at all. I just wondered if he might have gone to Chicago to buy an old Sieben's beer bottle.'

'Sieben's?' Cindy crooked a finger and beckoned me to follow her through the kitchen and down the basement steps. In the small room at the bottom of the steps, she turned on a light to reveal packing box after packing box. Something told me each and every one of them contained more memorabilia.

'Sieben's Beer.' She pointed to the neat writing on the side of one of the boxes. 'This whole box is filled with Sieben's bottles.'

'So Dean wouldn't have been all that excited about buying another one.'

'You got that right.' Cindy led the way back upstairs.

'But he was excited, wasn't he?' I asked her once we were in the kitchen.

'He couldn't even sleep that night. Bounced around here like a kid on Christmas Eve waiting for Santa to visit.'

'And he didn't tell you why.'

'I didn't ask.' She jerked open a drawer, found a pack of cigarettes, and lit up. 'I didn't want to hear it. Because I didn't care. More junk is just more junk and Dean, he was like a junkie. He had to have another fix, no matter what it cost.'

'So now what are you going to do with it all?' I asked her.

Like maybe she'd never thought of this until that very moment, Cindy froze and held in a lungful of poisonous smoke. 'I guess I get to sell it, huh?' A slow smile spread across her doughy features and smoke streamed out of her nose. 'Yeah, I could sell it all and finally get the money that should have been mine all these years. Every last penny of it!' She practically skipped into the dining room where she turned on the lights and went from display to display. 'All of it gone. And me gone, too. Back to the suburbs where I belong.'

'I'm sorry I have to ask.' I wasn't, but hey, had I really been working with the police, I think that's what I would have said. 'I need to know where you were last night, Mrs McClure.'

'You and that good looking cop who already asked me.'

Of course Quinn had. Like I said, thorough.

She stuck the cigarette in her front teeth so she could open one of the drawers on a buffet against the wall. There was an envelope there from a bank, and she pulled out a short stack of tens and counted them. 'Six hundred,' Cindy said, more to herself than me. 'I'm surprised. I thought this was the money Dean took with him to spend in Chicago.'

'Does that mean he didn't buy anything when he was there?'

She went into the living room. 'He sure acted like he did, he was that excited. But what the hell . . .' She put the money in her purse. 'At least he left me something, something other than bad memories and a boatload of anger.'

'Which is why I asked . . .' I tried to get her back to what I needed to know. 'About last night?'

'Last night. Yeah. I was out. With friends. We went to dinner. And I never got home until . . .' Cindy glanced over her shoulder at the area rug that had been thrown over the dark red stain on the wall-to-wall. 'That good looking cop, he was still here. You must have been gone already by the time I got home.'

'I was.' That much was true. 'I'm sure Detective H—' I coughed away the rest of the name; I wasn't taking the chance that Cindy might have seen that damning letter to Margaret Roadhouse. 'I'm sure the detective asked where you'd had dinner.'

'Sure. Absolutely. That new place, that Max's over on Madison. I had pasta.'

I made a mental note of this. Not the pasta part.

'And the people you were with?' I asked.

Like I should have known all along, Cindy shrugged. 'Peggy and Mary Jean and Carole. Like always. We go to dinner every month. We went last night. Like always.'

I remembered the car still running in the driveway. 'And now?' I asked.

'Now?' Cindy breezed past me and up the stairs. 'I'm just here to get a few things. You don't think I'm going to spend another night in this house, do you?'

I couldn't say I blamed her.

Upstairs, I heard her rummaging through drawers and dragging something – I guessed it was a suitcase with wheels – out of a closet.

But then I heard something else, too, and it was so loud, I practically jumped out of my skin.

'I know you're in there!' a woman's voice screamed from the front porch right before that same woman pounded on the front door. 'Open up, McClure, you son of a bitch. Let me in!'

NINE

The woman at the door was maybe forty and wearing nondescript black pants and a gray North Face jacket. She was half my height, about as big around as a strand of angel hair pasta, and she had brown eyes, a long nose, and dark hair that was not as luxurious as it was simply long. It hung over her shoulders in sad little clumps and, though I had plenty of other things to think about at that particular moment, the benefits of deep cleansing and really good conditioning automatically popped into my mind.

Since Cindy was still upstairs rummaging through closets, I took over the role of hostess, and when I asked the woman what I could do for her, I thought maybe her eyeballs were going to pop right out of her head.

'You can let me in the house, that's what you can do for me.' She didn't wait for the invitation, she wedged herself between me and the door jamb and pushed her way into the McClures' living room. 'Where is he?' she demanded, her hands curled into fists and her cheeks the same fire-engine color as her fingernails. 'Where's McClure, that son-of-a-bitch?'

This, I couldn't say since I knew better than most that the *where* of where a person went after death wasn't as simple as the heaven or hell most people expected.

'It's complicated,' I told her.

'Yeah, well it better get uncomplicated, and fast.' Did I mention that this woman was no taller than a minute? The way her jaw worked up and down and she pulled in breath after stuttering breath, she reminded me of a little gray mouse on speed. All she needed were the whiskers. As if she was reinforcing my impression of her, she zipped around and gave each of the items in McClure's living room display a quick once-over, and I guess she didn't see whatever it was she was looking for because her top lip curled and left a smudge of red lipstick under her nose.

'I need to see him.' She stomped one foot against that area rug that had been tossed over the stained carpet, and I wondered what she'd say if she knew how truly close she was to all that was left there in the house of Dean McClure. 'I need to have a talk with that scumbag.'

'And you are?'

She didn't expect this interruption of her tirade and, for a few moments, she choked on her outrage. 'I'm . . . I'm . . .'

'Well, come on, spit it out! Who are you and what are you doing here?'

She raised her head and stuck out her pointy chin. 'I'm Angie Triccorio, that's who I am!'

The name was vaguely familiar, or at least the Triccorio part was, and to figure out why, I did my best to sort through everything I'd learned in the last couple days. The pieces finally clicked, and I stepped into the dining room and looked at the framed birth certificate that was set on the buffet and leaning against the wall.

'Aha!' Like she was a heat-seeking missile and had found her target, Angie zipped right over to the birth certificate. She wrapped her bony fingers around the gold-colored frame. 'This is mine!'

'Hold on there, lady!' I yanked the birth certificate out of her hands and just so she'd know it wasn't going anywhere anytime soon, I wrapped my arms around it and hugged it close to my chest. 'You just can't come waltzing in here and start grabbing stuff. What gives you the right to—'

'What gives me the right?' She was breathing so hard, I waited for her to keel over. 'Triccorio! Triccorio!' Though I had the birth certificate turned toward me and she couldn't see the writing on it, she stabbed a finger toward it. 'Joseph Anthony Triccorio was my great-grandfather.'

This, I admit, was mildly interesting.

Which didn't mean that I was about to relinquish my hold on the birth certificate.

'So?' I asked.

In return I got the outraged sputter I expected.

'Joseph Triccorio was my great-grandfather,' she repeated as if I hadn't heard her the first time. 'That means that his birth certificate . . . that birth certificate . . .' When she poked a finger in my direction again I was glad I had the birth certificate pressed to my midsection. Her fingernails were long enough to do serious damage. 'That birth certificate belongs to me, to my family.'

'So how did McClure get it?' I asked her.

'What, you're going to play stupid?' Apparently, she figured I was, because Angie went right on. 'There was an auction. Six or seven weeks ago. And all my great-grandfather's stuff was included. Don't ask!' I wasn't going to, but she flipped up a hand like she had to stop me before I did. 'My father had three brothers, and one of my cousins, Jason, he ended up with all Great-Grandpa's things. He's a loser, and he's up to his ears in gambling debt. He sold all the Triccorio stuff. He sold my heritage!'

'And let me guess, Dean McClure bought it.'

'Well, you should know!' She tossed her head, but thanks to the absence of that deep cleaning and good conditioning I mentioned, her tresses did not bounce in response. 'You're his wife, right? You're Mrs McClure?'

I let her go on believing it and eased into my interrogation. If there was one thing I'd learned in my time as PI to the dead, it's that sometimes going in with guns blazing gets me nowhere. It's not like there are any rules about how these things work, it's more of a gut feeling. At that moment, mine told me that taking it slow and easy would produce more results with Angie.

'How did Dean get your great-grandfather's birth certificate?' I asked Angie.

'I . . . I told you.' It wasn't hot in there, but she fanned her face with one hand. 'My stupid cousin, Jason, he sold it. He sold everything.'

'And why did Dean McClure buy it?'

'Really? You don't know?' She paced a little pattern over to the buffet and back again. Since the room was minuscule, it didn't take long. 'My great-grandfather was Joey Ice Cube.'

'Sounds like a hip-hop mogul.'

'Well, he wasn't,' she snapped. 'There was a reason they called him Ice Cube. He iced people, get it? He was a hit man.

You know, a mobster. Family legend says that he used to do Al Capone's dirty work.'

Which explained why Dean McClure was interested in Joey Ice Cube.

I nodded. 'So McClure bought this and—'

'And a pair of Great-Grandpa's shoes, and one of his fedoras. A tie tack, an address book, the racing form he told my grandfather was lucky and every time he took it to the track with him, he won.'

'And Jason sold it all.'

'Jason is a jerk.'

'And Dean McClure bought it all, fair and square. Dean McClure owns it.'

She kept her gaze on the floor.

'Sounds to me like this is staying exactly where it is.' I set Joey Ice Cube's birth certificate on the buffet and made sure it was centered.

'But I tried to buy it, see.' Like it was a magnet and she was a helpless piece of metal, Angie took a step toward the certificate, but she stopped cold when she saw the determination in my eyes. 'First I tried to buy all the stuff from Jason, and I offered him a fair price, too. And you know what he told me? He told me he knew that there were collectors out there who would pay a fortune for gangster stuff. He told me he was going to sell to one of them. And then, that's what he did. He put the stuff in an auction, and I went to that auction and, before it started, I heard people talking and they said that Dean McClure was sure to snap up every bit of gangster stuff there. I talked to him. I explained. I begged him to stay out of the bidding.'

'And Dean told you to take a hike.'

'No.' Angie shook her head. 'No, he told me that he understood, that he wouldn't bid, that I could have the whole lot of Great-Grandpa's stuff and that he didn't care. But then the bidding started and—'

And I didn't need Angie to supply the details. I could tell what happened from the anger that flared in her eyes.

'As soon as I put in my first bid . . .' When Angie looked my way, her eyes were bright with tears. 'Every time I put in a bid, McClure bid, too. I went up and up and up on my bids even though I couldn't afford it. And McClure, he met my bid again and again and again.'

'It was a game for him,' I said.

Angie brushed a hand over her cheeks. 'Joey Ice Cube lived to be an old man, and I know he did some bad things in his life, but that's not the man I knew. I remember the man who took me for walks and bought me ice cream and told me stories about what his life was like when he was a kid back in New York. Those things, they're important to me. I thought maybe if I came around here I could talk some sense into McClure, get him to see what was right and how I couldn't help myself that I lost my temper over the whole thing. It ain't right, not this, not him having something that belongs to me. So that's why . . .' The right corner of her mouth pulled tight. 'That's why I came over here. To tell him he's not going to get away with this. He's not going to buy my family heritage. It don't mean nothing to him. Nothing except that it once belonged to somebody this McClure never even knew. It's my family.' Angie's voice trembled with emotion. 'My family. And I'm not going to let McClure do this.' She sniffled and marched over to the kitchen and looked in, then spun back around and came at me like a bullet. 'So tell me where he is. Maybe I can talk some sense into McClure.'

'I'm afraid it's a little late for that.'

She gave me a blank stare, and I knew it was time to reveal the ace up my sleeve. 'I'm not Cindy McClure,' I told her and added a little lie for oomph. 'I'm here in an official capacity. I'm working with the police.'

Angie staggered back against the nearest dining room chair. 'I didn't mean nothing. No matter what Dean McClure told you. I didn't—'

'He didn't tell me anything. Dean McClure is dead.'

'No!' She shook her head. 'That's not possible. He can't possibly be—'

'As a doornail!' I pointed toward the bloodstain on the living room carpet. 'Happened right there. Just last night.'

Angie had bad coloring to begin with and her blusher – too purple for her sallow complexion – didn't help. Now, what little color there was in her face drained away completely and left her as pale as most people think ghosts are. She back-stepped toward the front door and waved her hands in front of her as if that motion could brush away the bad news.

'It isn't possible,' she said. 'You're lying. You gotta be lying. No way McClure is dead.'

'Saw the body myself,' I told her. 'But don't worry. Word is, McClure's wife is willing to sell his entire collection. If you keep your ear to the ground, no doubt you'll hear about it and be able to swoop down and get your great-grandfather's stuff.'

I thought this would cheer Angie right up, and maybe it did but it was kind of hard to tell. Because while I was still talking, she raced outside and slammed the door closed behind her.

Cindy picked that moment to clunk, clunk, clunk her rolling suitcase down the stairs. 'Who was that?' she asked.

'Nobody important.'

Yes, this is what I said, but the more I thought about it, the more I wasn't so sure. See, there were a couple things about Angie's visit that got me to thinking, and what it got me thinking was this: Angie was awfully upset about how McClure bought her great-grandfather's stuff out from under her and to me, upset equals motive.

But there was something else, too. See, whether she realized it or not, Angie had said something damning there in the dining room. She said she wanted to explain to McClure why she'd lost her temper about the whole thing, but when she told me the story about going to the auction and talking to McClure, she never said that they'd exchanged angry words. Something told me that meant that Angie and McClure had talked before – or since – the auction.

This was all good news, right? I finally had a suspect, one with a motive and a temper, and I should have been all thrilled that the mystery was finally starting to clear up.

I was thrilled, honest.

Until I realized nothing is that easy.

Because on my way home, I realized something else. Cindy – Mrs Dean McClure – told me she had an airtight alibi for the night of Dean's murder. She was at dinner with friends at

Max's. Only on my way home, I drove right past Max's, and it was pretty hard to miss the fact that the windows were covered with brown paper and someone had written a message on it in bright blue letters: Opening soon.

I'd gone from no suspects, to one, to two and while I could see why either Cindy or Angie might have conked Dean over the head with that pen holder with the marble base, I could not see any reason either one of them might have done it and then walked off with Eliot Ness's ashes. Since Dean was dead, the ashes officially belonged to Cindy, so she didn't have any reason to spirit them away. And Angie didn't strike me as anything like the HITmen I'd met at the old church. Unless she was related to Eliot Ness, I didn't think she'd care.

And then, of course, there was the matter of that note Dean McClure had written to Quinn's lieutenant.

These thoughts played over and over in my head the next day as I went through the motions over at Garden View. I typed up the latest version of Chet's newsletter and accepted a whole lot of undeserved kudos when Ella proofread it and praised me to the high heavens because it was so interesting and so well written. I took a busload of people from the Parma Heights senior center on a tour of the high points of the cemetery, the chapel, and the memorial to a long-dead president (oh, if they only knew that he and I had once solved a murder together!). I consulted with Albert, my ghostly accountant, who gave me some advice on how to forecast my budget for the next fiscal quarter, and though I didn't understand a word he said, I did what he told me to do and was glad to be done with it.

After a day like that, a long soak in a hot tub sounded like the perfect way to spend the evening.

At least until I had a better idea.

Long day? Overstressed? Tired and frustrated by a case that was going nowhere?

I knew the perfect antidote.

Quinn.

I texted him and told him I was making dinner at his place. Don't worry, this didn't scare him. At least not too much. He knew that when push came to shove, I could make a decent pot of spaghetti sauce and that I considered bags of salad God's gift to the culinary world. I stocked up at the grocery store and headed over there.

Quinn lives in a seventh-floor loft where the floor-to-ceiling windows afford a killer view of the river and the downtown skyline. From the kitchen, I could also see a smidgen of Lake Erie shoreline and as I opened cans of tomatoes and tomato paste and sprinkled oregano and basil and fennel into my concoction, I watched the evening sunlight glint against the water.

I set the table and chose a bottle of wine from Quinn's extensive and expensive stash, lit some candles, and waited.

Quinn had promised he'd be there, and I knew his word was golden, but I also knew that there were times he got waylaid by bosses and crime and bureaucratic red tape. By the time he showed up, I'd already opened that bottle of wine and started in on a glass, but he didn't hold that against me. I poured for him, we clinked glasses, and he sipped and savored.

'This is terrific.' He breathed in the scent of the spaghetti sauce and gave me a kiss and that made it official – I couldn't dispute what he said, things were terrific. Well, except for that note I'd found over at McClure's.

A funny sort of rat-tat-tat started up inside my chest even before I told myself there was nothing to worry about. Whatever had happened at that downtown bar with Dean McClure, I knew Quinn had a good reason for everything he did. Just like I knew he'd give me a sound explanation – for that and for why he'd shown up at my office the day before and told Ella he was going to surprise me when number one, he said it wasn't possible for him to leave work and number two, there was nary a surprise in sight

He strolled into the living room. 'This is exactly what I needed. It was a long, long day.'

'I've been working, too.' When he sat down on the sleek leather couch and loosened his tie, I snuggled close. 'For one thing, I've been trying to figure out what the surprise is.'

He gave me a look that clearly told me he didn't know what I was talking about.

'The surprise. The one you told Ella you were leaving in my office. You know, yesterday when you—'

'Oh, that.' He laughed, but not like it was funny, more like he was anxious to change the subject.

'Even though you told me you couldn't get away from work,' I pointed out.

'Well, that was the surprise, wasn't it?' Another chuckle didn't exactly convince me but, hey, I wanted an explanation, right? And at least I was getting one. 'I was going to leave you a note and invite you to dinner tonight, but I dunno . . .' His broad shoulders rose and fell. 'That felt so impersonal. Then you beat me to it when you called and said you were coming here tonight, anyway, so it worked out just fine.'

It did, and I knew in my heart of hearts that the whole I-can't-come-see-you-but-then-I-did thing would turn into the big ol' nothing it did.

Grateful, I sighed with relief. At least until I remembered Dean McClure. 'This whole Dean McClure thing doesn't make sense.'

'McClure.' Quinn put his glass down on the mid-century teak coffee table in front of the couch. 'One less creep in the world. Good riddance.'

I suspected his attitude had something to do with what had happened in that downtown bar, but Quinn didn't know that I knew. I played it cool. 'You never talk about a victim that way, even the ones you know are bad guys.'

'Yeah, well, McClure was . . .' A shiver snaked over his broad shoulders. 'All I'm saying is that without people like McClure in it, the world is a better place.'

'Does that mean you found something in his place that proves he was a bad guy? That he was going to do something he shouldn't have done?'

'Found something? I wish. We've got a dead body and a lack of clues.'

'What about . . .' I knew the time was right. Since it was impossible to explain, I got up and took the note from McClure out of my purse. 'This was in his desk,' I told Quinn and, curious, he sat up and tried to see what I had, but I held on to the paper. 'You didn't take it with you when you searched.'

'I didn't have a chance to search McClure's place until this morning,' he admitted, and before I could even ask he added, 'Yeah, I know, I should have done it Monday night when I was there, but after you left, I don't know, I felt as if all the energy had drained out of me and my head pounded like a jackhammer. I knew it wouldn't do any good to search, I couldn't even think straight. So I kept the place locked up tight and—'

He sat up and aimed a laser look in my direction and his eyes shot green fire. 'But not locked up tight enough, am I right? Pepper, were you poking around at McClure's? You can't compromise evidence like that.'

'I was with Eliot Ness, doesn't that make it all right?'

He either didn't get the joke or he didn't care. 'No, it's not all right.' Quinn got up and stalked over the fireplace and back again. 'You can't screw around with my crime scene.'

I fluttered the paper in his direction. 'Except this doesn't have anything to do with your crime scene. At least I didn't think it did. I figured you'd already searched the house and that's why you left this in McClure's desk, because it didn't mean anything and you didn't care who saw it.'

He held out his hand and instinctively, I pulled the paper closer.

'McClure was going to tell your lieutenant,' I said. 'About what happened at that bar a couple weeks ago.'

'And what?' Quinn threw his hands in the air. 'When you found that stupid note, you thought it wasn't anything and now you think . . . what? That I killed Dean McClure to keep him quiet?'

Quinn is not one to jump to conclusions and this time he'd gone in with both feet.

I sucked in a breath of surprise. 'I didn't say that.'

'You didn't have to.' Quinn scraped a hand through his inky hair. 'Give it to me,' he said.

'What if it's evidence?'

'I said, give it to me.' He didn't wait for me to offer the note, he yanked it out of my hand and when he was done looking it over, he ripped it into a hundred little pieces and let the scraps rain down on the hardwood floor. 'There. Now it doesn't matter. I just did what I would have done if I'd found that at McClure's the night of the murder. It's done. It's over. You don't have to think about it anymore.'

'But, Quinn . . . is it true? If McClure was going to contact your lieutenant—'

'Like I told you, McClure was a jerk, and I don't know why you care. I also don't know why you'd believe some stupid letter from him when you don't believe me.'

'Maybe because you haven't explained your side of the story yet.' Was that my voice, high and tight and loud enough to bounce around the loft?

'Maybe I don't need to.' He grabbed his glass and downed the rest of the wine in it. 'So are we going to eat or what?'

I swallowed around the knot in my throat. 'You can eat, I'm not very hungry.'

'Don't be so sensitive.' Quinn took a step toward me and I stepped back. I was in no mood for an apology, not right then.

'I'm going to . . .' I refused to cry in front of Quinn because if I did, he'd think I was upset rather than just out-and-out pissed so I turned and raced across the loft and into the master bathroom.

There I allowed myself a couple minutes of hot, furious tears, then splashed cold water on my face and considered my options. Dinner with Quinn wasn't one of them.

My mind made up, I left the bathroom and was almost out into the hallway, headed for my purse and the door when something in his bedroom caught my eye. It was nothing more than the sparkle of the last of the sunset against the waters of Lake Erie, but it flashed through the windows and across the room and landed on Quinn's open closet door.

I am not a neat freak and, any other time, I would have ignored that open door. But hey, an open door gave me something to slam, and I marched into the bedroom all set to take out my anger and my frustration.

I didn't, and I had that stream of sunlight to blame again. Because it oozed across the floor and into the closet and landed on something that glimmered in light.

I bent for a better look and was instantly sorry I did. For one thing, I was pretty sure I'd never be able to get up again, that my legs wouldn't hold me and my heart wouldn't start up again and if it did, it would be with a thump that Quinn could hear. I checked over my shoulder to make sure he wasn't around before I got to my knees for a better look at the object tucked in the back of the closet.

It was a fountain pen holder on a marble base with a brass elephant on it.

And it still had Dean McClure's blood smeared all over it.

TEN

The flowers were on my desk when I arrived at Garden View the next day. Two dozen roses, and their colors reminded me of the vivid reds and pinks of the sunrise I'd watched that Thursday morning since I couldn't sleep and I'd spent the night staring out my third-floor apartment window.

Yes, the flowers were from Quinn.

Yes, there was a card and on it, he said he was sorry for what had happened the night before and that he could – and would – explain everything.

I recognized his handwriting, which meant he didn't call the florist, but made the time to stop and place the order himself and, I'll admit, this melted some of the ice that had solidified around my heart the night before. Some. Not all. Flowers or no flowers, a total thaw wasn't going to happen until he told me what was up, and why just mentioning that note that McClure had written to Quinn's lieutenant had made him so defensive.

And then, of course, there was the not-so-small matter of the murder weapon in Quinn's closet.

I hadn't said a word to him about it that Wednesday night. But then as soon as I rushed out of the bedroom, I was pretty busy hightailing it out of his place, my heart in my throat and unshed tears stinging my eyes so that I could barely see to drive home.

Even the next morning, just thinking about that fountain pen holder and the blood caked on it in nasty, rusty-colored streaks caused my heart to jump and my pulse to pound along with it. I'd seen the pen holder on the floor of McClure's living room the night of the murder, and I remembered that it was there when I went upstairs with Quinn. It was gone when I came back downstairs. I'd assumed that it had been bagged and tagged by the crime scene people, but that will teach me.

That pen holder never left McClure's with the technicians. It had never been entered as evidence.

Because Quinn had snatched it up.

Bad enough when thinking all this through already had me feeling queasy. Worse when my phone rang. I checked the caller ID and I knew a losing cause when I saw it, so I picked up on the third ring.

'Hi, Mom!'

'Hi, honey! I know you're working and I don't want to bother you, but I just thought I'd check in and see what you're planning to wear on Saturday.'

It took a few moments for me to figure out what she was talking about, and when I did, I groaned.

'I'm not being pushy,' my mother told me, as pushy as ever. 'But I figured it's important. You'll want something comfortable and something easy to take off and put on if you're trying on gowns at the bridal fair.'

This time, my groan was accompanied by a well-deserved curse word.

'Really, Pepper!' Mom sloughed the whole thing off as if it was meant to be funny. It wasn't. 'A bride is always much classier than that.'

'Except I'm not a bride.'

'Not yet you're not.'

I glanced at the vase on my desk and at the flowers and greenery and tiny sprigs of white baby's breath that overflowed from it, and I couldn't help myself, I sighed.

'What's that?' Call it mother's instincts, I pictured Barb sitting up, cocking her head, eager and interested. 'What's wrong, Pepper?'

'Nothing's wrong.' I lied like a champ. 'It's just that Quinn and I, we're—'

'Of course you're fighting! That is what you were going to say, right?' Before I had a chance to ask how in the hell she knew, my mother breezed right on. 'It's only natural that there would be tensions between the two of you at a time like this. You're doing important work, figuring out the rest of your lives. You're bound to get on each other's nerves once in a while.'

If she could have seen me, she would have known that I shook my head. 'That isn't it, Mom.'

'Then it's the actual wedding, isn't it? Who you want to invite, who he wants to invite. And music! My goodness, I remember the squabbles your dad and I had about the music when we were planning our wedding. He always loved Motown. And that crazy, psychedelic rock. And my Grandfather Livingston, well, he was paying for the reception and it was at his country club. He insisted on a twelve-piece orchestra and all the old standards. Your dad, he slipped the band a hundred dollar bill and had them play that old song, that *Sugar Pie, Honey Bunch*. You know the one.'

She sang a couple bars just in case I didn't, then laughed. 'Oh, I thought my grandfather was going to have a coronary right then and there! Of course things are a little easier these days because you have DJs and you can pick any kind of music you want. Remember that, Pepper, it isn't worth fighting over. You can pick any kind of music you want, honey.'

'We're not fighting over music, Mom. We're not talking about music. We're not even talking about a wedding.'

'Well, then that explains everything, doesn't it? You need to talk! You need to get your ideas out in the open. If you just bottle it all in, of course you're both going to snap.'

Snap is what we'd done.

Or at least what Quinn had done.

Thinking back to the night before, I still wondered how things had gotten out of control so quickly. It wasn't like Quinn and I had never had a fight before; we were people with intense opinions, and his were usually wrong. But even when he was being his usual strong-willed, pig-headed, hard-nosed self, he'd never gone off the deep end. Not like he had that Wednesday evening.

'I think we're both just tired.'

I didn't realize I'd even said it out loud until my mother replied. 'Just wait! Once we're into the planning full swing, things will really get hectic. Lots of sleep and plenty of hydration. That's what you need.'

'I don't have to wait for things to get hectic, they're already hectic, Mom. Quinn and I, we're investigating a murder.'

Barb sucked in a breath. 'Oh, is there a ghost involved?'

'Sort of. Kind of. But not in the murder, more like in the robbery that took place during the murder. Maybe.'

'Well, no wonder you're feeling out of sorts!' Since she'd just figured out the problems with my love life – if only it was that easy . . . my mother had the luxury of imparting her maternal wisdom. 'You two have a lot going on. You'll see. I guarantee it, honey, you'll see how things will smooth out once you get this murder out of the way. Now, what did you say you were wearing on Saturday?'

'I'll find something,' I assured her and before she could question me further, I told her I had to go and ended the call.

As it turned out, it was a good thing I did, because Eliot Ness picked that moment to materialize.

'I couldn't help but overhear,' he said. 'You and that detective—'

'Something's going on,' I admitted. 'Quinn knew Dean McClure.'

I don't know why, but I could picture Ness nodding. 'I knew that. Because of that note we found in the victim's office. But I also know that the night of the murder, he never bothered to mention that he was acquainted with the victim. Not to you. Not to his fellow cops.'

'Yeah, well, it gets worse.' I flopped down into my desk chair. 'Quinn's got . . . I mean, he doesn't exactly have it, it was more like it was just there. And maybe he doesn't even know it's there. That's possible, isn't it? Maybe somebody's messing with him.'

The flurry that was Ness had been hovering on the other side of my desk. Now, it fluttered over and right in front of my face.

'Explain,' the G-man ordered.

It was hard to get the words out, I mean what with the lump of panic in my throat. 'I found the murder weapon. It was at Quinn's,' I told him. 'It was . . . It was hidden in his closet.'

The cloud scuttled back across the desk and over to one of my guest chairs. 'It's just like I said, corruption within the department. It always comes down to corruption within the department.'

'And it's just like I said,' I told him in no uncertain terms, 'that isn't possible. There's got to be some other explanation. Quinn isn't covering up for anyone, and he's sure not the murderer.'

'So his explanation, what is it?'

Ah, that was the question, the one that had kept me awake and pacing all night. 'I thought he didn't care about McClure's complaint to his lieutenant. I thought it didn't mean anything.'

'But it did.'

I shrugged. 'That note was still in McClure's desk because Quinn never saw it. He hadn't searched the house yet. If he had seen it . . .' I remembered how Quinn had ripped up the complaint. 'Well, I'm guessing if he had seen it, it never would have been picked up as evidence because he would have destroyed it.'

'Exactly.'

I didn't like the way Ness said this so I made sure I gave him a sour look. 'I can wrap my brain around the complaint. It didn't mean anything. It couldn't have. But the murder weapon . . .' I swallowed hard.

'A fountain pen holder with a brass elephant on it.'

It wasn't a question, but I nodded anyway

'Al Capone collected elephants. Did you know that? He had elephants carved out of marble and ivory and wood. He had brass ones like the one on that pen holder. He liked elephants, but they always had to have their trunks raised in the air. He claimed that meant the elephants were good luck.'

'Not so much for him, huh? He's the one who ended up in prison.'

'He didn't think he ever would. He thought he was golden. Sounds like that detective of yours and Capone have some things in common.'

'Not a chance.' I made sure the glare that went along with this statement told Ness everything he needed to know. 'I told you before, Quinn is honest. Sometimes, too honest.'

'An honest man doesn't walk away from a crime scene with the murder weapon.'

'Which means there has to be some explanation. I mean, a really good explanation for what Quinn did.'

'I'd like to hear it.'

'So would I.' My mind made up, I grabbed my phone and called Quinn, but he didn't answer. I liked to think it was because he was busy, not because he was avoiding me. Without leaving a message, I tossed my phone on my desk. 'So where does this leave us?' I asked Ness.

'Still looking for answers. The only question is—'

'Where can we find some?'

Too antsy to sit still, I picked up my phone, all set to tuck it into my purse, and saw that *The Hit List,* the gangster collectors' newsletter, was still in there where I'd put it after the meeting the other night.

So was the roster of HITmen names, addresses, and phone numbers.

'I have suspects,' I said and though I was talking to Ness, I was already heading to the door. I didn't have a tour coming in to the cemetery until that afternoon and until then, I had enough time to follow a few leads, and enough stories to tell Ella to provide me with some cover for my absence. 'You'll see,' I told him on my way out the door. 'I'm going to figure out who really killed Dean McClure. And I'll show you that there's no way Quinn is mixed up in any of this.'

As it turned out, I found out when I called him that Nathan Armstrong was at work that day and rather than wait for his shift to be over, I met him at the gift shop at a park nature center. He was a big guy with wide shoulders and close-cropped gray hair. His short-sleeved Cleveland Metroparks polo shirt showed off bulging biceps and a stomach that was as flat as the proverbial pancake.

A guy who collected gangster-related memorabilia didn't strike me as the type who would be a nature lover, but then over the years of being PI to the dead, I'd learned that people are full of surprises.

'You said when you called that you're working with the cops?' Armstrong stuck out a hand and shook mine and I side-stepped a display of hoodies that featured pictures of songbirds on them and his question, too.

'Pepper Martin,' I said and if he noticed that I didn't answer him, he never let on. 'I just have a few questions.'

'Sure.' The gift shop was one of those out-doorsy sorts of place that I do everything in my power to avoid. Timber ceilings, wide windows that looked out over a deck and parkland beyond, a variety of small animals in aquariums: snakes and turtles and lizards. With a wave, he invited me over to a counter against a wall decorated with posters that featured photos of the park, and he slipped behind the counter and a display of stuffed toy critters.

'Cute,' I said, stroking a little fox with big eyes and fuzzy ears.

'If you like this sort of nature crap.'

'You don't? You work at a park.'

'Hey, a paycheck is a paycheck. I got my regular full time job over at the airport – I'm a baggage handler. And I got this gig part-time. It's the only way I can keep my wife happy. You know how it is. The HITmen told me you were at the last meeting so I guess you must understand. My wife gets all bent out of shape if I spend what she calls our living money on my gangster stuff.'

'Ah.' I did my best to give the single syllable all the importance it deserved and thanked my lucky stars that Armstrong had steered the conversation in the direction it needed to go. 'Gangster stuff. Like Dean McClure collected.'

The word Armstrong grumbled is best not repeated. 'I knew you'd want to talk about him. You asked the other guys, right? At the meeting the other night?'

'You weren't there.' It never hurts to get the ol' ducks in a row. 'Was there a reason you were avoiding the group?'

'A reason like I killed McClure and I wasn't ready to face the world?' He barked out a laugh that was as big as those bulging muscles of his. It bounced around the high, timbered ceiling for a couple seconds and startled the lizard in the nearest aquarium. It scuttled under a rock and, even though I knew it couldn't escape the aquarium, I took a step away from the scaly creature.

Rather than have Armstrong think I was as anxious for info as I actually was, I forced myself to look away from the lizard and eased into my line of questioning. 'Tell me about him.'

'McClure?' He grumbled that word again, and good thing

Armstrong kept his voice down because there was a grandma with a couple kids checking out the display of animal footprint pictures not too far away. Armstrong leaned over the counter and lowered his voice. 'The world is a better place without Dean McClure in it.'

It wasn't the first time I'd heard that opinion.

'The HITmen think he might have stolen something from you.'

'You found the report?' Since I didn't have the authority to even look for it, I was glad when Armstrong went right on. 'Then you know the details. The guys were over for a little Christmas cheer, and when they left' – his hands out at his sides, he lifted those massive shoulders and let his arms drop – 'my Al Capone arrest record was nowhere to be found.'

'And you think Dean McClure took it.'

'I don't think it, I know it. McClure, he was that kind of a greedy creep.'

'It's not in his house, not with the other things he has on display.'

'You searched, huh?' He actually seemed impressed by this information so I didn't want to burst his bubble and mention the breaking and entering. 'Well, it's not much of a surprise that the arrest record is nowhere to be seen, is it? He wouldn't just put it out on display. Not considering how he stole it.'

'But there are lots of other things in his collection.' Like I actually had to think about what I'd seen, I paused for a moment. 'Did you and McClure often bid against each other at auctions?'

'Me, McClure, everybody else in the collector community. We all want the same stuff, and there's not much of it to go around.'

'What about Angie Triccorio?' I asked him.

'Who?' he asked, but then the confusion cleared from his blue eyes. 'That crazy skinny dame? The one who was at the auction a couple weeks ago?'

'That's her. Why do you think she's crazy?'

'Because she wanted that stuff. You know, the stuff that belonged to Joey Ice Cube. And the way she was acting, she would have done anything to get it.'

I remembered what Angie had said about how she'd lost her temper when she talked to Dean. 'You're talking about when she and Dean McClure had that big fight.'

Armstrong pursed his lips. 'I was there the whole time, and I never saw a fight. No, no, that's not what I meant. I meant she was crazy because she was pleading with McClure before the auction. Begging him. She was crying so hard, her mascara was running down her cheeks.'

'But she wasn't yelling? She didn't lose her temper?'

'No yelling. In fact, it was kind of pathetic. I pulled her aside and I told her so. I told her the last thing she wanted to do was let McClure know how desperate she was to get that stuff. I told her that once he knew someone else wanted it—'

'McClure was sure to bid on it.'

'You got that right. That's just the kind of guy he was.'

It was no wonder no one liked Dean McClure. 'Do you know why McClure went to Chicago last weekend?' I asked Armstrong.

'I know he called and told me he was headed there.'

'Did he say what he was planning to do?'

'He didn't have to. Anytime McClure knew he had a line on something that would make the rest of us jealous, that's when he called.'

Just like the HITmen said.

'But this time . . .' Thinking, Armstrong drummed his fingers against the glass countertop and the motion-activated raccoon in the critter display started an electronic, high-pitched chatter. 'This time he was real excited, I mean more than he's ever been before, even when he went off to Vegas to buy Capone's phone from some collector out there. He did mention that he was going to stop by Mount Carmel Cemetery, but that, that was no big deal. McClure, he stopped there every time he went to Chicago.'

If I was half the cemetery geek Ella thought I was, I would have known more about other cemeteries and their residents, but Armstrong, he didn't know that. 'Why?' I asked him.

He lifted a silvery eyebrow. 'Why Mount Carmel? You don't know? That's where Al Capone is buried.'

I guess this shouldn't have surprised me. Except . . .

'He went to the cemetery every time he was in Chicago?' I asked Armstrong.

'You bet. Sometimes, McClure, he'd leave a bottle of booze on Capone's grave. Sometimes, he'd take pictures. I went with him once, back when we first met and before I knew what a jerk McClure was, and one time was enough for me. I swore I'd never go with him again.'

'Because . . .'

The way Armstrong shook his shoulders made me think that even after all this time, the thought made him suddenly cold. 'It was weird. McClure, he was weird. We went to the cemetery and yeah, I'll admit it, it was interesting and all. I mean, I'd never been there before, and it was kind of a kick, seeing Capone's grave. And there were flowers on that grave. Imagine that, after all these years, people still leave flowers. That time, McClure took a bottle of Sieben's Beer. Sieben's, that's—'

'The brewery Capone once owned. Yes, I know.'

I could tell by the little smile he aimed my way, Armstrong's opinion of me rose. 'Well, he put the bottle of beer there on Capone's headstone, and McClure, he took a couple pictures and so did I. And then I figured we were done. I mean, how much else can you do at a cemetery? It's really a pretty boring place.'

My opinion of him rose a tad, too, but that didn't distract me from the matter at hand. 'So there you were at Capone's grave, and McClure, what did he do?'

'He sat right down. Can you believe it? He sat right there on the ground next to the headstone,' Armstrong said, amazement in his voice. 'And it was like he was carrying on a conversation with the guy. He told Capone about all the stuff of his that he'd collected over the years, and if that wasn't weird enough, he even asked questions. Things like, *Was that phone I bought really from your headquarters at the Lexington Hotel?* And, *That collection of carved ivory elephants, I've read about it and wonder what happened to it. You don't know who has it, do you?*' Like he still couldn't believe it, Armstrong shook his head.

'I'll tell you what, Detective Martin,' he said, 'I'm just as serious about collecting as McClure ever was. It's history, you know? These things are history and there's stories attached to them, and it's all interesting stuff. But McClure, he sat there chatting away and every once in a while he'd stop and cock his head. You know, like he was' – Armstrong gave me a quick look designed to see how I'd react – 'I know it sounds crazy, but it was like Capone . . . it was like Capone was answering his questions.'

Since I knew more than most about things that go bump in the night, I doubted if this was true, but that didn't mean listening to Armstrong's story didn't send shivers up my spine. 'There's no such thing as ghosts,' I told him, because I figured that's what I was supposed to say.

'Well, I know that,' he replied, 'and you know that. But McClure? I'm not so sure he knew it.' Maybe Armstrong was doing his best to scatter the weird vibes that tingled through the air when he mentioned Capone's ghost, because he waved a hand in my direction. 'McClure was nuts, and he was a liar, and a thief.'

'And you had every reason to be angry at him.'

He shot me a look. 'You don't think I—'

'I don't know what to think, not until I have all my facts straight. Where were you Monday evening, Mr Armstrong?'

'You're asking me for an alibi?' I wondered if he really was surprised, or if he was just stalling for time. Either way, it didn't take Nathan Armstrong long to make up his mind. He reached into his back pocket, pulled out his wallet and slapped it on the counter, then rummaged through a small pile of receipts he pulled out of it.

'There.' He shoved a paper across the counter to me. 'That's where I was. That's my receipt from the hotel in Houston. You cops are good at checking these things. Go ahead, call the airlines and check my flights. I left here Friday evening and didn't get back until Tuesday afternoon. I was visiting my brother. So you see' – he whisked the receipt out from under my nose – 'I may have hated Dean McClure, and I might actually be a little happy that he's dead. But I sure as hell am not the one who killed him.'

ELEVEN

I would love to report that I made great progress with the case over the next few days except even I'm not that good of a liar. Sure, I spent the rest of Thursday (when I wasn't showing old folks around the cemetery) thinking about what I'd learned from Nathan Armstrong. That hotel receipt from Houston proved that he wasn't the one who'd killed Dean McClure, but truth be told, it didn't help a whole bunch. I eliminated a person I thought was a really good suspect, and that left me back where I'd started from when I first went to talk to Nathan.

And where I'd started from made me as nervous as hell.

Could Quinn have had something to do with McClure's murder?

A thousand times, I told myself no. A thousand times I told myself I'd just come out and ask him. But when I called (not a thousand times, honest), Quinn never answered. And when I stopped by his place that Thursday evening, he wasn't home and I was in no mood to wait around.

By Friday, my head was in a whirl and my stomach was tied in so many knots, it was like my Aunt Lucy (a former hippie and proud of it) was in there showing off her macramé skills.

I didn't like feeling that way. And I sure didn't like questioning the motives and honesty – and the guilt – of the man I loved.

With no other options, I did an online search for Angie Triccorio's address (not such a hard thing considering how singular her name was), told Ella I had a dentist appointment, and headed over to where I'd started out that morning – Little Italy, my own neighborhood.

Cleveland's Little Italy is a hometown gem. The neighborhood is right outside Garden View Cemetery (that is not the gem part), and was established back in the day because a fancy cemetery needed fancy monuments and fancy monuments could only be cut into granite and marble by skilled craftsmen and many of those skilled craftsmen were Italian.

They came to this country and they brought along their families and their traditions. The neighborhood they established is still vital and hopping, a haven for foodies, a place where the entire city parties in the summer for the Feast of the Assumption, and in my case, home sweet home. Not because I had Italian ancestors or because I was much of a foodie, but because rents in the area were pretty reasonable, and when my dad went to prison, I was all about looking for a bargain.

As long as I was going to Angie's and staying that close to home, I parked in my usual place behind my building and thanked my lucky stars that I had a reserved spot. It was a gorgeous Friday afternoon with the sun shining and temps high enough that I didn't need a coat. The sky was blue, and Clevelanders were ready to shake off their winter doldrums. The neighborhood was jumping. The cafes had tables and chairs set up outside. The art galleries displayed their wares along the sidewalk. Tourists abounded, and the bars had their music cranked. The smooth tones of Frank Sinatra accompanied me on my walk over to East 123rd Street.

Angie lived at the end of the street and that street—

I stopped as I neared the house and groaned. Was my life destined to always end up in the same place?

Angie's backyard butted up against the northern edge of Garden View Cemetery.

I ignored the symbolism, or the curse, whichever it happened to be, and rang the bell.

Since Angie looked green and like she was going to throw up at any minute, I was surprised she made it all the way to the door to answer.

'I'm ready,' she said. She stepped back from the door to allow me inside and for reasons I couldn't fathom, she held both arms out in front of her. 'You can take me now. I'm' – she swallowed so hard, I heard the gulp, and a tear cascaded down her cheek – 'I'm ready.'

In situations like this, I have found that it's always wise to play it slow and careful. If I just came out and admitted I didn't have a clue what she was talking about, I might miss out on some interesting information.

Playing it slow and cool, I stepped farther into a living room with blue carpeting, a nondescript brown couch, and a gray recliner that leaned to one side.

It looked as if Angie and I shopped for furniture at the same Goodwill store.

'There's no hurry,' I told her. 'You look a little shaky. You want to sit down for a while?'

She sank onto the recliner and, since she was facing the window that looked out over the street, the late morning light revealed smudges of sleeplessness under her eyes. 'I knew you'd come eventually. I mean, I could tell when I met you over at McClure's that you're a smart woman. I knew you'd figure it out.'

'I am smart,' I admitted. 'But I don't know everything. Nobody does, do they? How about if you fill me in on the details.'

She brushed the back of one shaky hand over her cheeks. 'You mean about me. Me and McClure.'

'Yeah. That's what I mean.' I settled myself on the couch. 'You said you lost your temper with him, Angie. But the people who saw you and McClure at the auction said you were anything but mad. You did your best to be nice to McClure, to try and get him to see why it was important for you to win the auction for Joey Ice Cube's things.'

She nodded, and that stringy hair of hers drooped over her shoulders, sadder looking than ever that day. 'I tried so hard. I wanted him to understand, to see things from my point of view. He wouldn't listen. He just wouldn't listen. What kind of man is that cruel?'

This I couldn't say, but I did know that what Angie had to say lined up with what Nathan Armstrong had told me. 'The auction was six weeks ago,' I said. 'And if you didn't lose your temper with McClure then, when did it happen, Angie? Did you see him some time after the auction?'

'McClure . . .' She sucked in a breath that trembled through her scrawny body. 'McClure died just this past Monday.'

Was she saying what I thought she was saying?

A little thread of hope tangled around my heart. This was what I wanted, wasn't it? A lead that would stand up, one that made sense, and pointed me in a direction – any direction but the direction of the detective who was the love of my life.

'Are you telling me—'

'It was Monday. You know that. Of course you know it was Monday.' She sniffled and clutched her bony fingers together at her waist. 'You knew all along, didn't you? That's why you came back here today.'

'I suspected,' I said. Oh, how I could cover when I had to! 'I wanted to make sure you had a chance to tell your side of the story.'

'That's really nice. It's not what I expected from you cops.'

'It's the least we can do,' I told her, playing the good cop role for all I was worth. 'As long as you're willing to tell me the truth.'

She hung her head, and when she spoke, her voice was so low, I had to lean forward to hear her. 'I went over to McClure's on Monday evening.'

'The night of the murder.'

'Yes.' She dared to look up at me through the tangle of her dark hair. 'I . . . we . . . all I wanted to do was talk to him, to explain again, you know? He remembered me. He knew what I wanted.'

'And he told you no again.'

'I offered him more money than he paid at the auction!' Her voice high and tight, Angie popped out of her chair and went over to a picture of a man and a woman that hung on the wall. He had a huge mustache. She was wearing a trim, dark suit with a nipped waist and a slim skirt, and carrying a bouquet of flowers. Angie laid a hand on the frame of the picture 'This is the wedding picture of Carmella and Joseph Triccorio, my great-grandparents, and when I left here last Monday evening, I stopped right here, right where I'm standing now, and I made him a promise. I told him I was coming home with all those things that had belonged to him. I' – she drew in a shuddering breath – 'I let him down.'

It seemed counterproductive to remind her that, at this point, he probably didn't much care so instead I said, 'Let me guess, when McClure turned down your latest offer, that's when you lost your temper.'

'I tried not to. Honest! But when that bastard refused to listen—' Her hands curled into fists. 'I just couldn't help myself. I looked at my great-grandfather's birth certificate sitting there in the house of this stranger, and it was like my head exploded. That's when I did it.'

My blood buzzed, and I had to force myself to keep my mouth shut. I didn't want to distract Angie from what I knew she was about to say.

'I popped him in the nose,' she announced. 'There was an awful lot of blood.'

I remembered what Quinn had told me, that when the crime scene techs turned McClure over, there was blood on his face. 'And once you punched him, that's when you picked up the fountain pen holder, right?'

Like I was suddenly talking Chinese, Angie blinked at me in wonder. 'What fountain pen holder?'

'You might not have known what it was,' I said, because let's face it, I wouldn't have known it was a fountain pen holder, either, because these days, who would? 'It was about this high.' I held my hands about a foot apart. 'And there was a brass elephant on it. The whole thing sat on a heavy marble base.'

She shook her head. 'Why would I want that? It never belonged to Joey. Are you saying you think I stole it?'

Now I was the one getting confused. I rose to my feet, the better to intimidate Angie into telling the truth. 'You used the fountain pen holder to bash in McClure's head.'

'No! I never did. I just punched him, and his nose started bleeding. It bled and it bled and the sight of all that blood, it made me feel like I was going to puke. That's when I turned around and ran right out of the house.'

'You didn't kill him?' I asked her.

'Well, sure I did. Only I didn't know it at the time, I mean, not until I went over there on Tuesday to talk to him again and you told me he was dead. And that's when I realized I must have hurt him more than I thought I did, that I killed him. I never meant to do it, but I couldn't help myself. I punched

McClure in the nose and he bled to death. That's why you showed up right? Go ahead.' Again, she held her wrists out to me, her pointy chin firm and her scrawny shoulders thrown back. 'I know what I did was wrong. Slap the cuffs on me. Arrest me.'

I won't bother to report how Angie reacted when I told her that McClure's death did not result from a good whack to the nose. To say she was relieved and grateful and teary is putting it mildly. I had to pry her arms from around me to escape her appreciative hugs.

While Angie was thrilled, what I'd learned from her left me in a bad, bad place.

It didn't help that the next day was Saturday. Yes, the dreaded Saturday.

The bridal fair.

Every time I think about it, I get queasy. For a whole lot of reasons. A hotel filled with vendors eager to sell their wares, brides-to-be (most of them younger than me) and over-anxious mothers (in my opinion, mine took the cake) was not the best place for a woman who might be almost-engaged to a might-be murderer.

I soldiered on.

But then, there was a bar, and a Bloody Mary on a Saturday morning seemed like the thing to do.

'Oh, look at that!' My mother and I were hemmed in on all sides by booths of photographers who wanted to create the perfect memories for me and florists who wanted to make my decorating dreams come true and bridal shops whose smiling representatives told me in no uncertain terms that they would make my wedding into the fairy tale I'd always imagined.

As if.

That being said, when Barb gushed for the umpteenth time since we'd entered the bridal fair, I wasn't exactly sure what the gushing was all about.

I thought it over while I sipped my Bloody Mary.

'Look at what?' I asked her.

'That dress, of course.' She made a beeline for a mother of the bride display and a little number with a deep V-neck, a slinky purple undersheath and an over-dress studded with multi-colored sequins in a fishscale design. Barb touched a loving finger to the scalloped hem that hit the mannequin it was modeled on well above the knee. 'Wouldn't this make a statement!'

'It certainly would.' Since my drink glass was clutched in one hand, I grabbed her by the shoulder with the other and propelled her on to the next vendor exhibit and wondered what had happened to the woman I had grown up with, the one who'd always had such terrific taste. Maybe those years in the Florida sun had fried her brain. 'We might want to think about something with a little less bling,' I told her.

'Well, of course.' Mom sipped a mimosa, but I don't think that accounted for the two spots of bright color in her cheeks that matched the vibrant red of her (and my) hair. 'I get it, Pepper. I really do. It's going to be your special day and I have to play second fiddle.'

Just as she knew it would, the comment hit me right in the heart. 'You'll never play second fiddle to anyone,' I reminded her. 'And I don't expect you to. I just think that something a little more understated . . .' For the first time since we'd entered the sixth circle of hell, I actually looked around with interest. Another bridal shop had a display nearby, and I piloted Mom over and to a rack of dresses that seemed more in keeping with the persona of a sixty-something mother whose husband had once done time in federal prison and whose daughter talked to the dead.

'Gray is pretty,' I told her, my hand on an age-appropriate dress with a long skirt and a lace top. 'It would look good with your coloring.'

'Well, that all depends on what color your attendants are wearing.' She gave me an expectant look and, since Mom is barely five feet tall, she had to look up at me to do it. 'You have thought about bridesmaids, haven't you? And a maid of honor?'

I hadn't. Just like I hadn't really thought about a wedding. Just like I couldn't possibly think about a wedding now when I wasn't sure what was going on with Quinn.

My sigh would have given me away if I didn't follow it up

with a quick, 'I really don't have that many friends. The girls I hung out with in school—'

'All dumped you like their mothers dumped me when Dad went up the river.' Was that bitterness I heard in Barb's voice? It made me love her all the more, in spite of the fact that she'd bought into this whole bridal fair nonsense. 'With friends like that,' she said, 'you don't need enemies. And why would you want any of them as bridesmaids, anyway?' She glanced through the rack of understated dresses. 'There's always Ella and her girls,' she said.

Had I really come to that point in my life when the only person I could find to stand up for me at the altar was my boss and her kids?

I groaned and sipped and when my plastic glass was empty, I tossed it in the nearest trashcan.

'You're not making this any better,' I told my mother.

'Really?' She smiled because she didn't believe me. 'Well, I think this is the most fun I've had in a long time. So' – she finished her drink, too, got rid of her cup, and wound her arm through mine – 'if not Ella, is there someone else? Maybe a . . . you know . . .' She glanced all around but really, the women who chattered around us like a barnyard of chickens weren't paying any attention, anyway. 'Maybe a ghost.'

I pictured Jean Tanneman in pink taffeta. 'I don't think so, Mom. That would be pretty hard to explain to our guests.'

'You've got a point there.' Mom and I strolled past a display of white roses, orchids as big as dinner plates, and some weird spiky flowers in colors that reminded me of Skittles. 'We'll worry about attendants another time, and like you said, there's no hurry. Maybe by the time you and Quinn set a date, you'll have some new friends.'

This did not seem likely.

Either setting the date or finding friends who would understand when I told them I saw dead people.

Mom pulled me into a quick hug. 'It's not easy, this Gift of yours, is it?'

'You got that right.' We were at a point in the hotel where the vendor booths went up a hallway in one direction and down the hallway in the other. There was an open area where the hallways converged, and a few plush chairs for weary fair-goers. I dropped into the closest one and slapped a hand on the arm of the one next to it, just so some other footsore mother-of-the-bride didn't get any ideas.

'So what is happening, Pepper?' my mother asked and slipped into the saved chair. 'You said you had a case. Does it involve' – she mouthed the word – 'ghosts?'

'It involves ghosts, it involves a dead guy. It involves a dead guy who delivered a bottle to me at the cemetery right before he died and I can't for the life of me figure out why.'

'Hmmmmm.' Barb drummed her fingers against the arm of the chair. It was upholstered in pink-and-white-striped brocade that wasn't particularly appealing but seemed appropriate to the occasion. 'I never realized this PI business could be so tough. But no matter.' Cheered, she sat up and smoothed a hand over the black skirt she wore with a lightweight green sweater. 'Once we get some other cases, ones that don't involve ghosts, things will look up. Your dad and I are really looking forward to joining you in our PI firm.'

'I'm not so sure about this whole PI business. It just seems to get me in trouble.'

Barb made a face. 'I don't like the sound of that. But by trouble, you mean . . .'

'Ella tried to run me over the other day,' I told her and even though I still thought it was plenty weird, I dismissed the whole thing when my mom's face went pale. 'I'm sure it was an accident. You know Ella, she gets distracted so easily.'

'Well, let's hope that's all it is. I can't imagine Ella would ever do anything so terrible. How could she be your matron of honor if she tried to run you down?'

'Exactly, and exactly why it's weird. And then there's . . .' Honestly, I had no intention of baring my soul, not to the woman who just about fainted from apoplexy when one of the young models who was part of the show came by in a bridal gown dripping in white lace. But no one else knew I talked to ghosts, no one but my dad who had wisely chosen to stay home even though my mom said she'd tried to bring him along.

And Quinn, of course.

'There's something going on,' I told my mother, who heard the worry in my voice and turned concerned eyes on me. 'Something weird is happening with Quinn.'

'You don't think he's going to call off the wedding, do you?'

'Not what I'm talking about,' I told her. 'It's more serious than that.'

This, I think, took her some time to work her way through. For one thing, she was in that crazy state of mind where her daughter's wedding was the only thing she could think about. And for another . . .

Barb's eyes went wide. 'You don't mean . . .' She clutched the arm of the chair. 'Are you telling me it has something to do with this case you're working on?'

'It does. At least I think it does. He's acting strange, Mom. For one thing, he knew the victim and he never bothered to tell me about it after I found the body. For another . . .' I could barely make myself say it. 'He took the murder weapon from the scene. I found it hidden in his bedroom. Between that and Ella, well, I don't know. I just can't figure any of it out. It reminds me of that time back in Chicago that I told you about. You remember, when my friend Dan's dead wife's ghost showed up and possessed me so she could use my body.'

Barb chafed her hands up and down her arms. 'It gives me the willies every time I think about it. You could have been hurt, honey. I hate thinking about it.'

'So do I. But every time I think about how strange everyone is acting—'

'Well, it isn't everyone, is it? And really, just because a ghost possessed you . . . I mean, that was just you, right? And it was probably because of your special Gift. And this is Ella and Quinn, and they don't have your Gift, and it doesn't make any sense that a ghost would want to possess either one of them, and it makes even less sense to think that a ghost would possess two people at once. I don't know very much about the paranormal, but that doesn't seem possible.'

'You're right.' I sloughed off the worry that had been nibbling away at my composure these past days. 'There has to be some other explanation. Some logical explanation.'

'And you'll find it. Believe me!' Barb stood up and I did,

too. 'Now, how about if we do a taste test on some of those cupcakes we saw earlier? I'm thinking the sugar will improve both our moods.'

She was right. The sugar worked wonders and so did the fact that I displayed enough patience for Mom to try on not two but three different mother-of-the-bride outfits. She ruled out the pantsuit immediately, but she liked both a long black skirt that came with a sparkling jacket in a color like paprika and a tea-length flower print dress. She took the card of the sales rep at that booth and promised she'd stop in.

'Your turn now,' she said.

We were in front of a double-wide display of bridal gowns and I automatically took a step back. 'I don't know, Mom. I don't think I'm in the mood.'

'Oh, come on.' Mom dragged me into the display with its plush, champagne-colored carpeting and a crystal chandelier overhead. Soft music played from an iPod. 'This is going to cheer you right up and it will make you forget all about that horrible gown you had the last time you almost got married.'

In the great scheme of things, trying on dresses should have improved my mood. After all, bridal gowns were pretty much just fancy (and pricey) party dresses, and there wasn't much I liked better than trying on fun dresses. Still, the weight of my worries felt like a physical thing. Lucky for me, I found a rack of dresses toward the far end of the display and a spot behind it between the dresses and the back wall where I could be alone. With Mom on the other side of it, I took a moment to breathe deep and try to control the stress I could feel building into the mother of all headaches.

'Well, there you are.' Mom found me, and to make her think I was actually enjoying myself, I pulled a gown off the rack. It wasn't bad, actually, an ivory dress with a satin ribbon for a belt and some tasteful beading at the neck and on the skirt.

'Pretty,' Mom said, and she ran a hand over the gown. She slipped the satin belt from its loops and ran it through her fingers. 'You know, Pepper,' she said, 'sometimes there are things we just can't help. We don't have a choice. Sometimes we have to do things. I hope you understand that. This is one of those times.'

There is no way in any universe I could have moved fast enough to get out of her way because, let's face it, there is no way in any universe I could have imagined that my mother would have wrapped that satin belt around my neck and pulled tight.

'I'm sorry, my sweet,' she crooned, her face red and her eyes bulging and that satin belt crushing my windpipe. 'I'm so sorry, but you have to die.'

TWELVE

No matter how many times I tried to block the memory from my mind, I couldn't get rid of it.

Barb Martin—

She of the Ann Taylor clothing and the porcelain skin I had always been so grateful I'd inherited.

The woman who could have kept any one thing when her life was auctioned off to pay Dad's federal tax bill and had chosen her Marc Jacobs bag.

A person who was kind to small children and animals, who had a great sense of humor and a sweet smile and terrific taste.

My mother tried to kill me.

Over the next thirty-six hours, the scene played over and over again in my imagination and by Sunday night even though my head still throbbed and my stomach was still topsy-turvy and my throat was sore inside and out, I couldn't help myself, I saw it all again, happening as it had happened back at the bridal fair – in slow motion and colors so vivid, they made my eyes ache.

I thought about how in that one electrifying instant when I realized that my mom wanted me dead, I'd been grateful for the height I'd inherited from my father's side of the family and how that, at least, gave me the physical advantage over my short, slim mother.

I'm not sure where my chutzpah comes from, maybe my Aunt Charlotte or my Grandma Martin, the women my mother once told me had also chatted it up with ghosts, and who'd passed their questionable Gift down to me.

Wherever it came from, both the fact that I tower over my mother and my tendency to be anything but a shrinking violet came in handy. As soon as my total, complete, and absolute surprise faded into fear and panic, as soon as it hit me that I couldn't breathe, I reared back and braced my hands against Barb's arms.

She was surprisingly strong, and as determined as any opponent I'd ever faced.

I struggled to claw her hands away from my neck.

She hung on.

I fought to rip the satin belt away.

She wound it tighter and pulled harder.

Stars burst behind my eyes, and I would have screamed for help if I could have gotten out anything more than a pathetic gurgle.

And through it all, the only thing I could think was that my mother – my slightly crazy, sweet, funny mother – was determined to see me die.

I blacked out, then snapped back to, and found myself staring into Barb's eyes, and that's when I was more afraid than ever.

There was no one in there looking back at me.

The next day, the memory still filled me with horror, and I rubbed my hands up and down my arms to try and keep from shivering. It didn't help. Nothing could erase the memory of my mom's eyes – there was no sign of a soul in them.

That did it. Now and then. Now, it sent me off on another crying jag. Back at the bridal fair, it officially scared the wits out of me and gave me the extra shot of adrenalin I desperately needed. I gathered my strength, grabbed her around the waist, and did the unthinkable – I lifted my mom out of her size-six sling-back pumps and flung her as far from me as I could.

She landed against that rack of bridal gowns that had shielded what just happened from the crowd, and though she is not a big woman, she was moving at a pretty good clip. The rack went down. So did Mom. By the time our fellow bridal fair attendees realized there was something happening and gathered around, curious and bug-eyed, Barb was on the floor in a pool of silk and lace and I had unwrapped that scrap of satin from around my throat, breathing hard and wondering what the hell had just happened.

My legs were jelly but I managed to stagger over and kneel next to where she lay, her eyes closed and her breathing shallow. Sure, I was the one who'd just pitched her into a display of expensive gowns. Sure, she was the one who'd told me she was sorry but I had to die. But she was my mom.

'Are you all right?' I put a hand to her cheek. It was icy. 'Mom!' I yelled for someone to call EMS which shouldn't have been all that hard considering how many people had their phones out and were taking pictures of what they probably figured was either an accident or the result of too many mimosas.

I twined my fingers through Barb's. 'Mom, it's me. Can you hear me?'

'Pepper?' Her voice was no more than a whisper, and her eyes fluttered open. There was a spark in them that had been missing just a minute before and, realizing it, I let go a breath that felt like fire in my throat.

'Mom, are you OK?'

She tried to sit up. No easy thing considering two sales clerks were already flapping around us, clucking about their merchandise, plucking gowns off the floor.

When they tried to pluck the one Barb was on top of, I warned them away with a look and put my arm around her shoulders to help her sit up.

'What . . .' She glanced at the crowd gathered around us and the ruins of the display. 'What happened?'

My throat hurt bad enough, I didn't need to add a knot of emotion to it. I swallowed and winced. 'You don't remember?'

Someone had the good sense to bring Mom a cup of water, and she sipped carefully. 'We were looking at the gowns and then . . .' Her voice faded. Her eyes clouded. 'I must have fainted,' she said. 'That's what happened, right? I . . . I fainted.'

I didn't have the heart to tell her any different.

The paramedics who showed up were kind and attentive. They didn't find a thing wrong with Mom and, of course, I turned up my shirt collar to hide any sign of the attack and never breathed a word about how my windpipe was just about crushed. I took Mom home and Dad put her to bed. When I called on Sunday night, that's where she still was.

'She says she can't sleep, that she's got a really bad headache,' Dad told me. 'I'm thinking it's a migraine, but I've already called and gotten her in to see her doctor tomorrow morning just to be sure. You said she just blacked out and landed in the middle of that clothing rack?'

Yeah, it was what I said. But then, it was pretty hard to tell my dad the truth when the truth was so ugly even I still had trouble believing it.

My mother tried to kill me.

The thought settled and I got chilled all the way down to my bones. I told Dad I'd check in again later and realized after I ended the call that it was already later. It was long past dark and I hadn't bothered to turn on the lamp next to the couch. I did and groaned when the light hit my eyes. I groaned some more when I realized how much groaning made my throat hurt.

I dragged myself into the kitchen and put on water for tea, then took a gander at myself in the bathroom mirror. Forget my messy hair and my red-rimmed eyes! On the outside, my throat looked as bad as it felt on the inside, and I wondered if I had a turtleneck that would cover the band of raw flesh and bruises.

I would have to make up some excuse for my raspy voice and my swollen eyes and my red nose when I went to work the next day, just like I would somehow have to come to grips with what had happened and, in doing so, figure out what I was going to do about it.

My tea made, I took it back to the living room and flopped onto the couch. If I could close my eyes for more than a minute without seeing Barb's face, red and ugly and dead set on destroying me . . .

I guess I fell asleep, because I woke up with a start when my phone rang.

It was Quinn.

I didn't answer.

He'd know instantly that something was wrong – he had those kind of instincts – and I wasn't ready to tell the story.

I checked the clock, and though I'd slept only thirty minutes, even that little bit of rest had helped some of the horror dissolve from my brain and with it, my inability to think past what had happened.

In that moment, I was reminded of the time I'd told my mom about, when Dan Callahan's first wife (deader than a doornail and a bitch besides) had possessed me. Could something like that have happened to Mom? All this, of course, made me think about Dan. Back when I first met him, I thought Dan was a medical researcher, but I found out soon enough that the cute, shaggy-haired guy was actually a paranormal researcher who not only believed in my Gift but wanted to find out how it worked. He knew more about the paranormal than any other person – any other living person – than I knew.

That was the moment when I knew exactly what I had to do.

Because there was definitely something weird and spooky going on, and I needed help.

Dan's help.

When I called into work on Monday morning and told Ella I had the flu, I hardly had to fake it. My nose was stuffy, my voice was gravelly, and since I'd spent most of the night crying off and on, I sounded like hell.

I forced myself to take a shower, to eat something (toast, and it almost didn't stay down), to get into my car and drive to the hospital where I'd first met Dan after I fell at the cemetery, hit my head on Gus Scarpetti's mausoleum, and started seeing ghosts.

From the outside, Dan and I looked like old friends, but if we were, my stomach wouldn't have been fluttering and my knees twitching as I made my way through the maze of hospital hallways to his office. Dan and I, see, might have been on our way to a serious relationship at one time if not for that aforementioned dead wife of his. Oh yes, and his second wife, a woman who'd tried to kill me when I was working a case out in New Mexico.

So much for Dan's taste in women.

What he lacked in judgment, Dan made up for with his unexpected martial arts skills, an unwavering belief in the paranormal, and maybe – I crossed my fingers – enough experience with the strange and the odd and the unnatural that he could help me figure out what was going on.

I found the office door with *Dan Callahan, PhD* printed on the sign in front of it and knocked.

There was no answer.

This didn't stop me, the door wasn't locked and I stepped inside and—

'Oh!' I pulled up short; there was a man in a wheelchair sitting next to Dan's desk sorting through a pile of papers, and that was unfortunate. Not about the wheelchair, about the fact that I didn't have a few minutes alone to dig around Dan's desk and see what he'd been up to in the year or so since I'd last talked to him.

'I'm looking for Dan Callahan,' I said.

The man spun his chair around so that he was facing me instead of the desk. He was in his thirties, with the kind of face I bet had tempted many an angel to sin, close-cropped dark hair, eyes the color of strong brandy, a day's worth of whiskers, and a smile that not only could charm the birds out of the trees, but would have them dancing to his tune.

'Caleb Beauchamp.' He stuck out a hand and I shook it and tried to place an accent that dripped Spanish moss and Tabasco sauce. 'And who did you say you are?'

'Pepper Martin.' I didn't realize our fingers were still entwined until I felt mine burning. I pulled my hand away. 'I'm looking for Dan, and—'

'You're Pepper Martin? Ooohwee!' He tipped back his head and let out a laugh. 'You are not what I was expecting.'

Someone had obviously been talking about me, and it was just as obvious who that someone was.

'If he's around . . .' I glanced around the office. It was small and cluttered with books and files and Dan's many diplomas lined up on the walls. 'There's something I need to talk to him about. It's really important.'

'Maybe I can help you.'

Caleb had powerful arms and they were covered with tattoos: a skull, an eagle, a lightning bolt, the words *Semper Fi.* He was dressed in jeans and a black T-shirt that had seen better days. Graduate student, I decided instantly, and I'd bet anything he thought Dan was exactly what I'd thought Dan was when I'd first met him: a scatterbrained scientist who studied peoples' heads.

'It's kind of personal,' I said, before I realized he was bound to take that completely the wrong way. 'Well, not exactly personal, not like that. It's personal in a professional way, and I can't discuss it with anyone except Dan. I don't know you and—'

'It might not be a bad idea,' he said.

'You mean for you to find Dan.'

'I mean for you fixin' to get to know me.'

The smile I gave him was tight around the edges. 'If you could find Dan for me, I'd appreciate it.'

That smile of his never wavered. Neither did the very level look he gave me. Or the spark of amusement in those dark eyes of his. He sat perfectly still for one second, two, then excused himself and wheeled around me and toward the door.

'If you wait, I'll see if I can find him,' he said, and Caleb left the office.

Fine by me. It gave me a chance to glance over Dan's desk at the same time I shook off the discomfort that prickled over my skin for no good reason.

I twitched the thought away, bent my ear to make sure I didn't hear anyone coming, and did a quick sort through of the papers Caleb had been looking through when I walked in. There wasn't much of any use: a couple reports written in scientist-ese, a folder that contained someone's brain scan, a desk calendar that didn't have anything filled in on any of the dates – nothing for the coming months, nothing since the first of the year.

I had just slapped that date book shut and put it back where I found it when I realized Caleb was sitting in the doorway.

'Dan wouldn't mind,' I said by way of explanation. 'We're old friends.'

'That's not the way I heard the story.' He rolled farther into the office. 'Dan says—'

'What?'

'You're a little defensive, aren't you?' His grin was as hot as lava and, no, I don't know exactly how hot that is and I bet the big brains there around the hospital do, but I don't much care how much smarter they are than me. 'Don't worry. Dan, he's not the type who kisses and tells.'

I crossed my arms over my chest and leaned back against the desk, trading Caleb nonchalant smile for nonchalant smile. 'That's a good thing. Because there's nothing to tell.'

'He was right about you!' He checked me out slow and easy, toes to tip of head, then back down again. 'He told me you were pretty. He forgot to mention the red nose, though.'

I hated myself for it, but I automatically slapped a hand to my nose and cursed myself for not doing a better job with my makeup before I left the house.

'You have troubles, cher? Something you need to talk about?'

'Yeah. To Dan. He's the only one who can help me.'

'Lucky man.'

'Can we just get serious for a minute, please? If I was looking for lame pick-up lines, I'd go hang out in one of the downtown bars.'

'Was it lame?' Caleb's face twisted with regret. 'You'll have to pardon me, ma'am. I'm a little out of practice.'

'With any luck, you'll find an audience that's a little more appreciative.'

'Your mouth to God's ear. Though I will admit, I'm a little partial to redheads. It's all that fire.'

I shot him a look that would have leveled a lesser man. 'And all that temper. Not to mention impatience.'

'Are you in that much of a hurry?' When he rolled over to the other side of the desk, I had to stand up and turn around to see him. 'That's too bad. I was going to suggest lunch.'

'I'm not hungry.'

'On account of the . . .' He wiggled one finger in my direction to indicate my raw, red nose. 'I understand, and it don' madda. We'll do lunch another time. Or dinner. I make a mean pot of beans and rice.'

'I won't be hungry then, either,' I told him at the same time a voice inside my head reminded me that if I didn't do something soon about the strange happenings in my life, I might not be alive whenever then was. 'I don't eat much.'

Like he didn't believe me, he had the nerve to pucker up and wrinkle his forehead and, no matter how cool I tried to play it, I couldn't help the spurt of annoyance that shot through me.

'Not criticizing!' he said, one hand out as if to stop me coming at him (which I wasn't going to do, but then, he was in a wheelchair and that wouldn't have been fair). 'I just gotta say that a woman with a little bit of a shape to her is way more attractive than those skinny little sticks a man sees everywhere. If I offended you' – he bent from the waist – 'I beg your pardon.'

I was just about to accept the apology when he added, 'But I don't take back what I said, or what I think. Dan might have talked about you, but he forgot to mention that you're one beautiful woman.'

'Dan must have better things to think about.'

His laugh filled the office. 'You think? Some of us around here wonder if he thinks at all. Everyone's pretty sure he's the absentminded professor.'

'He can be.'

'Still, women find him attractive. Maybe because he is so scatterbrained.' As if he actually had to think about this, Caleb tipped his head. 'Do you think scatterbrained is attractive?'

'I never said I thought Dan was attractive.'

'Touché.' His laugh was easy and honest. 'Other women have. You know he was married a couple times.'

'You obviously know the story.'

'His first wife was killed in Chicago. His second wife had an unfortunate accident on a mesa out in New Mexico. She was involved in some sneaky stuff, dealing in stolen antiquities, and I hear nobody suspected her except some tall drink of water with red hair from Cleveland who happened to be out there at the time.'

'I'm surprised Dan talks about it,' I said. 'He's not exactly the type to open up to people.'

Caleb shrugged those broad shoulders of his. 'We're colleagues.'

It was the perfect opening, both for what I wanted and to get me out of a conversation that felt more uncomfortable by the moment. 'And you told your colleague I was waiting for him?'

'No.'

When my mouth fell open, he grinned.

'Dan isn't here,' Caleb said. 'Not right now, anyway. But here . . .' He grabbed the top sheet from a notepad on the desk and scrawled something on it.

'Eight o'clock tonight,' he said, his smile gone and his expression suddenly stony. 'Be there.'

THIRTEEN

Like it or not, I've learned a few things about Cleveland history since I started my job at Garden View Cemetery. Never interested in the past, I'd pretty much been swallowed up whole by it, and not just by the dead I'd seen and talked to, but by those thousands of Garden View residents whose last resting places I saw each and every day I went to work.

When I took visitors on tours, I had to know who was who and what was what and why it was important (well, Ella said it was important) so people could get to know more about these dead peoples' lives.

History went along with the package, and history told me that the building I'd been sent to at eight o'clock that Monday night was the city's famous Terminal Tower.

Here's all anyone ever needs to know: the Terminal Tower is a Cleveland icon, fifty-two stories high and smack dab at the heart of what we call Public Square, the center of downtown. Once upon a time when it was built (back in the 1920s), it was the tallest building in the country except for the Empire State Building. It was built by two brothers, the Van Sweringens, who back in the day were movers and shakers in the city and had a few billion dollars to their names. Originally, the tower was part of a huge complex that stood on top of a railroad station, but these days, there are no more trains in and out except for the city's local rapid transit cars. There's a mall at and below street level that includes shops and restaurants and offices in the tower.

I stepped out of the elevator on the tenth floor of the Terminal Tower and glanced around. Like pretty much every other office building I'd ever been in, this one was predictable, and except for the marble floors which said something about the age of the building, pretty much uninspired. The walls were white, the offices I passed had glass doors that led into reception areas and signs outside that said they housed things like attorneys and engineers and architects.

The scrawled note Caleb had handed me told me to go to the end of the hallway and that's where I found myself, convinced that Dan had opened some sort of private practice (for what, studying peoples' brains?) and that, as usual, he was working crazy hours.

Unlike the other offices I'd seen, this one had a solid wood door, and it was locked. I knocked and got no answer.

Just as I raised my hand to knock again, the door was pulled open just enough for me to see Caleb standing on the other side.

Standing being the operative word in that sentence.

'You're early,' he growled.

'I found a parking space faster than I thought I would.'

He wasn't listening. But then, his head was bent and he was looking over his shoulder, obviously trying to catch something coming from another room. A second later, he yelled, 'Who is Mel Brooks?'

I can be excused for being just a tad confused. 'He makes movies, right?' I asked.

But again, Caleb wasn't listening. Balanced on each of the canes he held, the kind that had braces that went around his forearms, he called out again, 'What is a sylph?'

'Uh . . .' I'm not exactly sure what I was going to say and I guess it's a good thing because he shouted, 'What is tweed?'

'I can come in, right?'

I think he actually forgot I was there, because he flinched and turned to me. From somewhere behind him, I heard the distant, droning sound of a car commercial. 'Sure, yeah.' He stepped back and opened the door all the way. 'Come on in.'

I didn't. Not right then, anyway, but it's not like I didn't have a good excuse. With the door fully open and Caleb standing back, I toed the doorway, totally stunned and feeling like Dorothy must have when she plunked down into a Technicolor Oz.

I looked back the way I had come, at the white walls and the offices arranged like soldiers, one after the other. I turned to Caleb and the hallway that stretched behind him for what looked like miles. The entire hallway was paneled in rich, dark wood, including the ceiling. The furniture was old and substantial, there was a mahogany table against the wall with sumptuous wingchairs on either side of it. There were silver sconces on the wall and, overhead, a crystal chandelier threw patterns of light all around.

Caleb closed the hallway door and, each step slow and obviously painful, he turned and disappeared into the first room down the hallway where I heard the sounds of a TV.

Still stunned, I followed along and found myself in a room with a fireplace on one wall and windows on another that provided a million-dollar view of downtown Cleveland.

It turned out the view didn't interest Caleb in the least.

The commercial break was over, and *Jeopardy* was back on.

'Who is the Duke of Wellington? What is a flyby? What is Dublin?'

Completely ignoring me, he answered each of the show's questions rat-a-tat, long before any of the contestants even had time to ring their buzzers and attempt to answer.

'What is the bourgeoisie? Who is Mel Tormé?'

'Is Dan here?' I dared to ask.

I guess he did remember I was there because he shot me a look, but he didn't answer. Well, he didn't answer me, anyway. What he actually said was, 'What is flax?'

While he kept his eyes glued to the super-sized flat-screen, I held my temper (barely) and took a seat on a black leather couch. There was a desk across the room with three computers on it, each with its own giant-sized monitor and each of those opened to a different webpage. Next to them was what looked like a police scanner, a couple walkie-talkies and (I swear) some gizmo that reminded me of those radar devices they use in the UFO movies, the kind with a round screen and an arm that sweeps around it and beeps when aliens are close at hand. There was a framed photo there, too, of Caleb standing in full combat gear and holding a gun big enough to do major damage, a dusty landscape in the background. There were piles of papers on the desk and, on the table in the center of the room along with a couple beat-up books, more than a few empty beer bottles, and an empty bag from Taco Bell.

When it came to organizational skills, it looked like Caleb and I had something in common.

When Alex announced that the day's Final *Jeopardy* category was Nineteenth Century American Literature, I knew I had a small window and I'd better act fast.

'So . . .' I got up and marched over to where he stood in front of the TV. 'What happened to the wheelchair?'

He looked down at the braces on his arms. 'What, you think I was trying to pull some kind of scam back at the hospital?' I guess he knew that's exactly what I was thinking because he didn't give me a chance to answer. 'It's easier to use the chair when I'm out, but I need the exercise. I use these around the house.'

'House?' I checked out the twenty-foot-high ceiling, the chandelier that hung at the center of the room. I peeked out into the hallway again and all that rich, dark wood. 'You live here?'

I should have known better than to expect an answer. I mean, any answer other than, 'What is *The Purloined Letter*?'

As soon as the words were out of his mouth, he turned off the TV.

'Don't you want to find out if you're right?' I asked him.

For the first time since I walked in, he flashed that hot-as-hell grin I'd seen back at the hospital. 'I'm always right. So . . .' It took some effort and obviously some skill, but he managed to pivot around and joined me near the doorway. 'We should get down to business.'

'Yes, we should. So where's Dan?'

'Callahan?' Caleb stomped over to the other side of the room and turned that photo of himself facedown on the desk before he shuffled through some papers. He didn't fool me. He wasn't searching for information, he was stalling for time, and when he was done, he had the nerve to give me a look that was all about innocence. 'Tibet,' is all he said.

'What?' I'd already flown at him so it was a little late to stop myself, but I didn't knock into him or knock him over, and I figured that was something, especially considering how easy it would have been. 'What do you mean, Tibet? He can't be in—'

'Tibet.' He was sure of himself so he could afford to watch me seethe. 'Dan . . .' He propped himself against the desk so he could slip one arm out of the brace and run a hand along the back of his neck. 'That boy's long gone, just about a year now.'

'But why did you . . . Why didn't you . . . I said I wanted to see Dan and you said . . .'

'That you should stop by.' He gave me the same kind of careful up-and-down look he had back at the hospital. Now that he was standing, I saw that Caleb and I were the same height. We were eye-to-eye. Which meant I couldn't help but catch the way his were touched with flecks of amber that caught the gleam of the chandelier.

There was no way he could miss the flames in my eyes, but apparently, the guy was fireproof. As if I hadn't said a word, he headed for the door. 'Come on,' he said. 'I'll show you around.'

He was out of the room faster than it should have been possible for a man with two canes, and I scrambled to catch up with him. I found him outside a room with yet another fireplace and wallpapered in an amazing swirl of spring green and white.

'Dining room,' he briefly glanced inside before he hobbled to the next room.

'Gym.'

Except for another fireplace and chandelier, this room was sleek and modern and complete with a treadmill, weights, and a platform that was about ten feet long and had railings on each side. I had no doubt he used it to practice walking.

I glimpsed a kitchen, too, with plenty of stainless appliances and couldn't help but ask, 'Where do you sleep?'

Caleb glanced up at the wood-paneled ceiling. 'Twelve bedrooms upstairs on floors eleven and twelve. If you'd like a tour . . .'

He knew I didn't or he wouldn't have grinned that way. I breezed past him and farther down the hallway to where it opened into a wide foyer, a stairway on one side and a wall of leaded glass windows on the other.

'Great room's right here,' he said from behind me, and the

room he led me into was the size of the house I'd lived in before Dad got sent up the river. The timbered ceiling was two-stories tall and, not one, but two huge crystal chandeliers hung over an Oriental rug as big as a football field. There was a fireplace on the far wall that was taller than me, and a sort of gallery, like a choir loft, above the double doors where we'd walked in.

'That's where the musicians used to play,' Caleb said, looking up to where I was looking. 'You know, when they had parties here.'

It was beyond amazing. 'What is this place?' I asked him, and then answered before he could, 'I mean besides where you live.'

'It's where the Van Sweringens used to live.'

'The brothers who built the building.'

'Pretty and smart.' He nodded. 'They had a home in the suburbs and an estate in the country and they kept this here little apartment for business guests and for when they worked late and didn't want to leave the city.'

'And now you live here.'

'Home sweet home.'

'And Dan lives here, too?'

'Dan's in Tibet.'

'Yeah, you told me that. Which means I paid twenty bucks to park for nothing.'

'You think?'

One entire wall of the great room was lined with leaded glass windows, and Caleb went and leaned against it, easing up on the braces as he did, and some of the tension eased from his shoulders, too. The glass in those windows was old and smoky and there was no clear view, but the city lights winked at us from the other side, muted and blurred like stars someone had tried to erase.

The hell with ambiance; I headed straight for the door.

'You're not leaving, are you?' Caleb called after me.

I was already standing in the double doorway under the musicians' gallery so it wasn't like he was some kind of genius, even if he did know all the answers on *Jeopardy*. 'I told you, nobody can help me but Dan.'

'And you told me it was personal, too,' he called over because really, the room was huge and by this time it seemed like we were miles apart. 'But you're going to have to do something and do it quick, cher. With or without Dan. You know, before someone tries to kill you again.'

I froze and I guess I stood there quite a while because when I snapped to, Caleb was right in front of me. 'You want to tell me what's going on?'

I looked away. 'You wouldn't understand.'

'Try me.'

'You think Dan's an absentminded professor.'

'I do, but I also know he's one of the few people in this country doing serious scientific research on the paranormal.'

My gaze shot to his. 'You know?'

'Oh, darlin', I know a whole lot of things.'

'Like all the *Jeopardy* answers.'

A smile touched his lips. 'Every night. Every single one of them.' Caleb walked past me and back out into the foyer. There were a couple chairs there and he sank down in one of them. Rather than look like I was giving a presentation to a class, I sat down in the other.

'Now,' he said quite simply, 'tell me.'

I shrugged and wondered if I would have felt just as confused if Dan was the one asking for the details. 'I don't know where to begin.'

'At the beginning.'

'The beginning . . .' I shook my head in wonder. 'You mean, the first time someone tried to kill me recently?'

It was hardly a laughing matter, but something about what I said set Caleb off. He slapped a knee. 'Recently! I knew I was going to like you the moment I clapped my eyes on you, sugar. Yeah, tell me about how someone tried to kill you recently.'

I didn't mean to do it, but my hand automatically drifted to my neck. 'Yesterday . . .' I hated sighing. It made me look like some stupid heroine from some stupid romance novel. I sighed, anyway. 'My mother tried to strangle me.'

He nodded. 'That explains the red nose. And the turtleneck. But it doesn't explain why you wanted to see Dan. Unless you think there's more going on than just your momma being miffed at you.'

'Of course there's more going on!' It was suddenly so obvious to me, I sputtered out the words. 'My mother tried to kill me, and last week, my boss tried to run me over.'

Thinking this through, he pursed his lips. 'He doesn't like you?'

'*She* does like me. She says I'm like one of her daughters. And just for the record, my mother likes me, too. I'm her only child.'

Maybe he knew how painful it was to even talk about what had happened at the bridal fair because he controlled a smile, but just barely. 'When did all this start?'

I didn't have to think about it. 'Last Monday. At the cemetery. The same day I met—' I swallowed the name.

We were seated side by side, and Caleb put a hand on my arm. It was a cool evening and I was wearing skinny jeans and a tawny-colored sweater that didn't prevent the heat of his skin from seeping through. I slipped my arm out from under his hand and stood up. 'So you see why I need to talk to Dan,' I said. 'He's the only one who will understand. If you've got a cell number . . .'

One corner of his mouth screwed up. 'In Tibet?'

I threw my hands in the air. 'Well, I've got to do something! There's something weird happening and, yes, it's something paranormal. And I can't just stand back and let it happen to the people I love.'

'I get it. Really, I do.' It took him a bit to get to his feet. 'But you're in boo-coo trouble if I'm not mistakin', and you're going to have to trust someone if you're going to get out of it. I may not be Dan, but right now, it looks like I'm all you got. Unless I'm not.' He gave me a steady look. 'Why don't you ask your boyfriend for help?'

'How do you—' I gave myself a mental slap; this wasn't the time for games. 'I can't,' I admitted. 'There's something weird going on with him, too.'

'Your boyfriend.'

I didn't so much shrug as I did twitch. 'It sounds so high school, doesn't it? Quinn isn't just my boyfriend, he's—'

'Your lover.'

I looked Caleb in the eye. 'Yes.'

I didn't see a clock anywhere nearby but I swear, I heard the seconds tick away – one, two, three – before he said, 'Lucky man.'

'I'm lucky, too,' I said, and I believed it with all my heart. 'He's wonderful. The best. But . . .'

'But?'

I don't know what possessed me. Maybe it was keeping secrets and bottling up emotions. Maybe there was something about the strange apartment that no one would guess even existed and the silence that pressed around us. Maybe it was Caleb himself and maybe it didn't matter. When I let go a breath, it felt as if I'd been holding it in all week long.

'He's a cop, and we were at the scene of a murder and he took the murder weapon. I don't mean he took it like he took it so it could be entered in as evidence, I mean he took it. Really took it. I found it in his closet.'

Caleb whistled low under his breath. 'And this all happened since last Monday?'

My blood pounded and my heartbeat did, too, and I couldn't stand still if my life depended on it. I zipped over to the huge double doors of the great room and back again, my fingers folded into fists and pressed to my sides. 'All of it has happened since last week when I got this package at the cemetery.' As soon as the words were out of my mouth, I realized how weird they sounded and explained. 'I work at Garden View. And I was there last Monday and this big old Buick drove through, and the driver brought me a package and inside the package was an old beer bottle, and I don't know why anyone would send me an old beer bottle, but somebody did, only Quinn dropped the bottle as soon as it was out of the box and it broke so it really didn't matter, anyway, and then the guy who brought it . . . well, that's the person I found dead when I went to see him and he was murdered, you see, and the murder weapon was this big old fountain pen holder on a marble base and it was there when Quinn got there with the other cops, and then it wasn't, and of course I figured they'd taken it, you know, the way they do. Only they didn't. Because, like I said, I found it at Quinn's.'

To Caleb's eternal credit, he didn't bat an eye at this crazy story. 'He's an honest cop?'

'As the day is long!'

'And Quinn, he hasn't tried to kill you, too, has he?'

The very thought made me feel as if I'd been punched in the solar plexus. 'No. Not him.'

'But he doesn't know you saw the fountain pen holder.'

I sucked in a breath. 'You think if he did—'

'I can't say. Not for sure.' I guess I looked like I was going to keel over, because Caleb put a steadying hand on my arm. 'We need to get to the bottom of this,' he said.

I didn't miss the *we*. I don't think Caleb intended me to. When I looked his way, I realized there were tears in my eyes and, annoyed at myself for showing even that much weakness, I dashed my hand across my cheeks. 'How?' I asked him.

'I don't have a clue!'

At least he was honest, and I couldn't help but smile.

'That's better.' He met my smile with one of his own. 'But we're never going to get anywhere if you don't tell me the whole story, cher. You said it all started last week when you met someone, only you haven't told me who that someone is.'

I made a face. 'You won't believe me.'

He gave me a wink. 'Try me.'

I could, and find myself laughed out of the apartment.

Or labeled a nutcase.

Or considered a threat to my own and others' safety.

But there was something in Caleb's steady gaze that told me there might be another possibility, too.

I drew in a breath for courage. 'Eliot Ness.'

Even if he didn't believe me, I'd hoped he'd be a little impressed. Instead, without a word, he moved past me and into the gym and when he came back out again, he was in his wheelchair. When he rolled by, he grabbed my hand. 'Come on,' he said. 'We're going upstairs.'

I held back, but he was determined, and plenty strong. I shuffled beside him and found myself in front of the private elevator that served the apartment, and when he hit the door open button and backed into it, I got in, too.

Honestly, I wasn't sure what I expected, but I was relieved

when he didn't punch the buttons for either floor eleven or twelve.

He hit thirteen.

The door slid closed and I found myself with my back to him, wondering where we were headed and why.

'We must have a long way to go,' I said, trying for conversation to cover a sudden onset of jitters. 'You needed your chair.'

Behind me, he laughed. 'The chair? Hell no, cher. The chair is just so I can enjoy the view.'

FOURTEEN

Maybe it was the altitude.

Or maybe it was knowing that there in the elevator barely big enough to accommodate his wheelchair, Caleb was checking out my butt.

My brain went into overdrive. I needed to think about something – anything – else, and somehow my gray cells glommed onto a detail of the case I'd completely blocked from my mind.

The elevator doors swished open on the thirteenth floor, but I didn't move. Instead, I blurted out, 'My sweet!'

Behind me, Caleb chuckled. 'It's about time you fell under the spell of my charming personality and realized how wonderful I am!'

'No! No, not you!' I stepped off the elevator into a foyer similar to the one outside the great room three floors below, the better to whirl to face him. 'My sweet. That's what people have been calling me.'

'That doesn't surprise me.'

He wasn't getting it. But then, I wasn't explaining. Not clearly, anyway. 'Well, it should surprise you,' I told Caleb. 'Because I'm not sweet. And that's what people have been calling me, anyway. That's what Ella said after she almost ran me down. And Saturday, that's what my mom called me, too. You know, when she was trying to strangle me.'

If he was chuckling before, he sure wasn't now. His eyes narrowed, Caleb wheeled off the elevator and gave me a searching look. 'Anyone else?'

'Yes!' I remembered like it was yesterday and like it was yesterday, the memory hit like a punch at a Smackdown. 'Quinn. When we were at the murder scene. I thought . . .' I swallowed down the sudden sour taste in my mouth. 'I thought he was trying to be funny. See, earlier that day . . .'

This time the memory that slammed into me sent me staggering back. That gave Caleb the opportunity to roll up closer.

'It was Wally,' I told him. 'Wally Birch, the maintenance man in the administration building at the cemetery. You've got to know Wally.' I wasn't big on eye rolls, I mean, not unless they were absolutely necessary to get a point across. This was one of those times. 'He's the crankiest guy on the face of the earth. He never has anything nice to say to anyone. And last Monday . . .'

I thought back through it all. 'It was after I opened that package delivered by Dean McClure, the murder victim. Before he was killed, of course,' I added for clarification even though I had a feeling Caleb didn't need it. 'I opened the package and took out that bottle and Quinn dropped it and it shattered. Wally came in to clean up and I expected him to moan and groan because that's what Wally does. Always. But he didn't. Not this time. When I thanked him for his help, he said, "No problem, my sweet." Or, "That's all right, my sweet." Something like that.'

'And when Quinn said it . . .' The way Caleb sent me a laser look, I knew this was important and he wanted me to concentrate. 'Was that before or after the murder weapon went missing?'

'Before, I think. Yes, I'm sure of it. The pen holder was on the floor in the living room when we went upstairs to look around. That's where we were when he called me "my sweet." And the pen holder wasn't there when I got back downstairs. And Quinn, he went downstairs before I did.'

Caleb scrubbed a hand over his chin. 'Where did you say that old bottle came from?'

'Chicago. It was from some old brewery there. McClure, the murder victim, he went to Chicago the weekend before and he was all excited about bringing something home. At least that's what he told the other HITmen.'

Sure, Caleb was confused, and I couldn't blame him so I gave him the 411 on the collectors' group.

He took it all in, nodded slowly, and asked one more question. 'And this was all after you met the ghost of Eliot Ness?'

Something in my expression must have told him all he needed to know because Caleb grabbed onto my hand and, together, we went over to a set of double doors very much like the ones downstairs in the great room. I mean, they were just as big. And just as solid. And just as ornately carved as the ones downstairs.

But there was something very different here.

I stopped three feet from the doors and eyed them carefully, not seeing anything different, but feeling it. There was something on the other side of the doors, something heavy and important. Something very cold.

Was it something good or something bad?

Before I had a chance to decide, the doors clicked open and I found myself face to face with a man with a receding hairline, wire-rimmed glasses, and a neatly trimmed beard and mustache. He had on one of those old-fashioned sorts of shirts like I'd seen Albert, my dead accountant, wear, the kind with the stiff collars that tied on, and he had a dark cravat looped around it.

As fashion statements went, this one was right up there with dead and gone, but I didn't need that to tell me the man at the door was, too.

He floated two feet above the floor.

'Hey, Dewey, quit wasting time. We've got a visitor and we need to get to work.' Like talking to a ghost was just part of an ordinary day, Caleb rolled into the room and took me along with him. 'Give me everything you've got on possession. And while you're at it, let's look at containment spells, too.'

I didn't even realize how much I'd tightened my hold on Caleb's hand until I saw him wince. 'You . . .' I wasn't sure if I was accusing him or congratulating him. 'You can see this guy? You're like me, you can see ghosts?'

'Not me, cher!' Something very much like regret touched his expression. 'I'm not lucky in that way. Not like you. Me and Melvil here . . .' He sneered at the ghost who sneered right back. 'We've got work to do together. Which is the only reason I can see him. And the only reason he can touch things and move things. At least within these four walls.'

The walls he was talking about were even more amazing than those of the great room downstairs. This room was nearly a twin of it, but while the room down on the tenth floor was elegant and refined like the grand party room it once was, this one was cavernous and filled with shadows. It was also jammed wall to wall and floor to ceiling with bookshelves, and every one of those shelves was packed with books.

I stepped up to the closest shelf and took a gander at a book that was two feet tall and six inches thick. The binding was broken, the red leather cover worn smooth. There was a title written on the spine in gold letters, but not in any alphabet I'd ever seen.

'What is this place?' I asked Caleb.

'Hopefully, it's the place that will help us find the answers we need.' He glared at the ghost. 'Let's get crackin', Melvil. We got us a situation here and we need answers.'

'Certainly.' His shoulders shot back, and the ghost bit the word in two. 'Possession, did you say?' He turned and drifted into the nearest aisle of books. 'That might be in with the 100s, philosophy and psychology. Or perhaps the 200s, religion. As far as containment spells . . .' He sniffed his opinion and disappeared into the endless, shadowy maze.

As for me, I was still too stunned to move. 'Why didn't you tell me?' I demanded of Caleb.

'Seeing is believing, sugar, and I f'sho didn't think you'd believe me if you didn't meet ol' Melvil for yourself.'

'He's a . . .' I peered down the long, murky aisle but there was no sign of the grim-faced ghost. 'What's he, like your research assistant or something?'

'More like the albatross around my neck,' Caleb admitted. He scratched a hand along his neck. 'Me and Melvil, well, we've been assigned to a sort of project, and I gotta tell you, it is not a match made in heaven. I mean, not like you and me, sugar. But since I'm pretty good with information and he's got this thing about classifying it all . . .' He looked up at me, a question in his dark eyes. 'You've heard of the old guy, right? Melvil, Melvil Dewey?'

The name was vaguely familiar but it took a moment for the pieces to fall into place. Ella's daughter, Ariel, remember, is in library school and once upon a time, I'd spent a very long evening with her, half-listening while she regaled me with stories about the libraries she knew and loved and all the fantastic (her word) classes she was taking.

'The Dewey Decimal System?' I asked Caleb and stabbed my thumb over my shoulder. 'He's the guy?'

'One and the same, and he's been dead since 1931 so you'll have to excuse him if he doesn't have much of a sense of humor. Then again, the way I've heard it, he didn't have much of one when he was alive, either. What he did have was an eye for the ladies, so I'd suggest you watch your step around him. It's been a mighty long time since the old guy has been around a pretty woman.'

'Ghosts I can handle,' I assured him, though with all that was happening in my life, I wasn't so sure. 'But what about possession?'

'You know about that. Dan's wife, Madeline, she took your body.'

'The bitch.'

Caleb tried not to smile and lost, but he sobered fast enough. 'I can't say for sure, not without doing some research, but I think that might be what's happening now.'

I'd considered the possibility, too, but listening to someone else confirm it sent ice water through my veins. 'Ella and my mom and Wally Birch and . . .' I swallowed hard. 'And Quinn? But why?'

'Ah, that's always the question, ain't it?'

Out of nowhere and as quiet as a . . . well, as a ghost, Melvil Dewey floated over and tossed a small book at Caleb. When he caught it in one hand, a puff of dust rose off the black leather cover.

'Containment spells,' the ghost said simply and disappeared back into the stacks.

'This might take a bit,' Caleb said. 'If I could talk to you in the next couple days . . .'

'Sure.'

I'd already started backing toward the door when he rolled up next to me. 'Oh, no, cher! What sort of gentleman would let a lady walk back to her car at night all by her pretty little self?'

So it turns out Caleb had a big brain, too, just like Dan. I mean, he must have, right? Otherwise he wouldn't be consorting with some big shot library ghost and doing research out of dusty books.

I am not one to kid myself. I knew I didn't have that kind

of big brain. I didn't need one. Brains that aren't filled with useless facts and focused on dusty books have time to think about other things.

Like murders.

And how the whole 'my sweet' thing fit into the puzzle that was my life.

I put my not-so-big-but-just-right-anyway brain to work on that the next day and sometime between when I took a busload of old folks around to see the various and sundry angel statues in the cemetery and when I had to make a presentation to the board about my budget for the upcoming quarter (they declared it perfect, by the way, and I had Albert to thank for that), I made up my mind. I might not know what was what when it came to libraries, but I sure knew how to investigate. As to where I was planning to start . . .

'I don't know, Pepper, I'm just worried. That's all there is to it.'

I shouldn't have been surprised when Ella trailed into my office when I already had my purse over my shoulder and was watching for the clock to officially hit five. She must have known she'd end up worried when she got up that day because Ella was dressed in a somber gray pantsuit. She ran one nervous hand along the big buttons down the front of her jacket. 'I've called a few times and he hasn't answered,' she said.

I can be excused for being a little confused. Ella often has that effect on me.

'Wally!' she said, apparently reading my mind. Or maybe just seeing the look of complete and utter confusion on my face. 'Wally Birch didn't come to work today. And he didn't call in. I know, I know what you're going to say, Wally's an old curmudgeon. And you're right. And come to think of it, he's not very thorough when it comes to his job, either. But Wally and I . . . Wally and I started here at Garden View on the very same day. Did you know that? We've worked here together forever, and I know one thing about him, he is dependable. Well, most of the time, anyway, when he's not hiding in the employee locker room or taking a nap in that unused mausoleum he doesn't think I know about. If he was sick, Pepper, I'm sure he would have called to tell me.'

Me, I wasn't so sure. But I was plenty curious.

Rather than explain, I scooted around Ella with a mumbled story about a follow-up dental appointment and how I had to hurry and how she shouldn't worry because I was sure Wally was fine.

Only as it turned out, he wasn't.

Once upon a time when he was celebrating some big birthday (I think it was sixty but don't hold me to it), Ella had me take a big bunch of balloons over to Wally's. It should come as no surprise that he answered the door, snatched the balloons out of my hand, and closed the door in my face. Fine by me since I didn't want to chat with the guy anyway, and finer still because, thanks to that little adventure, I knew where he lived. I pulled up to his oh-so-humdrum home in an equally humdrum suburb west of the city, and I knew something was up as soon as my knuckles hit the front door.

It swung open.

I might not have a big brain, but I'm nobody's fool and I'd seen plenty of horror movies.

I knew this was not a good sign, but just like all those heroines in all those horror movies, I went in, anyway.

'Wally!' I toed the edge of a green shag carpet that was out of date before I was born. 'Hey, Wally, it's me, Pepper from the cemetery,' I called out. 'You here?'

I didn't get an answer.

What I did get the moment I stepped from the tiny entryway and into a living room was a bird's eye view of the biggest mess I'd ever seen.

My own apartment included.

The green couch was turned over and the cushions were tossed around it and slit to pieces by the knife that lay on the floor beside them. A bookshelf across the room was completely emptied, and the ancient issues of *Playboy* and *Popular Mechanics* that had once been on it were all over the floor. The kitchen was worse. Every cupboard and drawer was open, and everything that had once been in them or on them was scattered. I stepped over the remains of broken dishes, kicked through a stack of silverware and what looked like a dozen rolls of paper towels that had been torn to shreds.

Even the walls hadn't been spared.

The one next to the fridge (open and emptied, its contents on the floor in globs that were quickly turning stinky) was kicked in and the plaster torn out in chunks so that I could see the wooden studs behind it.

It didn't take a big brain – mine or anyone else's – to see that something was very wrong.

'Wally!' I tried again and who can blame me? I'd already found one body just a little over a week before, and I wasn't happy with the thought that there might be another one around. I made a beeline back through the living room and up a stairway that had once been carpeted. Now, the carpet was torn away and lying in chunks, like the skin some gigantic lizard had shed.

There was a bathroom at the top of the stairs and it, too, was in shambles. The medicine cabinet was open and emptied, the trash can was dumped. The shower curtain had been torn from its rings and was wadded up in the bathtub. Yes, I looked underneath it. Just in case.

By this time, my stomach felt pretty much like Wally's house looked. Ripped to shreds and turned upside down. When I tried one last, 'Wally!' my voice shook.

This time, though, I heard what almost sounded like a reply.

The groan came from the bedroom on my right, and I rushed in there and found more destruction. Every wall of the room was torn apart like the one in the kitchen and there was plasterboard in hunks everywhere. The closet had been emptied, and the mattress had been pulled off the bed and tossed on the floor.

Another groan came from under the mattress.

'Wally?' I lifted the mattress and shoved it back on the bed. Beneath it, Wally Birch lay on his back and if it wasn't for the fact that his eyes fluttered open and he let out a moan, I would have thought he was dead.

Wally's face was ashen. His shirt gaped open. His pants were torn and his hair was a mess. His fingernails were gouged and all of him – skin and clothing and hair – was painted with a gooey mixture of plaster dust and blood.

Wally had torn apart his own house.

The realization settled in me like ice, and for a few moments, I was frozen along with it. That is, until Wally groaned again.

I got on my knees and swallowed down the funny feeling in my stomach when I took his hand and my own fingers were instantly slick with blood.

'Wally, it's me, Pepper. Don't worry. I'm going to call for help.'

I did, and while I waited for it to arrive, I reached for a pillow that had been thrown on top of the dresser next to the bed and gently slid it under Wally's head.

'What happened?' I asked him.

Wally's eyes flittered open and he stared like he couldn't bring me into focus.

'What did you do, Wally?' I asked him. 'What happened to your house?'

When he turned his head to look around, he let out a yelp, and I settled him and told him not to worry, that we'd sort things out later and everything would be fine.

Only I wasn't so sure.

The paramedics arrived along with a couple grim-faced cops and I gave them the song and dance I'd prepared while I waited for them: friend from work, concerned about Wally when he didn't show up that day, came over just to check. Found this.

The cops took notes and looked around.

The paramedics loaded Wally up on a stretcher and told me they were taking him to the nearest hospital.

'I'll make sure Ella knows what's going on,' I told Wally when they were carrying him out of the bedroom. 'I'll let her know where you are and that everything's OK.'

Only it obviously wasn't.

I knew this as I navigated those giant chunks of carpeting on the stairway and, if I didn't, I would have gotten the message loud and clear when I walked out to the ambulance at Wally's side.

Just as they lifted the stretcher, he grabbed my hand.

'It's not OK,' he said, his voice thready. 'It won't be OK. Not ever. Not until I find . . . I've got to find the ashes.'

FIFTEEN

Ashes.

Possession.

Containment spells.

The thoughts didn't just float through my head and swirl through my dreams all that night, they pounded around inside my brain like they were wearing steel-toed boots.

Was it any wonder I was a little bleary-eyed the next morning?

My head thumping, I dragged into the office. Surprise, surprise, I perked up instantly as soon as I was inside my door.

Quinn was there waiting for me!

My all-out happiness at seeing him lasted about as long as the heartbeat that reminded me of what Caleb had talked about the night before. He said there was a possibility that Quinn was possessed.

'Hey!' My favorite boy in blue (who happened to be wearing a charcoal suit that day) was perched on the edge of my desk, a bouquet of flowers in his hand. I knew from the plastic bag they were in that he'd stopped to get them at a grocery store rather than at a florist, but I didn't hold that against him. There is something about a macho cop in a killer suit carrying a perky bunch of pink, lilac, and yellow daisies that can't help but melt a girl's heart.

He slid off the desk and gave me the smile that never failed to make me sizzle, his arms wide open. 'What, after all these days of not seeing me, you're just going to stand over there and not come here and give me a kiss?'

I snapped out of the dark thoughts that had kept me frozen near the door. This was Quinn smiling at me, not some stranger. His amazing green eyes weren't devoid of emotion like my mom's had been at the bridal fair when she attacked me. There was love shining in them and in the smile that warmed me down to my toes.

And besides, he hadn't once called me *my sweet*.

'I'm just surprised to see you, that's all.' I darted over and gave him that kiss he wanted, and the second my lips touched his, I realized how much I'd missed him. When we were done (it took a bit, but like I said, it had been a while) and he handed me the flowers, I slipped them out of the bag and put the bouquet on my desk next to the vase of roses he'd sent me a few days earlier. 'I know you've been busy. I didn't think you'd have a chance to stop by.'

'And you . . .' he tapped the tip of my nose with one finger. '. . . haven't been answering your phone. What's up?'

I covered up a shrug when I slipped out of my leopard-print raincoat. 'I didn't want to bother you.' I didn't want to admit to him that my mother had tried to kill me, either, because that was a story for another time. 'I figured you were knee deep in the Dean McClure investigation.'

'Exactly what I've been doing.'

There was so much enthusiasm in Quinn's voice, something that felt very much like hope tangled around my heart. I thought back to what he'd told me when we'd first discussed the case. 'You don't think McClure is the scum of the earth and the world is better off without him?'

Quinn laughed. 'Yeah, well he was the scum of the earth. And he was trying to cause trouble for me with my lieutenant. But that half-baked accusation of his never would have flown.' He sloughed it off as nothing. 'Even if he did have a serious beef with me, you don't think I wouldn't work hard on McClure's case, do you? That wouldn't be right. Every victim deserves justice, and annoying or not, McClure was a victim.'

Spoken like the Quinn of old, the true-blue cop with a moral code that was as solid as the Rock of Gibraltar!

Relief swept through me like a wave, and I threw myself into Quinn's arms and kissed him so hard, I knocked him back onto my desk.

When we came up for air, he laughed. 'What was that for?'

I couldn't tell him it was for proving that Caleb was dead wrong. Back when Quinn said those things about McClure, when he destroyed the note McClure had written to his lieutenant, he wasn't possessed, he was tired, overworked, stressed.

And when he walked away from the crime scene with the murder weapon?

A shiver slipped up my spine and raced across my shoulders and, before he could notice, I backed out of Quinn's arms.

I was one hundred percent positive that he had an explanation for that, too, and that he'd tell me when the time was right.

'Dinner at my place tonight?' he asked.

I pretended I had to think about it. 'What are you cooking?'

'It depends how much time I have on my hands. I might be just finishing up with the McClure case.'

This was good news and, at the same time I wondered if it could have anything to do with Wally Birch and his mention of the missing Ness ashes, Quinn grinned.

'Cindy McClure,' he said quite simply.

There was a vase on the bookshelf across the room and I went over and retrieved it and plopped the flowers in it. I'd get water for them later. For now, the trip across the room gave me a moment to line up what I remembered about the Widow McClure. 'I'm not surprised,' I admitted. 'She hated that Dean spent all their money on gangster memorabilia. And she lied about her alibi for the night of the murder, too.'

I almost felt guilty for taking the wind out of Quinn's sails, but I couldn't help but grin.

'She told me,' I explained. 'She told me that she was out with friends at the time of the murder, but the restaurant she said she was at hasn't opened yet. I bet she told you the same thing.'

He nodded. 'She did. Which was dumb, because she should have known that was an easy thing to check. Turns out she was actually with the guy she's been seeing on the side. What she didn't mention . . .' I have to admit, sometimes when Quinn looks so pleased with himself, it drives me nuts. He's a competitive guy and he loves to win and when he thinks he's one-upped me (I know it's hard to believe, but it's actually happened a time or two), the left corner of his mouth pulls into a satisfied little smirk that drives me crazy. Sometimes I want to slap that smile off his face. Sometimes I think it's as sexy as hell. This time, I swear, I was so relieved to see him acting like Quinn and talking like Quinn and not being mysterious or trying to kill me like some other people had done lately, I didn't much care. He grinned and I grinned back and, yes, all was right with the world.

'She'll be able to sell all McClure's junk now,' I said, though I was sure Quinn didn't need the reminder. 'That's why Cindy killed him, right? She couldn't stand him collecting any more gangster stuff.'

'Wrong.'

He laughed, but hey, Quinn is nothing if not a good sport. He knew it wouldn't be fair not to provide an explanation. 'McClure had been buying up gangster memorabilia for years, and he already had an extensive collection when he married Cindy. That was six years ago. That collection . . . well, you saw it, Pepper. You saw how carefully he had everything displayed. His collection was the most important thing in his life. From what the people I've interviewed told me, it was even more important to him than his marriage.'

I can't exactly say the pieces fell into place because there were still plenty of gaps, but I can say I was beginning to get a better picture. I gasped. 'He started collecting a long time ago. He wouldn't risk losing that collection, not for anyone or anything. They had a prenup, didn't they?'

'Sexy and smart!' Quinn gave me a quick kiss. 'Their prenup specifies that Cindy takes possession of Dean's collection on the event of his death, but if they were ever to divorce—'

I swear, if I wasn't so happy to see Quinn acting like the man I was crazy about, I would have slapped my forehead. 'Dean was talking to an attorney?'

'The papers were about to be filed. Cindy had to act fast, or she was going to be left with nothing.'

'You're brilliant,' I told him, but Quinn being Quinn, he already knew that. 'So she killed Dean before he divorced her and left her with nothing. Now that he's dead, she can sell off his collection and get all the money. But what about . . .' Honestly, I hated to ruin a special moment, but I couldn't help myself. 'So what did she do with Eliot Ness's ashes?' I asked Quinn and didn't bother to add, 'And why is Wally Birch looking for them?' because I was still pretty fuzzy about that part of the equation.

He sloughed off my question. 'My guess is that she took

those first thing, right after the murder. Or maybe before. Maybe McClure found out she'd taken them and they fought about it, and maybe that's how she ended up killing him. I don't know the details, not yet. But don't worry, once we arrest her, she'll start talking. Then she can tell us who she sold the ashes to, we can get them back, and you and Eliot Ness . . .' As if he thought he actually might see him somewhere in the office, Quinn looked around. 'Well, that's what you said he's after, right? He wants his ashes sprinkled at the lake so he can rest in peace.'

'Exactly.' I did my best to sound upbeat. Not so easy considering the thoughts that still pounded through my head. How did Wally know about the ashes in the first place? And why did he care? Why was Wally looking for them?

I didn't have the heart to put the kibosh on Quinn's good mood so I told myself this was all a subject for another discussion and I was sure that when we had that talk, he'd explain about the fountain pen holder, too.

Possession schmussession!

Quinn was Quinn, and I was a woman in love. There wasn't anything or anyone who could ruin my mood.

I hoped the sizzling smile I sent him told him just that, and in case it didn't, I closed in on Quinn, step by slow step. 'Did you say what time tonight?' I asked him.

'I was thinking six.'

'And is this a formal occasion?' I fingered the lapel of his suit jacket. 'I mean, should I get all dressed up? Or would you rather I wear nothing at all?'

He wrapped his arms around my waist and slid his hands down my hips and across my butt, pulling me closer. 'Nothing at all sounds perfect to me,' he growled in my ear. 'We'll light a fire, open a bottle of wine and—'

'I sho'do hope I'm not interruptin' anything.'

Just like that, the heat inside me changed to ice and, still caught in Quinn's arms, I turned to find Caleb sitting in my office doorway.

'Good mornin'!' He had the nerve to act casual. Yeah, like he hadn't been eavesdropping and hadn't heard all that about fires and bottles of wine and no clothes at all. If I had any doubts, all I had to do was look at the wide smile he gave me when he looked me up and down like he could picture the whole thing. 'Nice to see you again, Mizz Martin.'

He wheeled his chair into the office and, when I slipped away from Quinn, Caleb introduced himself.

I cleared away my mortification with a little cough and wished it was just as easy to get rid of the fire I felt burning my cheeks. 'Caleb is a—'

'Librarian,' he interrupted me and explained to Quinn, his accent so thick that morning I imagined needing a machete to cut through the swamp. 'Mizz Martin here is preparin' a new tour for the cemetery and I'm helpin' her with a little bit of research.'

'Then I'll leave you to it.' Quinn moved toward the door, but not before he gave me a smile that heated me through to the soles of my peep-toe pumps. 'And I'll see you this evening,' he said, and left the office.

'You think that's smart?'

The good old boy who'd rolled into the office suddenly sounded a whole lot more like the Marine I'd seen in the photograph at Caleb's place.

I spun away from the door. 'Do you think it's any of your business?'

As if he had every right, he rolled around to the desk and looked over the papers I had piled there. Newsletters, tour requests, phone messages. He didn't fool me one bit, I knew he wasn't reading any of it. He was stalling for time. Giving me the chance to reconsider what I said.

I did and decided I was right in the first place.

'This isn't something you can take lightly,' he said.

I knew what he was talking about but pretended I didn't. 'You barging in here, you mean?'

Finished looking over my desk, he smoothly moved over to the bookshelf and rolled along the front of it, scanning the few books alongside the files, magazines, and stacks of old newspapers Ella was sure I'd use – someday – for research. 'Me and Melvin have been busy,' he said, not looking my way. 'You want to hear what we found out? Or are you gonna be pigheaded just because some guy has an expensive suit and a big' – he looked over at me, the soul of innocence – 'bunch of flowers.'

Honestly, there was nothing in my desk I needed, but if I didn't do something and do it fast, there was a chance I was going to leap across the room and do some serious damage to Caleb, so I sat down, opened the top desk drawer, and rummaged around.

'It ain't that easy.' When I looked up again, he was right next to me. Lesson to be learned: wheelchairs can be pretty quiet. 'You might want to ignore it, but it ain't that easy. In fact, if I'm right—'

'You told me you're always right.'

I didn't mean it as a compliment so he had absolutely no reason to smile. 'Afraid I am this time, too. Which is why you need to set aside your emotions and listen to reason.'

I grumbled a word I didn't apologize for, slammed my desk drawer closed, and plunked back in my chair. 'Get it over with,' I ordered him. 'What's going on?'

'I'll tell you, but you tell me . . .' Caleb glanced around the office. 'Is Ness here?'

Maybe he had been all along because Eliot Ness picked that moment to sparkle right in front of my desk.

'He's here,' I told Caleb. 'Can you see him?'

He looked where I was looking. 'No, ma'am,' he said, 'but there are some things I need to talk to him about. If you'd be so kind as to help?'

I did, and I won't report all the back-and-forthing that went on, what with Caleb asking questions, Ness answering, me telling Caleb what Ness said. It pretty much went something like this:

'You knew he was trouble from the start, didn't you, Mr Ness? I mean, even after you got word that he was dead, you knew there was a chance he could still cause serious harm.'

'Of course.' That cloud that was Eliot Ness glittered. 'When a person is that vicious—'

'You're the one who arranged for the containment spell?'

The cloud moved up and down, nodding.

'I give you a great deal of credit, sir. From what I've been reading, a spell like that ain't easy and finding the right person to work it . . . well, that's a whole other thing, am I right? Near as I can remember, there ain't a listing in the Yellow Pages for witches and warlocks. You put a lot of effort into making sure it got done and got done right. And that spell worked. Worked like a charm for going on seventy years now. Until . . .'

I wasn't part of the conversation. I mean, except for being the go-between, but I couldn't help it, if I didn't find out what he was talking about, I was going to jump out of my skin. 'Until what?' I asked and I didn't care which of them answered, I looked back and forth between Caleb and Ness.

'Let me explain,' Caleb said. 'Just like you got this ol' Gift of yours, there are people who have other . . .' He turned the thought over in his head. 'Other talents.'

'Like you and Melvil Dewey.'

He acknowledged that I was right with a curt nod. 'And there are others whose jobs are a little more . . . let's say esoteric. See, if a person is really bad, I mean a real son-of-a-bitch, and that person dies then comes back in spirit, he can cause a whole bunch of trouble. You've found that out.'

I thought of Madeline who had taken over my body, and the ghost of a former police officer who'd tried to make trouble for Quinn and would have succeeded if I hadn't destroyed his spirit permanently.

'That's why some ghosts are kept in their place so to speak,' Caleb went on. 'With containment spells.'

'To make sure they don't come back and cause trouble.'

He nodded. 'But it's possible . . . not common, mind you, but possible . . . for a spell to be broken. If the timing is right. If the conditions are perfect. And if a living human can be found who's willing to help out.'

I wasn't exactly sure where he was going with all this, but wherever it was, I knew I wasn't going to like it. I swallowed hard. 'And all this has something to do with Ness's ashes? And Dean McClure's murder?'

'And with all them trips ol' Dean took to Chicago. See, he started out going there because he was interested in history and in collecting. But once he got started, he couldn't stop. He had to keep going back. It wasn't that he was just interested in more memorabilia or excited to see all the old gangster stomping grounds again. Ol' Dean, he was obsessed, and according to the books Melvil found for me, it wasn't his fault. It's easier for a spirit to take over a mind than it is for him to take over a body and ol' Dean had the perfect mind. Too focused on one subject and just a little weak.'

It was cold in the office, and I shivered and chafed my hands up and down my arms.

'When a spirit has that kind of control, he can make a living person do almost anything. In this case, he wanted to end up right here.' When Caleb tapped a finger against my desk, I jumped at the sound. 'Right here at Garden View Cemetery.'

'But why?' I asked.

Caleb spread his hands. 'Can't say fo'sure. Won't know fo'sure until whatever he's planning happens and, by then, I'm thinkin' that it's gonna be too late. But we can pretty much guess. He took over McClure's mind, and he made McClure bring him here, and that there bottle that was delivered to you . . .' Caleb caught my gaze and held it. 'His spirit was inside it.'

'And escaped when the bottle was broken!' My stomach got queasy and I pressed a hand to it. 'So that spirit . . .' Like I actually expected to see it, I looked into every shadowy corner of the room. 'It's on the loose?'

'It's lookin' that way,' Caleb conceded.

'But why?'

He couldn't see Ness. Not like I could. But he'd seen where I was looking as I conveyed what Ness had said to him, and Caleb turned that way. 'It all started when Mr Ness here showed up.'

'Because someone doesn't want my ashes to be returned,' the G-man said and when I told Caleb this, he said he was pretty certain Ness was right.

'Like any spirit, this one needs a physical form to accomplish things in this here world,' Caleb went on. 'So he's taken to slipping in and out of peoples' bodies. People like your mom, Pepper, and your boss. Like that Wally fella you told me about.'

'Who said he had to find Ness's ashes!'

'And I'm sorry to tell you, but the same applies to your friend, Quinn. That would explain why he made off with the murder weapon. He doesn't want anyone to find out what really happened to Dean McClure.'

'Not because he killed him,' I insisted, my shoulders back and my chin raised even before I realized I'd moved. I had no proof that Quinn was innocent, of course. I didn't need any. I knew this was true down deep in my bones. 'Quinn didn't kill anybody.'

'But the longer the murder goes unsolved, the more time our ghost will have to find the ashes, and my guess is he'll destroy them. Beggin' your pardon for being so blunt, Mr Ness, but you understand. Because if Eliot Ness's ashes are all in one place, all at one time, he can manifest himself and he'll have his old get-up-and-go back and then our bad guy, well, he won't stand a chance. This is his ultimate revenge. I mean, for all you done to him, Mr Ness.'

By now, my heart was pumping like a piston, and the blood whooshed through my head. In the crazy version of the universe where I existed, it all made sense.

Except . . .

I think it's called grasping at straws.

I wasn't so sure about the straws, but I knew about the grasping. I held on for all I was worth.

'But Quinn's fine,' I said and pointed toward the doorway Quinn had walked out of ten minutes before. 'You saw him. He's fine. He's acting regular. Normal. He didn't call me—'

'My sweet, yeah.' I already knew that Caleb didn't give a damn about my feelings, and he sure didn't mind delivering bad news. Still, he scratched a hand along the back of his neck and his mouth screwed up into a look that might have been regret on anyone else. 'I'm afraid that "my sweet" thing, it sealed the deal. Found that out when I was researchin', too. See, our slippery ghost, the one who arrived in the bottle, that's what he called his wife. My sweet. He always called her "my sweet."'

'And Quinn didn't. Did you hear me when I told you that? He didn't call me "my sweet" today.'

'Nope, he didn't. Which means he's fine. For right now.' I

couldn't tell if Caleb thought this was a good thing or not. 'But that don't mean it will last. What it does mean is that we need to find those ashes before he does because when he does . . .' Again, he looked across the room, but he didn't know that Ness had floated closer. He was right in front of Caleb now, and Caleb was looking right through the little effervescent cloud. 'He's going to destroy you, sir.'

'Stop it!' My nervous energy got the best of me and I popped out of my chair. 'You're making it sound so scary.'

'Oh, believe me, darlin', it is,' Caleb told me. 'Because if he can make your dear mother try to kill you and he can make a good cop walk off with evidence, then he can pretty much do anything he wants. And we've got to make sure that don't happen.'

It didn't take much convincing. But then, Caleb had done a pretty good job of scaring me.

I slipped on my coat and headed for the door. 'Then the first thing we need to do is find Ness's ashes,' I said to no one in particular. 'And then we need to find—'

Who?

At the door, I stopped and turned back around. 'Who's this ghost who's out to cause so much trouble? How do I know what to look for if I don't know who to look for?'

'That's an easy one, sugar.' Caleb nodded toward Ness. 'You want to tell her, sir?'

Like he didn't even want to think about it, Eliot Ness shivered. 'All the pieces fit. There's only one person it can be,' he told me. 'Al Capone.'

SIXTEEN

'Alphonse Gabriel Capone, 1899 to 1947. Nasty scar on his face.' It wasn't like Eliot Ness couldn't see the picture I was checking out on my computer screen, but I pointed, anyway. 'The two of you, you were like sworn enemies, right?'

'You've been watching too many movies, kid.' The cloud that was Ness hovered just over my desktop, and I pictured him sitting there on the edge of it, his legs casually crossed. 'Sure, my job was to investigate Prohibition violations. And Capone, he had quite a bootlegging empire. He made millions. But the fact is, I never even saw Capone in person until he appeared in court in 1931. Then, when he was finally convicted on tax evasion charges, I rode along in the procession of cars that accompanied him to the railway station on his way to prison.'

'So it's not like the movies?'

'Is anything?' Ness asked, and I guess he knew I didn't need to answer. I saw the cloud move nearer to the screen. 'He wasn't a big man, but he was heavy and powerful. Got his start as a bouncer in a bar back in New York. Back when we were compiling information on him, we figured he was personally responsible for ordering at least five hundred murders.'

I looked at the man in the picture, at his smiling face and pudgy cheeks, and I shivered. 'And he collected elephants?'

'And played the banjo. Did you know that?' Ness chuckled. 'Doesn't seem like the type, does he? But he did. In fact, when he was in Alcatraz, he joined the prison band. Imagine him strumming away there on that rock in the middle of nowhere.'

It had been more than an hour since Caleb had left the office and Ness and I had been doing research the whole time. I sat back and rubbed my eyes. 'I guess all that's interesting, but none of it tells us how to get rid of his ghost.'

'Would it help if you could see him?' Ness asked.

Sure, I'd checked out my office when Ness and Caleb first started talking about a malevolent ghost on the loose. And yeah, I'd checked it out a couple more times as I searched online and read about the life and times of Al Capone. But that didn't mean I couldn't look around again. Just to be sure.

Certain we were alone, I turned my attention back to Ness. 'At least I'd know what he was up to then,' I told him. 'And then maybe I could figure out what to do next.'

'You? Figure out what to do next? You're a detective, remember, kid. You know what's going on.'

I did. Or at least I thought I did. When Quinn left he said he was on his way to wrap up the McClure case, and by now, I pictured Cindy McClure in handcuffs, scared to death and singing like the proverbial bird.

'I guess I should be happy, right?' I'm pretty sure I wasn't asking Ness, just talking to myself. 'Dean McClure's murder is solved, and Cindy might even tell us what happened to your ashes and then you can manifest and take care of Capone once and for all.'

'So why the long face?' Ness wanted to know.

I hated sighing because, like Ness said, I was a detective, and I knew detectives weren't the sighing types. I sighed anyway and covered it up with a grumble, 'It's the whole thing with Wally and the ashes. It doesn't make sense.'

'Evil ghosts and containment spells and spirits possessing the living . . .' The sound that came out of Ness wasn't exactly a chuckle, it was more of a harumph of skepticism. 'There was a time none of that would have made sense to me, either. In fact, even when I arranged for that spell to be cast there at Capone's grave back in the forties . . .' Why did I have the feeling he was blushing? And running a finger around the inside of his shirt collar, too? 'I felt silly for doing it, I'll tell you that. But I figured what the heck, nothing ventured, nothing gained.'

'It looks like what you did gain was seventy years of peace. At least when it came to Al Capone.'

'And now that peace has been shattered.'

'What do you suppose Wally knows about it?' I asked him. 'And why would Wally tear apart his own house looking for the ashes? The only reason is that he thought the ashes were there.'

'Sounds right,' Ness admitted.

'But if he knew they were there, why would Wally have to rip his house apart to find them?' I drummed my fingers on the desk to the same cha-cha rhythm my heart was pounding in my chest.

'The answers aren't in dusty old books,' I said and wished Caleb was there to hear me at the same time I was glad he was long gone. The man made me crazy.

I grabbed my purse and my raincoat, told Ella I was heading out for an early lunch, and went right over to the hospital where Wally had been admitted when he was taken away from his house, bloody and jibbering.

In the gift shop, I bought one of those big Mylar balloons and I wound the string around my fingers and headed for Wally's room, holding my breath (well, figuratively, anyway) the whole time.

If Wally liked the balloon and thanked me for being his sweet, believe me, I was outta there.

'What's that for?'

When he glared at me from where he was propped up in bed and gave the balloon a death-ray look, I nearly jumped for joy. I tied the balloon to the rail on Wally's bed. 'It's from Ella,' I said because I figured that way he wouldn't grab the nearest sharp object and get rid of the balloon permanently. 'She asked me to come over and see how you're doing.'

'Ella, huh?' Wally had just finished his lunch, and he pushed aside the tray. The bowl of green Jell-O on it wiggled. 'She called, you know.'

I wasn't surprised.

'She said she was coming over here to see me. Why isn't Ella here?' Wally demanded, looking past me and into the empty doorway. 'Why did she send you to waste my time?'

Believe me, if I didn't have an ulterior motive for the visit, I would have been on the elevator and back downstairs before Wally could spit out the next insult. The way it was, I pasted on a smile and, though I hadn't been invited, I sat down in the green vinyl chair next to Wally's bed.

'I'm the one who found you, Wally. I'm the one who called the paramedics,' I told him.

He shot me a narrow-eyed look before he glanced away, one bandaged hand picking at the white cotton blanket that covered him. 'I guess I'm supposed to thank you.'

'No need.' Was that my voice, all perky and kind? I only hoped I could keep it up. 'All that matters is that you're feeling better. I thought maybe . . .' I leaned forward and laid a hand on the blanket next to Wally's right leg. Hey, he might be old and crabby and maybe even recently possessed, but Wally was a guy, right? And guys always notice when I pay them a little extra attention.

'I thought maybe you could tell me what happened.'

Wally made a noise from deep in his throat. 'Don't remember,' he said.

'Maybe I can help.'

'Don't see why you'd want to.'

'Because . . .' I almost slipped and told him it was because I cared, but let's face it, even a guy in a hospital bed with a silver balloon decorated with pink flowers on it tied to the rail wouldn't have believed that. Wally would know bullshit when he heard it. I guess that meant the two of us had something in common. 'Ella asked me to,' I told him, lying through my teeth. 'She told me the two of you started working at Garden View on the same day. She says because of that . . . well, because of that, she told me she's always had a special affection for you.'

He darted me a look. 'Really? Ella, she said that? Well, isn't she . . .' He coughed away the sudden warmth that tinged his voice. 'She's just asking because she's the boss and it's what she's supposed to do,' he grumbled.

'She is the boss. And she's your friend. And she asked me what happened over at your house yesterday, but I couldn't tell her. Because I don't know. What I do know . . .' My hand still on the blanket, I leaned a little nearer. 'I think it all started last week. The day that package was delivered to me. You remember, Wally. It was a bottle, and my friend, Quinn—'

'Made a mess of everything!' Wally's top lip curled. 'Made work for me, that's what he did. Like I don't have enough to do around that place. Emptying trash cans and keeping the restrooms clean and picking up after you.' He shot me a look. 'You're messy.'

My organizational skills weren't what I was there to discuss. 'You did a great job of cleaning up that mess, Wally. And I was just wondering about it. I mean, when you were doing it, after you were done, did you feel any . . . different?'

'Don't be silly, girl. How can cleaning up a mess make somebody feel any different? Only—' Wally's eyes clouded over and his expression went blank and, for a second, I was worried about what was happening and what he might say when he snapped back to. 'Only I got to admit, I don't . . . I don't know how I felt, because I don't remember much.'

I gulped down the sudden knot in my throat. 'You remember coming into my office to clean up the broken glass.'

'Yeah, yeah. I guess I remember that.'

'And then?'

'And then . . .' Wally was clearly not a man who was used to sharing his feelings. His ears turned red. 'I don't know,' he admitted.

'You don't remember . . .'

'None of it. There you are, telling me I cleaned up that bottle, but it's like I said, I don't know. My brain, it's all foggy.'

'What's the next thing you do remember?' I asked him.

Thinking, he wrinkled his nose. It was a wide nose and so fleshy it reminded me of a lump of bread dough. 'I guess I must have . . . I dunno. I guess I must be working too hard. That's why I needed a little nap. I'm always working too hard, you know. You people, you always make me work too hard.'

I was almost afraid to ask. 'So you left my office and you took a nap.'

'I guess so. Only I don't remember leaving the office. I only remember that I woke up at three or four. Only you can't dock my hours,' he was quick to add. 'It wasn't like I was loafing or anything. I was just tired. From all the work I do.'

'Absolutely. I understand.' Only of course, I didn't, so I asked, 'So is that what happened at your house last night, too, Wally? Did you forget what you were doing? Were you maybe sitting in your living room watching TV and then—'

'Yeah, that's it. That's it exactly. I was in the living room, I remember that part now. And I had this idea that I had to look for—' Wally's forehead folded into a million wrinkles. 'Well, I don't know what I wanted to look for. I only know that something was missing and I had to find it and it was real important.'

'And the next thing you remember?'

For the first time since I came in the room, Wally looked me in the eye. 'You,' he said. 'You kneeling over me, asking what happened, asking if I was all right. And then the paramedics came and they carried me downstairs and I had a chance to look around and . . .' His left hand was bandaged just like the right, and he passed it over his eyes. 'What happened to my house, Pepper? Because I'll tell you what, I sure don't remember anybody coming in and tearing the place up, but that's what happened, isn't it? Somebody ripped my house to pieces.'

'It's nothing that can't be fixed,' I said, sounding like the eternal optimist I am not. 'Wally, when the paramedics carried you outside, you told me you were looking for ashes.'

'Ashes? Did I?' He considered this. 'What ashes?'

'I was hoping you could tell me that.'

Wally was not a man who was used to thinking, so he didn't give it much of a chance. 'I dunno,' he said. 'The only ashes I know anything about are the ones out in the fire pit. You know, when me and my buddies get together on weekends and do a bonfire in the backyard. Why would I be looking for those ashes?'

This I couldn't say.

What I could say was that I was feeling like I was at a dead end. My feet leaden and my heart heavy, I got up and headed for the door. 'Feel better, Wally,' I told him. 'I bet you'll be back to work in no time at all.'

He grunted. 'Place would fall apart without me,' he said. 'And not one person ever notices. It's Wally do this and Wally do that, and Wally does it all, too, and he never forgets anything except—'

'Except you did forget, Wally. The day you came into my office to clean up the glass. And yesterday when you were at home, and you don't know what happened and how your house got turned upside down. Both those times, you forgot.'

'Yeah, you're right.' He wasn't happy about admitting it. 'And then there was that other time, too.'

Let's face it, as statements go, this one wasn't much.

But it sure packed a punch.

The room wasn't big so it took me no time at all to get back to Wally's bedside.

'What other time?' I asked him and when he didn't answer fast enough, I grabbed Wally's hand. 'What other time?'

As if he wasn't used to another person's touch, or maybe because his fingers still hurt, Wally flinched and one by one, he picked my fingers away from his hand. 'It's nothing,' he assured me.

'Except it might be.' I stopped just short of slapping one hand against the bed. 'Wally, you've got to tell me. This might be really important.'

'I don't see how.' He scratched a hand over his ear. 'It was that same day, that day that clumsy friend of yours broke that bottle in your office. You say I cleaned it up, but I dunno . . .' As if filling in those empty hours he couldn't account for, he paused. 'I woke up eventually 'cause like I said, I was tired from too much work. And I did a few more things. You know, things Ella asked me to do around the building. I cleaned the employee locker room and straightened those pamphlets out on the shelves in the lobby. That kind of stuff.'

'And you remember all that.'

'Sure I do,' Wally told me. 'And I remember leaving work, too. Drove home the way I always do. Stopped off at the Dew Drop for a shot and a beer just like always, too. And after that . . .'

I sucked in a breath. 'After that?'

'Woke up at home,' he said. 'A few hours later. Only, Pepper . . .' When Wally raised his eyes to mine, his were moist. 'There was . . . My clothes had blood on them.'

Honestly, I couldn't tell if I was going to get sick or jump for joy. If Wally was possessed by Capone's spirit, if he was the one who went to McClure's to steal the ashes, if McClure was home and got in the way . . .

Sick won out, and I had to sit for a minute until my stomach settled down and, when it finally did, I was able to cough away the tightness in my throat and say, 'When you got the blood on your clothes, Wally, you might have taken something. Not that you meant to do it,' I added quickly because I could see by the way Wally's lips puckered that he was about to deny it. 'But you weren't thinking straight. Just like that morning when you cleaned up the bottle. What you took, Wally, I think it was a box, a wooden box about this big.' I held my hands out to demonstrate. 'It had ashes in it, Wally.'

He scrunched up his nose. 'Why would I want ashes?'

'It wasn't you. Well, it was, but . . .' I shook off the rest of the explanation because, let's face it, crabby or not, Wally was a logical (well, mostly) human being, and he wouldn't have believed a word of what I could have told him. 'I think you took the ashes home with you, Wally, and you put them somewhere for safekeeping.' Yeah, I left out the part about how that must have been after Capone's spirit had left him and about how that same nasty ghost must have shown up again and demanded that Wally produce the ashes and when he couldn't, how Capone's energy and Capone's anger and Capone's spite drove Wally to destroy the house looking for them. 'I know you don't remember, Wally, but it's really, really important for us to find that little box.'

He shook his head. 'If it was in my house, I would have found it, don't you think? From what I saw, I must have looked everywhere.'

I knew this, and this did not bode well for finding Ness's ashes, but before I could consider what my next move should be, Wally grabbed my hand and held on tight.

'You ain't gonna tell Ella, are you? If she finds out I've been forgetting things, she might think something's wrong with me.'

'Don't worry.' I gave him as much of a smile as I could muster. 'I won't say a word to Ella. I won't say a word to anyone.'

OK, this was not exactly one hundred percent true, because now that I finally had a solid theory about the case, I would have to share the news with Quinn. It all made sense, about

Wally forgetting and Wally tearing his house apart and maybe even about Wally killing Dean McClure.

If he was possessed . . .

I gulped down my panic, said goodbye to Wally and, all the way back out to my car, I tried to line up what Wally had told me with what I knew about the strange things that had been going on since the day McClure had brought that bottle to my office. After Ella almost ran me down at the cemetery, she had no idea what had happened and slept the sleep of the dead when she got home. After my mom tried to choke the life out of me, she assumed she'd fainted and had taken to her bed for a few days after, exhausted and confused. After Quinn visited the murder scene, he'd snatched up the fountain pen holder and tucked it in his closet.

They'd all been possessed, and Wally had been, too.

I hated to rain on anyone's arrest-the-perp parade, but I had to let Quinn know, and I made the call as soon as I got back to my car and, since he didn't answer, I left him a message.

'I'm pretty sure Cindy McClure didn't do it,' I told him. 'And I'm pretty sure I know what happened to the ashes. I'll explain it all tonight.'

Nervous energy being what it is, I worked like a demon that day. I scheduled four tours for the upcoming weeks, talked to Chet Houston about stories for the next newsletter, and even managed to return a bunch of the phone calls that had been piling up on my desk.

The second the clock struck five, I headed right over to Quinn's.

Yeah, yeah, I know he said six, but I had a key, and I knew he wouldn't mind if I got there early. As soon as he got home, we could discuss what I'd learned about the McClure case and then get down to dinner and everything that I was counting on happening after.

At his door, I regretted not stopping home to change into something slinky. No matter, I told myself, shoving my key in the lock, with any luck I'd be out of these clothes soon enough and then their relative slinkiness wouldn't matter.

I pushed open his door and stopped cold.

Quinn's loft is a wonder. Glass, metal, views of the city, soft lighting, warm wood. I don't know beans about architectural styles, but sleek and modern always came to mind. Clean and slick and uncluttered. Like his mind.

Except that day, there was something new in the front entryway.

It was as big as an end table and, in fact, since the top of it was flat, I guess that's what it was supposed to be. Except this table was ceramic.

Hulking.

Gray.

Ceramic.

Elephant.

My heart was already pounding when I realized it was keeping beat to the soft music I heard playing from somewhere inside the loft.

'Quinn!' My voice shook when I called his name. 'Are you here?' I sidestepped around the elephant – its trunk raised in greeting – and stepped into the wide open great room with its floor-to-ceiling windows, it's killer view of downtown Cleveland.

And more elephants.

Dozens and dozens of elephants.

There were little stone elephants on the coffee table and more of them lined up on the fireplace mantel.

There was a giant, stuffed elephant on the couch. And a colorful elephant quilt tossed over the back of the nearest chair. An elephant stared down at me, its tusks gleaming and a cartoonish smile on its face, from a painting over the fireplace that had replaced the painting I knew Quinn had paid a bundle for – a sapphire, amber, and maroon splotchy mess that he'd told me was a perfect example of Lyrical Abstraction (whatever that is) and always reminded me of the stuff I'd done in preschool that my mom had hung onto.

Evening light crawled through the windows on the far wall of the room and dappled all those elephants – with all their trunks raised – with gold.

And that music, it kept on playing.

I'd been so stunned by the sudden (and don't tell Quinn I said it, but I have to add the word tacky) change in decor, I'd barely paid any attention, but now, the plinking, strumming melody wormed its way through my bloodstream and stopped my heart cold.

'Quinn?' I called out to him but didn't get an answer.

But then, I guess that was to be expected because I found him in the bedroom, sitting on the edge of the bed with a faraway look in his eyes.

He was playing the banjo, and he didn't even pay any attention to me until I was five feet from him.

That's when he looked up, grinned, and said, 'Hello, my sweet!'

SEVENTEEN

It's not like anyone could blame me for not moving fast enough. After all, I was speechless. And terrified. I was still rooted to the spot when Quinn tossed the banjo on the bed and stood.

'You don't . . .' What I almost said was, 'You don't want to kill me,' but the very idea didn't jibe with my handsome lover standing there in nice tight jeans and the button-down shirt with colorful parrots all over it that I'd bought him after we spent a few hours daydreaming about where we'd like to go on our someday honeymoon and narrowed down the choices to Costa Rica or Hawaii. The words refused to form in my mouth and, instead, I managed to stammer out, 'You don't play the banjo!'

'Of course I do, don't you remember?' The voice was Quinn's. So was the smile. But the eyes . . . those green eyes reminded me of the color of the lichens that grew on gravestones in shady parts of the cemetery. Like death. 'I've always played the banjo.'

'Sure. Of course you have.' I backstepped my way to the bedroom door and hightailed it into the great room. 'I guess I'm just so hungry, I wasn't thinking,' I called out, then realized I didn't have to; Quinn was right behind me. 'So what are you making for dinner?' I asked him.

He ducked around the breakfast bar with the amber-colored hand blown glass pendant lights hanging over it and peered into a pot simmering on the stove. 'Pasta. I know . . .' Like I was going to say something (and let's face it, I wasn't because I was still too horrified to put together anything that sounded even a little coherent), he held up one hand. 'It might not be as good as your sauce, but I had to give it a try. It's the least I can do for you, my sweet. We'll sit down and eat in a couple minutes.' Humming a couple bars of *Ain't Misbehavin'*, he rummaged around in a cupboard, grabbed a box of pasta and set it on the countertop near the stove, then sauntered over and took my hand. 'But first, we need to talk about that message you left on my phone this afternoon. You told me Cindy McClure didn't kill her husband.'

It wasn't a question and, damn, if it was, I wasn't sure I could have answered it, anyway. The way my heart pounded and my blood pumped made thinking a little tough. How I managed a smile was anybody's guess. 'Did I say that? Really? What on earth was I talking about?' I laughed and oh-so-casually untangled my hand from his. 'I was so busy at work today, I didn't have a minute to even think about the case. I must have been speculating, that's all. Just taking a little break and speculating and—'

As quick as I took my hand back, Quinn grabbed it again and this time, he held on so tight I would have winced, but I didn't want to give him the satisfaction. 'You told me you know where the ashes are.'

It wasn't what he said that flash-froze my stomach.

It was the way he said it.

It was the look he gave me, the one that was completely devoid of emotion.

And humanity.

Funny, at that moment, looking into the eyes of death shook me back to life. Adrenaline shot through me along with a big dose of recklessness. Then again, something told me that the way things were going, I didn't have a lot to lose.

I laughed. 'Can you believe it?' I asked, and when I tugged my hand from his and he refused to let go, I tugged harder. Finally free, I didn't waste another second. I spun around and stutterstepped my way around the herd of wooden, stone, and glass elephants between me and the door. 'I left my phone in the car. I'm going to run down and get it and I'll be back in two shakes of a lamb's tail.'

The real Quinn would have known something was haywire as soon as he heard that lame lamb's tail line that I'd learned from Ness. This Quinn didn't bat an eyelash. But then, Capone and Ness shared a common history as well as a common vocabulary.

He didn't move an inch, and relieved, grateful, and praying that the elevator came and came fast, I dashed out into the hallway, slammed the door behind me and poked a finger against the call button.

'Come on, come on!' Yes, I know, pounding the button over and over wasn't going to help. Like I cared at that point! One eye on the closed door to Quinn's loft and my heart in my stomach, I pounded for all I was worth. 'Come on, already!'

The elevator arrived, the doors swished open and I stepped inside the empty car and punched the button for the first floor. It was only a few seconds before the doors slid closed and when they did, I let go a shaky breath.

At least until Quinn stuck his arm between the doors and they popped back open again.

That would pretty much be when my heart stopped and my breathing did, too.

'I hate the thought of you going down to the car by yourself.' As smooth as silk, he joined me inside the elevator. I stepped back, but . . . well, elevator. There wasn't much room for retreat. 'It's . . . what would you call it? It's unchivalrous. And you know I'm anything but.'

The elevator doors closed and the car lurched.

I took another step away from the most important person in my life who was suddenly a stranger.

'So . . .' I was wedged into the corner of the elevator, and Quinn closed in. He braced a hand on the wall on either side of me. 'You were saying, about those ashes.'

I'm not sure what I hoped to accomplish since my mouth was suddenly as dry as sand, but I ran my tongue over my lips. 'What I was saying was that I wasn't saying anything. I told you, I was just speculating. How could I possibly know where the ashes are?'

'But you do.'

It was as simple as that, and he didn't move a muscle or say another word, not even when the elevator bumped to a stop on the first floor and the doors swooshed open. Damn, there was no one waiting in the lobby.

I stepped forward.

Quinn didn't move and I was forced to stay right where I was. 'Where are they?' he asked.

Somehow, I managed to meet his gaze. 'I don't know.'

The elevator doors shut.

Quinn moved a step closer and all the colors on all those parrots on his shirt blurred in front of my eyes. 'I have all the time in the world,' he said and there wasn't one scrap of doubt in my head who that *I* was.

'Being dead does have its advantages,' I told Al Capone.

'Who would have imagined it, huh?' Like we weren't discussing something so weird it would have made most peoples' brains explode, he threw back his head and laughed in a very un-Quinn-like way. But then, the New York accent he'd suddenly acquired was very much not Quinn, either. 'When you're alive, you think dying is the end of the world! You know what I mean? And then you find out it's not. That there's more out there. More time. More things to do and places to go and people to—'

'Possess?'

He cocked his head and studied me and the elevator car started moving again. 'It could be worse,' he said.

'I doubt it.'

'You would. From what I hear, that's part of your problem. You doubt. And that makes you ask questions, and that means you stick your nose where it don't belong. See, when you do stuff like that . . .' He glided one finger down my neck and to the collar of shirt and inched it down to touch the bruises that still ringed my neck. 'This is what happens when you ask too many questions. And see this?' He fingered his left cheek. Quinn's left cheek. And because I knew every plane and angle of it, because I'd traced it in the dark and covered it with kisses and because so many times I'd felt it against mine, I knew there wasn't a scar on it. Yet his fingers traced the shape of a wound. 'These here scars, this is what comes from sticking your nose where it doesn't belong.'

'Then you should have learned a lesson.'

'Oh, I have.' His smile was sleek. 'I've learned to survive. My way. No one else's. I proved that, didn't I? Eliot Ness . . .' He gave the name a sour twist. 'He thought he could keep me in my grave with that there stupid containment spell. You see how wrong he was? And once you tell me where his ashes are . . . well, that will take care of him once and for all. Finally, he'll find out who's really the boss.'

'I told you I don't know anything about the ashes.'

'And I told you the world works the way I want it to. It always has and it always will. Don't forget, my pretty lady, just because I have all the time in the world, doesn't mean your friend here . . .' He touched a finger to the front of the parrot shirt. 'Your friend doesn't.'

He reached back and hit the button on the door panel and the elevator bumped to a stop. The overhead light flickered.

'You're a pretty dame, but you're not fooling anyone.' He leaned nearer. 'You've been through this. You know exactly what I'm talking about.'

There was no use denying it. Like it was no big deal, I tossed my head. 'You'll notice that Madeline Callahan, that ghost who tried to take my body, isn't around anymore. I took care of her.'

'And you think you can do the same with me?' His chuckle was soft and guttural. 'She was weak.'

'And I'm a lot stronger than I look.'

'And I don't take no for an answer.' He pushed himself against me, his mouth near my ear. 'And I'll promise you this . . .'

He didn't touch the button, but the elevator started up again and my heart bounced into my throat. When the doors whooshed open, I recognized the hallway outside Quinn's loft.

'I'm staying,' he said, his breath hot against my ear. 'Until you bring me those ashes, I'm staying right here in this body, and the longer it takes, the less likely it is that there will be anything left of him to ever come back to you.'

He stepped off the elevator and into the hallway, but the doors didn't close, not right away. That gave him a chance to tip an imaginary hat to me.

'That is, unless you'd like me to jump out of this jamoke and into someone else.'

The doors slid shut, but not before he delivered his parting shot.

'Like maybe your mother.'

I didn't go home.

Quinn had a key to my apartment, and until I had a chance to get the locks changed, I wasn't going to risk walking in and finding him there. And it's not like I'd get a wink of sleep or a moment's rest, anyway, not if I was listening for every creak of the floor and the telltale sounds of the door opening in the wee hours of the night.

With no place else to go (let's face it, Mom and Dad's wasn't an option, not when the only talk I'd hear was wedding-this and wedding-that), I drove back to the cemetery and, since it closes at sunset, I entered through the back gate that the landscape and maintenance crews sometimes use when there's a problem and they have to come or go after hours. I'm not brainless, I knew there was no way I was going to get any rest in my office. That wasn't what I was looking for, and at that point, it didn't much matter. I was so keyed up, so worried, and so scared out of my mind, I couldn't sit still, anyway.

I paced.

And talked to myself.

I tried to sit still and ended up twirling in my desk chair until my brain spun and my vision blurred and my head ached, and when I couldn't pace anymore and I couldn't twirl for another second, and I had nothing left to say even to myself, I laid my head down on my desk and cried my eyes out.

Like tears usually do when the world is falling apart, it helped to let them flow, and when I finally stopped, and my eyes were red and swollen and my nose was sloppy, I made up my mind.

I had to find Eliot Ness's ashes.

Fast.

I grabbed a legal pad and made a list, talking to myself while I scrawled line after nearly unintelligible line.

Wally looking for ashes.

So he knows they exist.

So he could have been the one who took them.

And killed Dean McClure.

'It makes sense from an investigative standpoint.'

If I had even an ounce of energy left, I would have jumped at the sound of Eliot Ness's voice. The way it was, I simply glanced over to my right and at the cloud suspended over my desk.

'I need to find your ashes,' I told him.

Was it possible for a man as professional as Ness to actually click his tongue? 'I told you that right from the start.'

'But now—' I bit back the rest of the words that had almost slipped. How could I tell Ness that I wasn't looking for the ashes so that he could rest in peace, but so that I could hand them over to Al Capone? I cleared the heaviness from my throat with a cough. 'Where do we start?'

'We start by being logical. By thinking clearly and dispassionately. Those tears of yours . . .' He zipped in close, and I had a feeling he was looking me in the eye. 'You're upset.'

I wanted to tell him. Honest. But the words burned inside me like fire and it was too painful, I couldn't force them out. 'Quinn and I had a fight,' I said.

'Is he possessed like that friend of yours, that Beauchamp fellow, said he might be?'

'He's not my friend.'

If Ness noticed that I didn't answer, he didn't let on. 'I was married three times, you know,' he said. 'And I wasn't much in the way of a faithful husband. I always had an eye for the ladies.'

'That's not Quinn's problem,' I told him in no uncertain terms.

'I didn't say it was. I just meant that I understand these little . . . let's call them differences. We can't let our emotions get in the way of our duties.'

'Like finding your ashes.'

'Exactly.' He wafted toward the door. 'Shall we get started?'

Of course we should. We had to. Only . . .

At the same time I stood, I raised my arms in the air and let them flop to my sides. 'Where?'

'Like your list says, with Wally, of course.' Ness hovered near the door and I knew what he wanted. I opened it for him and allowed him to step . . . er . . . float into the hallway before me. 'I think Capone must have possessed Wally, at least twice, possibly three times. It explains why he wasn't acting like himself when he came in to clean up the broken bottle.'

'Because Capone had slipped into him.' I'd already thought of this, of course, but it didn't hurt to say it out loud, just to keep the facts straight.

'And I think Wally, with Capone's spirit inside him, must have known about my ashes being in McClure's home because now he knows they're missing. Otherwise he wouldn't be looking for them.'

'Not only that, but I think he killed McClure,' I told Ness because he hadn't been around when I went to see Wally in the hospital that afternoon so he didn't know this part of the story. 'Wally doesn't remember what happened for a chunk of the evening when McClure was killed, but he does remember that when he got home, there was blood on his clothes. If Capone possessed him, it isn't Wally's fault,' I added with surprising oomph. Sure, Wally was Wally and a big ol' pain in the neck, but I couldn't stand the thought of an innocent man being accused of a murder. 'Wally killed McClure, took the ashes, and then Capone must have de-possessed him. Or un-possessed him. Or whatever you want to call it.'

We'd been walking down the hallway as we talked, and we were in the reception area where Jennine usually greeted visitors. In the light of the security lamp outside above the door, I saw Ness sparkle above the maroon sweater she kept on the back of her chair. 'You mean because—'

'Because Wally stashed the ashes and Capone doesn't know where they are.' Before he could ask me how I knew this for sure, I provided him with the most logical answer. 'When Capone possessed Wally again and went to get the ashes, Wally couldn't find them. Capone has no idea where they are. It explains why Wally ripped his house apart.'

'So when he wasn't possessed—'

'Wally put the ashes somewhere for safekeeping. But he doesn't remember where because after a person's been possessed, he'd kind of out of it for a while. I saw that with Ella and with my mom. So Wally forgot what he did with your ashes, and now it's our job to figure out where he put them.'

And then do what with them?

The thought pounded through my head, but I couldn't let it distract me. I couldn't worry about Al Capone or about dashing Ness's hopes for resting in peace. That was phase two of this operation. Phase one was all about finding the ashes.

There was a hallway directly opposite Jennine's desk and I started down it and Ness followed along. 'You have an idea?' he asked.

I hated to admit I didn't. Not a solid one, anyway.

'Wally said he cleaned the employee locker room,' I told Ness. 'At least it's somewhere we can start.' I pushed open the doorway at the end of the hallway and headed down the stairs.

The Garden View employee locker room is one of those places I don't visit very often. Since I'd had an office of my own ever since I worked at the cemetery, I'd never needed a place to stash my coat or my purse. Each employee and volunteer (there was an army of them, and they're all history lovers or genealogist or cemetery geeks like Ella), has an assigned locker and the sign Ella had hanging just inside the door informed them that at the end of every shift, each locker had to be emptied and left open. (Yes, this does sound dictatorial, especially coming from warm and fuzzy Ella, but there's the story of the volunteer who broke her leg on the way home from Garden View one day. And the operation that kept her from coming back for six weeks. And the tuna fish sandwich she'd stashed in her locker before she left on the day of the accident. Believe me, Ella was onto something with the open lockers!)

And as it turned out, I was, too, because the open lockers made it easy for me to see that Wally hadn't tucked those ashes in any of the lockers.

'Other possibilities?' Ness asked when he saw my shoulders droop.

There were hundreds.

Together, Eliot Ness and I spent the next hours checking out every one of them. We searched every inch of the administration building. We rummaged through every desk. We checked out every office. Since he had the whole incorporeal thing going on (a definite advantage in this instance), I was the one who went through the trash – and since Wally had been in the hospital and it hadn't been emptied and Max in accounting had a birthday that day and someone had brought in cupcakes with gooey chocolate icing . . .

In the conference room that also served as an employee break room, I grabbed a paper towel, scraped chocolate from my hands and kept the 'Ew!' to myself.

'Nothing,' I told Ness.

'Not yet.'

I wondered if he was so annoyingly optimistic when he was alive or if it was a trait he'd acquired since. 'I could go back to Wally's,' I suggested, not nearly as optimistic as he was, but far more desperate. 'But I was there. I saw the way the house was torn apart. If the ashes were there, Wally would have found them. He obviously looked everywhere.'

Except . . .

'What is it?' Ness asked. 'You look as if you've thought of something.'

'The fire pit.' I raced to my office for my keys and, even though I knew I'd be coming back since I had nowhere else to go, I locked up the administration building when I left. Ella was always the first one in the office every morning and I couldn't take the chance that she'd find the building open when she arrived in just another hour or so.

Holding on to the fragile thread of hope, Ness and I arrived at Wally's just as the sun came up over the horizon. If any of the neighbors was an early bird, I was ready with a story about how I was checking on the house for my dear coworker, but as it turned out, I didn't need the lie. We walked out back and found the fire pit with four tree stumps set around it for chairs.

With one finger (and cringing the whole time) I poked through the ashes. They were heavy and wet.

'Like they've been here all winter,' I grumbled.

'And no sign of the box my ashes were in,' Ness added. 'So I'm guessing my ashes aren't mixed with those.'

It hit me like a brick there in Wally Birch's backyard. How tired I was. How scared I was. How worried I was about Quinn's safety and his health and his soul.

'It's an honor to work beside a person who takes the job so seriously,' Ness said, and he wasn't reading my mind; I think he could figure out how I felt from the way I dragged around to the front of the house and out to the car, my head hanging. 'We've got to keep working at it, Pepper. You'll see.

What we've accomplished tonight is to eliminate a lot of possibilities. That means we're getting closer and closer to finding the answer. And the ashes. And then . . .' In the morning sunlight, what there was of Eliot Ness twinkled like stars and, yeah, I know the guy wasn't living and he sure wasn't breathing, but the sound he made reminded me of a person drawing in a lungful of fresh morning air and letting it out again with a whoosh to welcome the new day.

'You'll have my ashes,' he assured me. 'And then I'll rest in peace.'

'But—' Honest to goodness, I wanted to explain that there were things going on that he didn't know about, things that made me wonder what I would do once I got my hands on the ashes.

Would I take them right out to the newly filled lake behind the chapel so they could be sprinkled as they were supposed to have been sprinkled all those years ago?

Or would I turn them over to Al Capone to save Quinn's life and give Capone the power to destroy Eliot Ness once and for all?

I was too tired to think through the problem and, besides, even when I tried, all it did was bring up more questions.

Like, who was I really working for?

Eliot Ness?

Or Al Capone?

EIGHTEEN

It was a long day, and I sleepwalked through it like a woman . . . well, I was going to say a woman possessed, but honestly, it was too horrible to even think about. I dragged through an early morning meeting about customer service. I hauled myself out into the cemetery when some folks from the Western Reserve Historical Society showed up to check out the grave of the first woman from Ohio to ever be elected to Congress. The fresh air should have done me some good. Instead, the day's sunshine only left me feeling like a balloon with a slow leak.

Which explains why I wasn't fast enough on my feet to dodge Ella when she met me in the hallway as I was making my way back to my office.

'I've got the best idea!' She herself was a sunbeam that day in a bright yellow dress with orange accents. It actually hurt my eyes. 'I've been thinking, about that idea you suggested for an article for the next newsletter. The one about how changing tastes in architecture have affected the look of the cemetery over the years.'

I, of course, hadn't suggested the article at all. The idea had come from Chet Houston and, when he proposed it, I thought it was a little lah-di-dah sounding. Chet liked nothing better than to get down and dirty with his stories, and the ones he'd written for me in the past were more in the way of human interest: the burlesque dancer buried in section seventeen, the disgraced politician in an unmarked grave near the front gates, the bank robber buried beneath the spreading limbs of a pine tree not far from the administration building.

Chet, though, wanted to spread his journalistic wings and at least to him, a more in-depth article sounded like a good way to do it. As I'd told him at the time, 'Knock yourself out,' and since I hadn't seen hide nor hair of his ectoplasmic self since, maybe that's exactly what he was doing.

'Architecture, sure.' It wasn't much of a response, but hey, the way I was feeling, I figured Ella was lucky to get even that out of me.

She shuffled into my office behind me, so full of energy and so enthusiastic about the article, she could barely stand still. 'I'm thinking front page,' she said.

I would be sure to let Chet know.

I flopped into my desk chair. 'I'll get to work on it,' I told her.

'Good. That's great. I'm anxious for you to get started.'

I stared at her through blurry eyes.

'I mean, right now,' she said.

'Right—'

'Get crackin'!' Ella laughed. 'The light is perfect this afternoon. You can start getting some pictures and with the sky being so blue and the daffodils in bloom . . . well, you couldn't ask for a better day. While you're at it and out on the grounds, you can start making a list of the various architectural styles you'll see. But you know that, don't you?' Like she hadn't meant to say it in the first place, she waved her hands in front of her like that could get rid of the suggestion. 'I'm sorry, sometimes I know I sound like I did back when the girls were in high school and I was trying to help them out with their term papers. You know, suggesting that first they take notes then make an outline and, oh, how many times I reminded them that they needed to focus on the most important aspects of a subject rather than try to write about every little facet because that's too overwhelming! You don't need that kind of advice from me. Not anymore. The newsletters you've been producing are wonderful, Pepper. I'm just as proud of you as I can be!'

Even the smile I had to fight to give her wasn't enough. Urging me on, Ella motioned toward the door. 'I'm thinking of a two-part article,' she said. 'Or maybe it should be three. You could do gravestones in one, statues in another. But let's start with mausoleums. Those are the most spectacular, and there are so many different styles. Come on, Pepper!' When I didn't move fast enough (actually, I didn't move at all), she zipped over, grabbed my hand and dragged me out of my chair. For a short, round woman, Ella can be pretty tough.

She put a hand to the small of my back and pushed me to the door. 'Get going while the sun is still bright! And don't come back until you have pictures. Lots of pictures. You'll need a couple dozen at least and make sure you get some of each kind of architecture – classical revival and baroque and Egyptian and Gothic and . . .'

I can't say for sure, but I think she was still talking long after I left the office.

So here's the thing – any other day I would have been happy to get out of administration building. I mean, there's always something I can find to do that has nothing to do with cemetery work, right? Sometimes it's investigating. Sometimes it's a long lunch. Sometimes it's a quick shopping trip that, more often than not, ends up eating up more time than I expect but gives me a much-needed breather from the humdrum of Garden View.

That day, a little humdrum would have been welcomed.

At least humdrum would have helped take my mind off the worries that ate away at my composure and tap-tap-tapped inside my brain like the woodpecker I heard knocking against a tree when I schlepped into the parking lot.

If I was thinking straight – *if* being the operative word – I would have meandered around near the administration building; there are plenty of mausoleums nearby. But my brain wasn't working and my body was on autopilot. I got into my car and headed to the other side of the cemetery where I knew I'd find plenty of what Ella was looking for.

I took pictures of Egyptian-inspired mausoleums, and classical revival ones, too, and in spite of Ella's advice, I didn't bother with notes because let's face it, anything I needed to know about the mausoleums and who was buried in them, she could tell me and I could tell Chet. Done with my first stop, I got back in my car and made three others, hoping the whole time that the warm spring breeze and bright sunshine would take my mind off my dark thoughts.

It didn't, and after an hour of picture taking and another hour of sitting on a bench and brooding near an especially grand mausoleum erected in honor of some train magnate from more than one hundred years ago, I knew there was only one place in the cemetery that matched my mood. I headed for a section where I knew I'd find many of the examples of mausoleum architecture Ella had mentioned along with silence, emptiness, and plenty of gloom.

Garden View is a privately owned cemetery and we do plenty of fund-raising to make sure we have enough money for things like grounds maintenance. As such, the roads inside the cemetery's walls are in good shape. Still, maneuvering around gentle curves and down a little-used road that led to a wide, grassy expanse that was on a lower level than the rest of the cemetery is hard enough when I'm alert and paying attention. What with the way my head throbbed, the narrowness of the road, and the fact that the trees that overhung it meant moving into deep shadow one second and out of it the next into bright sunlight, it was more of a challenge that day than ever.

I finally made it and parked my car near a monument where candles twinkled in glass holders and visitors had left old vinyl record albums. As always when I was nearby, I stopped to say hello to Damon Curtis, rock star legend who also happened to be a ghost I'd met – and fell in love with – in the course of one of my first investigations.

'Wish you could help me now,' I whispered, but Damon didn't answer back. After years of yearning for eternal rest, I'd helped him find it, and he'd left me feeling lost and alone.

Pretty much like I was feeling right now.

If only I could turn off the worry center in my brain!

Because I couldn't – because I knew I never would until I did something to help Quinn – I glanced around the little valley. There were a dozen mausoleums down there, and many of them were more than one hundred and fifty years old, as old as Garden View itself. I tramped from one to the other, snapping pictures from all angles. Most people don't live and breathe cemeteries – I mean, not like Ella does – so most people don't realize that mausoleums are really burial chambers. They're free-standing structures and, inside, their residents (it's an Ella word and I'd heard it so often, that's how I thought of them now, too) are either interred in niches along the wall or, in some cases, on a lower level with a stairway leading below ground.

Then and now, mausoleums cost a bundle, and only the wealthiest could afford them, but the ones here in the valley were so old, no one had been buried in them for many years, and anyone who'd ever come to visit was long dead, too. Some of them had metal gates across their doorways, and they were rusted shut. Stone steps were cracked, and two of the stained glass windows that graced a couple of the mausoleums had been broken.

It was sad, and if I wasn't so darned tired, I would have made a list to give to maintenance so they could get down here and get to work making repairs.

Tired.

Maintenance.

Something about those two words penetrated the fog in my brain, but for the life of me, I couldn't figure out what it was. I moved away from one Gothic-inspired mausoleum to one with a flat roof and sphinxes on either side of the door.

Tired.

Maintenance.

As real as if they'd been whispered on the wind, the words tickled my brain again.

Automatically, I glanced around, half expecting and more than half hoping that Damon had somehow shown up, but I was the only one down in the little valley.

And I was so, so tired.

Tired. Like Wally said he was from working so hard.

With a kick like a double espresso, the thought hit and I was suddenly wide awake.

Wally took naps in an unused mausoleum. Everybody who worked at Garden View knew it.

'Wally took naps in an unused mausoleum!' I called up to the blue sky, and to Damon, too, wherever he was, and I hotfooted it over to the road and started with the mausoleum closest to it.

Locked.

So was the next mausoleum. And the next. And the one after that.

But the next one . . .

When the mausoleum door moved at my touch, I let out a breath of amazement.

'Wally took naps in an unused mausoleum,' I told myself one last time, and with one breath for courage and another so that I could get a lungful of fresh air before I stepped into the land of the dead, I went inside.

After all the time and all the worry and all the wracking of my brain, it ended up taking no time at all to find Eliot Ness's ashes. They were still in the little mahogany box Dean McClure had made for them, tucked into a corner between where the remains of someone named Isaac Chamberline (1820–1877) were resting in a niche and the stained glass window that tinted the entire inside of his mausoleum a color that reminded me of blood.

I grabbed the box and hugged it to my chest, realizing as I did that it all made perfect sense. Wally was possessed when he killed Dean McClure and took the ashes. He wasn't when he stashed the ashes in the most logical of places – the place he often came to hide out from his job responsibilities. If I needed proof, it was there in the sleeping bag Wally had left on the floor, the stack of magazines next to it, and the coffee cup, too, the one that said *Wally is the Man!* across it in big green letters. The way I remembered it, Ella had given Wally the cup the Christmas before. I wondered how she'd feel if she knew he was using it while he loafed on the clock.

I stepped out of the mausoleum and took a deep breath of fresh air. I'd like to say I did a little happy dance on the way back to my car, but let's face it, just because the ashes were in my hot little hands didn't mean I was carefree.

I still had to figure out if I was going to sprinkle the ashes at the lake so that Eliot Ness could finally enjoy the eternal rest he'd earned.

Or use them to ransom Quinn's soul.

I hadn't realized how long I'd been out on the grounds; by the time I got back to the administration building, the shadows were long and most of the cars in the parking lot were gone. I grabbed the ashes and, even though there was no one around, I wasn't taking any chances, I held them close to my chest when I went inside to get my purse.

Where was I headed after that?

Honestly, at that point, I wasn't sure. I only knew that I needed to do some serious thinking and, while I was at it, I wanted to call Quinn. And my mother. I wanted to see who was and who wasn't possessed. Whoever wasn't . . . well, maybe that person could help me think my way to a solution to the problem that was Al Capone.

Jennine was gone for the day, most of the lights in the building were off and, though I didn't remember closing my office door when I left, it was closed when I got to it and the light inside the office was off.

I pushed open the door and sucked in a breath of astonishment and horror when every light in the room came on.

And who could blame me?

The light spilled over the pink and white bunting that had been hung across my bookcase. It glistened against the bunches of pink and white balloons tied to my desk chair and my guest chairs and to the table that had been dragged into the room where a sheet cake with pink and white frosting shared center stage with a variety of packages wrapped in colorful paper.

Ella's three daughters, Rachel, Sarah, and Ariel stood behind my desk and they gave me half-hearted waves and the kind of smiles people offer when they're not sure if their friends are going to love them or hate them or ever forgive them for what's about to happen.

I guess I couldn't blame them, because what was about to happen was that Ella and my mother jumped in front of me, paper party hats on their heads and balloons in their hands, and yelled, 'Surprise!'

NINETEEN

Oh, I was surprised, all right.

I clutched one hand around the casket that contained Eliot Ness's ashes and used the other one to put a hand to my chin to push my mouth shut.

'It worked! It worked! We really surprised you, didn't we, honey?' My mother grinned like a teenaged prom queen and wound an arm through mine so she could drag me farther into the office. 'I knew we could do it,' she told Ella who beamed me a smile.

'I don't really need all those pictures of all those mausoleums. Not anytime soon.' Ella was so pleased with herself, I thought she would burst. 'I just wanted to get you out of the office so we could decorate.'

'Out of the office to decorate for . . .' I looked around. There were finger sandwiches on china plates on my desk along with pink punch in a cut glass bowl I knew had once belonged to my grandmother. Now that I was close enough, I saw that the pink icing on the cake spelled out *Congratulations, Pepper*!

But Ella and my mom, they couldn't have known I'd found the ashes. So why would they congratulate me? They couldn't have known what I was going to do with the ashes, either, so that couldn't have been it. Heck, even I didn't know what I was going to do with the ashes.

I suspected I resembled a deer in headlights, and it's so not a good look for me, so I pulled myself together at the same time I made a move toward the door. Ashes, remember, and whatever I was going to do, I needed to make up my mind and do it. Fast.

'Oh, no!' My mother held on like a limpet. 'You're not going anywhere. We're here to have some fun!'

'But I've got to go . . .' I tried for the door again, but if there's one thing I should have learned years earlier, it was that the woman who'd given birth to me could be just as stubborn as I was. I gave up with a sound that was half grumble, half sigh.

'What's going on here, anyway?' I didn't bother asking my mother. Or even Ella. I looked at her daughters because something told me if I was going to get an answer that made any sense, it would come from them. 'What are you all doing here?'

Rachel glanced at her mother. 'Her idea.'

Sarah slugged down the rest of the punch in her glass. 'And you know how she gets.'

Ariel's mouth screwed into a grimace. 'You can't say no to the woman. You should know that by now, Pepper.'

I looked to Ella.

'It's a shower,' she squealed.

'A shower.' The words felt as uncomfortable as my insides suddenly did. 'But there's no wedding. Not yet.' And maybe never, the voice inside my head reminded me. Because even if I didn't know how to handle the ashes, I was one hundred percent sure I didn't want to marry a man who had Al Capone inside him calling the shots. 'That means there shouldn't be a shower, and that means I really should be going . . .' Once again, my mother grabbed on tight and refused to let go when I made a move toward the door.

'It's not a wedding shower.' Since she still had a hold on me, I had no choice but to go along when Barb dragged me over to the table, poured a glass of very pink punch, and handed it to me.

'It can't be an engagement shower, either,' I told her. 'I told you, Mom. Quinn and I, we're not—'

'Of course it's not an engagement shower!' Mom laughed. 'It's a pre-engagement pre-shower shower.' She actually said this with a straight face. 'You know, just a little gathering to help get you ready for when the big moment really does arrive.'

Which it never would if Quinn was still being held hostage by the meanest son-of-a-bitch ever to walk the streets of Chicago.

'That's terrific.' The words somehow formed on my lips. 'But I've got this thing I have to take care of and it's really important and—'

'Oh, no! You're not dashing off anywhere.' My mother actually hauled me across the room. Before she deposited me in a chair festooned with pink crepe paper, I managed to put the box of ashes on my desk. 'We've been planning this for a long time and we're going to enjoy every minute of it. We're going to play Bridal Bingo.'

'And take a quiz about romantic movie quotes,' Ella added.

'And don't forget!' My mother's smile was radiant. 'Wedding Jeopardy!'

For one second, I wondered if Caleb would know all the answers. In the next, I wondered how the hell I was going to get out of there.

Before I had the chance to figure out an escape plan, Ella looked at her daughters. 'What do you think?' she asked Rachel, Sarah, and Ariel who, it should be noted, looked as horrified at the goings-on as I felt. 'Do we eat first or open gifts?'

I didn't wait for them to answer. 'This is all really lovely and I really appreciate it, but—' When I stood up, my mother pushed me back into the chair.

'I told you she'd be embarrassed.' Ella's laugh filled my office. 'You have a wonderful daughter, Barb, and I told you she wouldn't want to put us out. What she needs to remember . . .' Ella came over and patted my hand. 'You need to remember that we're your friends and we love this chance to spoil you. So' – she reached for a gift wrapped in green and blue paper – 'Let's start with the presents!'

Thankfully, there weren't many. Rachel and Sarah went in together and got me a silver frame and said I could use it for a picture of me and Quinn.

I couldn't help but imagine Al Capone standing between us in the photograph.

Ariel got me a book (of course) about how to plan a wedding.

And I had to question how Melvil Dewey would classify it, and where he'd put it on the shelves.

Ella presented me with a CD called *Perfect Wedding Music* and told me that Quinn and I would have such fun choosing the songs we'd like for the ceremony.

And before I could stop myself, I checked the song titles and wondered if any of them included banjo music.

My mother, it should be noted, really did spend a whole lot of time and effort on her gift. It was a photo album that she created online, pictures of me as a baby and a toddler and a kid. 'You were so adorable,' she told me. 'As soon as Quinn sees this, of course he'll propose right away.'

Oh, how I hoped not!

I didn't exactly like the thought of being married to a mobster.

There were a couple other little gifts, too, and honestly, I would have appreciated them more along with all the time and effort Ella and my mom put in to surprising me if I wasn't so anxious and so nervous and so darned worried, I thought my heart would pound its way out of my chest.

I was grateful for one thing, though.

At least nobody gave me any elephants.

By the time it was all over, it was long past dark. Rachel, Sarah and Ariel left at the same time, but not before they'd each given me a hug and whispered a quick apology. I thanked them for being such good sports.

Mom, Ella, and I walked out to our cars together, and I set the box of ashes on the front seat next to me and closed my eyes, doing my best to get my brain back on track. It would have been easier if I wasn't on a sugar high from the punch and the cake. Ella left the parking lot with mom's car right behind her so Ella could lead her through the cemetery and out the back gate that Wally must have come in the night he killed Dean McClure and stashed the ashes in the mausoleum. Once they were on their way, I started my car and followed.

I've mentioned how twisty and turny the roads are in the cemetery, right? It all has to do with the notion from back in the day that cemeteries were places of peace and quiet and yes, of romance, too. I mean, really, more than one hundred years ago, guys used to bring their dates to the cemetery in carriages so they could drive around and enjoy the scenery.

Go figure.

With all that romancey stuff in mind, I guess I shouldn't have been surprised when I rounded a gentle curve and my headlights hit the figure standing in the middle of the road, blocking my way.

Quinn!

I slammed on my breaks just inches from where he stood, his expression blank, and for the space of a dozen heartbeats, I sat there like I'd been flash frozen, my fingers clutching the steering wheel and my stomach in my throat. Call me psychic (and I'm really not since I can't see the future or read peoples' minds, I can only talk to the dead), but one look and I knew he wasn't the Quinn I knew and loved.

That guy wouldn't be lurking in the cemetery in the middle of the night. He wouldn't be standing square in front of my car, either, legs locked, feet apart, his arms at his sides and his hands curled into fists.

I slammed my car into reverse, backed up and tried to remember where I was and what was around me.

Angel statue on my right. I knew that, even in the dark, just like I knew that if I mowed it down, our insurance rates would skyrocket and Ella would never speak to me again.

Row of mausoleums behind me that were historic and valuable so there was no way out in that direction, either.

Shrubbery on my left that edged a family plot and heck, as far as I was concerned, shrubbery was replaceable.

I put the car in drive and shot forward, intending to go around Quinn and over the shrubs. Don't ask me how he moved that fast, but before I got as far as squishing even one branch, Quinn was right in front of me.

This time when I hit the brakes, I lurched forward and my head knocked into the steering wheel. By the time I shook away the resulting fuzziness, Quinn stood at the driver's door.

'No!' I felt along the controls on the inside of the driver's door for the lock button, but my head didn't cooperate and my movements were jerky.

Quinn's were as smooth as butter when he grabbed the door handle and yanked.

Cool night air slapped me out of my stupor but not fast enough. Quinn unbuckled my seatbelt and hauled me out of the car.

'Where are they?' he demanded.

It's hard to play it cool with knees knocking like castanets. I did my best, and while I was at it, I raised my chin and sent a laser look at the man I loved.

'I don't know what you're talking about.'

'I know you have them. Where are they?'

'Well, how would you know I have them in the first place?' I demanded. 'If you've got a connection to some kind of 1-800 psychic line, then you would have found the stupid ashes all by yourself a long time before this. Unless—' The thought hit, and I swallowed hard. 'You've been following me.'

'Hey, when you've got a guy with skills like this guy's . . .' Capone was talking about Quinn. In Quinn's body. Using third person. It was enough to make my head spin. 'Hand them over, and we can all get on with our lives.'

'Except you don't have one.'

His laugh was anything but friendly. 'And you think your friend here will have much of a life left by the time I'm done with him?'

Funny (and not in a ha-ha way), but ever since I found the ashes, I'd been dithering about what to do with them. Here in the dark, surrounded by the dead and face to face with evil, I had a moment of clarity.

'You're a bully.' I put both hands to Quinn's chest and shoved as hard as I could. When he stumbled back, I closed in on him. 'You have no right to jump in and out of peoples' bodies and make them do what you want them to. In fact, you shouldn't be here at all. You're dead, Capone. Get it?' I glared into Quinn's eyes, grateful that it was dark and I couldn't get upended by whatever it was I might have seen looking back at me.

I spun around and stepped back toward my car. 'I've got a really good idea,' I told Al Capone. 'How about if you go back to whatever hell you crawled out of.'

It was a great parting shot, or at least it would have been if the parting part ever happened. The way it was, before I ever got back to the car, Quinn's arms closed around my midsection. He lifted me off my feet, spun me around, and shook me so hard my head rattled.

'The ashes.' His words were fire. 'I want them and I want them now.'

The way he was hanging on to me, I couldn't move my arms, but there was nothing that kept me from rearing back and giving him a good head butt. The hollow sound of my skull connecting with his chin made me cringe, but good news, it made Quinn loosen his hold.

I wormed out of his grasp and, while I was at it, slammed my foot down on his, and when he yelped and staggered, I put some distance between us.

I was almost to the car when he grabbed me again.

'You can't get away,' he said, and maybe he was right, because the way his fingers dug into my skin and held on tight, there was no way I could move.

'I need those ashes and I need them now.' This time, he didn't give me a chance to come up with a smart-ass reply. He backhanded me across the face, and I went flying.

The last thing I remember, I landed in a heap in those shrubs I'd planned to run over just a short time before.

I don't know how long I was knocked out. I do know that by the time I woke up, the night air was cold against my skin and drops of dew mixed with the sheen of sweat on my forehead. Fog hugged what was left of the shrubbery where I'd landed and, shivering, I sat up, picked bits of greenery out of my hair, and tried to put together the pieces of what had happened. When they fell into place, I went right on shivering and dragged myself to my feet.

My car was right where I left it, the engine still running, the door still open, and I staggered toward it and watched the cemetery around me turn to a water-color image of itself thanks to the tears in my eyes. I really didn't need to go over to the passenger side door and look. I knew I'd find the seat there empty, and when I did, my shoulders sagged and my heart ached and I laid my forehead against the door frame.

'Sorry, Mr Ness,' I whispered. 'I tried. I'm sorry I lost your ashes.'

I dragged around to the other side of the car and, ribs protesting with every breath, I got in. Not that it mattered anymore, but when I did, I made sure the car doors were locked.

The way my head spun, it wouldn't be easy finding my way out of the cemetery, but I knew if I did, at least I'd be close to home. And then . . .

I couldn't think that far ahead. Instead, I leaned forward, peering out the windshield and inching my way down the dark road.

Fog whirlpooled around the car, and the windows misted, and as I neared the chapel and the little lake where I'd first met Eliot Ness, I was forced to slow down even more. It was a good thing I did, or I never would have seen Quinn off by the side of the road.

Yeah, yeah, I know . . . considering what had happened (was it minutes ago or hours?) the smart thing to do would be to keep on driving. But nobody ever said love was smart or that I was either, and even though every bone in my body ached and I realized that my pants were torn and my left knee was bloody, I was out of the car fast.

Quinn was propped against the Ness memorial, his eyes closed and, like Wally when I found him under the mattress in his bedroom, his breathing shallow. I knelt down and grabbed his shoulders so that I could slide his head away from the cold granite and put it on my lap. When I took his hand, it was even colder and clammier than mine.

'Quinn, can you hear me?'

He didn't answer or even open his eyes. But he did move his head from side to side and groan and this cheered me no end at the same time it shot panic through my insides.

'Quinn!' I hated that I sounded fragile and afraid, that tears clogged my voice and my heart thumped loud enough to be heard in the next county. Whatever was going on inside Quinn, whoever he was at that moment, I owed him more than helplessness. 'It's going to be OK, Quinn,' I promised him. 'Only you have to open your eyes. You have to tell me how you're feeling.'

His eyes fluttered open, but not long enough for me to find out who might be in there looking back at me. They flickered shut, and his breathing slowed.

And I knew if I didn't do something fast, I was going to lose him.

Sure, I could have called 911 and gotten a team of paramedics over there to help, but let's face it, it's hard to explain ghostly possession. At least to anybody in their right mind.

Which meant the only person who could help Quinn was someone who wasn't.

TWENTY

Like the last time I'd been to Caleb's, I had no trouble finding a parking spot. Getting Quinn up to the tenth floor apartment was another matter, and I won't go into details. Let's just say that the folks from the hotel next door are probably still looking for the luggage cart they'd made the mistake of leaving outside.

When Caleb answered his door and saw me, his face split with a grin. That is, until he looked beyond me to that luggage cart and the unconscious man sprawled on it.

He was using his canes, and he stepped back, threw the door open, and shooed me in, then dragged the luggage cart – and Quinn – inside, and it wasn't until he had the door closed that he bothered to say anything.

Just for the record, those words were, 'What the hell?'

'It's kind of hard to explain,' I told him, my words punctuated with worry. 'But we've got to do something. We've got to help Quinn.'

'And you, too, cher.' He touched a finger to my cheek where Quinn had backhanded me, and I winced and wondered how bad the bruise was. 'I'll get an ice pack.'

'No!' I stepped in front of him. 'Later. For now, we've got to do something for Quinn.'

To his eternal credit, Caleb didn't need more than my word. He grabbed the luggage cart and rolled it toward the private elevator outside the great room. 'There might be something in the library that can help us,' he said. 'But . . .' He studied Quinn's face. 'Are you sure you want to? Is Capone still in him?'

I hated to admit that I didn't know. 'He was,' I said instead. 'I was leaving the cemetery and there was Quinn and he hit me and I blacked out and . . .' It was all too horrible to think about. 'The ashes are gone,' I said, because cutting to the chase was better than thinking about what had happened there in the cemetery. 'And I found Quinn when I was leaving the cemetery. Just like this. He was just like this.'

Caleb thought it all over. 'Now that he's got the ashes, Capone may not need your friend anymore.'

'That's what I'm hoping,' I said. 'Only I tried to wake him up, and I can't, and we've got to do something.'

'We will.' On his way past, Caleb touched a hand to mine. 'Only that luggage cart sure ain't going to fit in the elevator. I'll get my chair. We can lift him into that and then—'

'Oh!' I didn't mean to catch hold of Caleb as he hobbled by. Honest. But I couldn't help myself when Eliot Ness materialized right in front of me.

And I'm not talking a sparkling cloud.

I recognized him from the pictures I'd seen online. Six feet tall, brown hair parted in the middle and combed to each side. He had a dimpled chin and a round face and, instantly, I could see why the newspapers back in the day had called him the Boy Scout Cop or the College Cop. Ness was only in his thirties at the height of his career, and he had an open, honest face.

'What's wrong?' Caleb asked me, because of course, when he looked where I was looking, all he saw was the elevator door.

I swallowed down my amazement. 'What are you doing here?' I asked Ness. 'If Capone destroyed your ashes—'

'Ness is here?' It was Caleb's turn to be surprised. He turned and faced the blank space where Eliot Ness – dapper in a three-piece pinstriped suit – stood. 'You can't be here.'

Ness scratched a hand over his chin. 'It's the darnedest thing. One minute I couldn't materialize and the next minute . . . well . . .' He looked down at his shoes, spit-polished to a shine. 'Here I am!'

I told Caleb what Ness said. 'But if that's the case . . .' Caleb screwed up his face. 'Beggin' your pardon, Mr Ness, but from everything we know, for you to materialize, that means Capone couldn't have destroyed your ashes. It would have to mean he did to them just what you wanted done. Capone sprinkled your ashes over the lake.'

A chill crawled up my back, and I shook my shoulders but no matter what I did, I couldn't get rid of the feeling that there was suddenly a live wire inside of me. It tingled along my spine and heated my blood. I opened my mouth to speak, only when I did, the voice that came out wasn't mine.

'You're damn right I did,' I said.

I wasn't sure who was more surprised, Eliot Ness or Caleb. Not that it mattered. Looking at their dumbfounded expressions, I laughed like I hadn't laughed since the day I ordered the St Valentine's Day hit.

'You mortadells! I played you the whole time and you let it happen. Them ashes? I never wanted to get rid of them. You should have known that, Ness.'

'Then why did you want them at all?' Ness stared me down the way he must have stared down a hundred suspects in his day. Well, he might have scared them, but I wasn't shaking in my shoes.

They were so stupid, I would have laughed again if the Pepper dame would have stopped fighting what was happening to her. She had spunk, this one, more than I expected, and I knew I would have to impose my will.

But then, that was something I was good at.

I shoved aside her puny little soul to make more room for mine and then I lifted my chin and puffed out my chest. 'Don't you get it, Ness? Don't you know how these things work? I can't do no hocus-pocus spell. Not like that guy did who you sent to my grave to keep me in my place. Only that didn't work, did it?' I fingered the scars on my left cheek. 'It ain't so easy to make Al Capone do what you want.'

'But what you wanted—'

It was nice watching Ness sputter! I chuckled. 'What I wanted then and what I want now is to destroy you once and for all,' I told him. 'And you should know I couldn't do that, not while I didn't have no body. And you, Ness, you had to have a body, too. Now you do, and now, we got no choice. It's been a long time coming, but now, now we're ready. It's time for us, Ness, to fight to the death.'

I was still Pepper Martin deep down inside, still inside my own body but felt like I wasn't, like I was watching a movie through my eyes, listening to my voice speak words I never would have said. I wanted to scream, to fight, to resist. I tried, but Capone's spirit was strong and the anger that fueled it was powerful. In horror, I watched the scene unfold and I saw Eliot Ness waver.

I chuckled.

Well, Capone did.

Right before he closed in on Ness. Hey, he didn't care about getting chilled to the bone. Not when the bones that were getting chilled were Pepper Martin's. He stood toe to toe with the G-man.

'It's time,' he growled only the sound came from my lips. 'What are you going to do, Ness?'

Moving like the wind, Eliot Ness zipped over to where Quinn lay unconscious on the luggage cart and oozed into him. Quinn roused, shook his head, and sat up.

But hey, I ain't no mortadell, either. Before he ever had a chance to get to his feet, I leaped on top of him and pounded him with my fists.

He was bigger than the woman whose body I'd taken, stronger. But he was still groggy from when I'd used his body then cast it aside, and I had the upper hand. I landed a right to his jaw and another one to his midsection, and when he flinched and his head shot back, I got in another punch to his chin.

'Pepper, no!' Behind us, that chooch, Caleb, shot forward and called out, but hey, I knew there was no way he could get in our way, not a cripple like him. I spun, shoved, and he went down in a heap at the base of the stairs that led up to the musicians' gallery that overlooked the great room.

By the time I turned around again, Quinn – Ness – was on his feet, his legs braced and his arm cocked.

I threw myself at him, but he was ready for me, and he caught me, midair, and hurled me back against the wall. I crumpled like one of them rag dolls. But not for long. Never for long.

Like it had in my lifetime, hatred boiled inside this body I'd chosen. It fired my will and drove me to my feet.

'Oh, no!' The dame's voice – Pepper's voice – reverberated through her brain. 'I'm not going to allow this, Capone. I'm not going to let you use me to hurt Ness or Quinn.'

'Wanna bet?' I growled back and bumped aside her spirit.

By that time, that Caleb guy was back on his feet and hey, I ain't stupid. He had the sort of glint in his eyes that told me he was tough and he could be trouble. When Ness came at me, I played my cards right. He punched, I ducked. He punched again and connected with my chin, and I darted up a couple of them steps. Oh yeah, my plan worked, all right.

He came up after me.

Years working as muscle on the streets of New York and more years running the Outfit in Chicago and don't think I didn't know what was what. Still landing punches – and taking a few – I went all the way up the stairs and into that musicians' gallery, and so did Ness, and with all those steps between us, there was no way Caleb could get up there to get in the way.

The gallery itself was maybe twenty feet long and ten wide, just room enough for me and Ness to face off against each other and, when he stumbled up there, fists raised and breathing hard, I was ready for him. I slammed a foot into his stomach and watched him go down and once he did, I kicked him in the head.

'No! No!' Pepper's voice screaming inside this head I was using was as irritating as hell, but until I was done with Ness, there was nothing I could do to shut her up. I needed her body. 'Stop! Don't hurt him.'

'You're one stupid dame.' I could afford to step back for a second. Ness was on the floor, writhing in pain, and I could draw in a breath and shake off the hurt from when his fist had connected with my ribs and rub away the ache from the spot where he'd plugged me in the jaw. 'Didn't you see it would come to this? Don't you know this is what I have to do? If I'm going to get rid of Ness once and for all—'

'But he's not the one who took you down. Not really. Not finally. You did that yourself. It was your own greed that put you in prison, not Eliot Ness.'

'But everyone thinks it was him,' I told her, and I wouldn't have had to bother if she would just shut up in the first place. 'People think of him. And then they think of me. And they think he got the better of me. It's time to show them that's not true.'

I lunged at Ness, but he was quick on his feet. Then again, he had the body of a cop to help him, young and agile and in perfect shape, even if he was still a little out of it because of the earlier possession. He dodged the blow I aimed at his face and got in a punch that sent me staggering back against the waist-high wooden wall that overlooked the great room.

By now, Caleb had dragged himself in there, and he watched from his vantage point fifteen feet below us, worry etched on his face. He'd have plenty more to worry about in just a couple minutes. And a body to take care of, too.

I pushed myself forward and met Ness, chest to chest, my hand automatically going for his throat.

He gripped my wrists, fighting me off, and managed to push me away.

We circled each other like hungry lions, both of us breathing hard now, watching for any little show of weakness, smelling blood in the water.

'Talk about mixed metaphors!' Pepper had the nerve to sound perky. 'You're a real loser, Capone,' she snapped. 'And you'll never beat this guy. He's bigger than me. He's stronger than me.'

'And you think he's not pulling his punches? You think he's not afraid to hit just a little too hard and really hurt a woman?' I chuckled when she trembled inside me; she knew I was right. 'There's no way he's going to beat me. Because there's no way he wants to hurt you, my sweet.'

She shuddered, and her spirit got even weaker. It wouldn't be long before I owned her completely and, just to show her how delicious it would be when the moment finally came, I raced at Ness and, when he slammed a fist into me, I never even flinched. I pummeled him and backed him against the far wall. He recovered and got in a punch to my solar plexus that sent me reeling backwards.

'Careful, Pepper!' Caleb called from downstairs. 'Don't let Ness get too close. He could push you over the gallery wall!'

Only he wouldn't. I knew he wouldn't. It was why I'd chosen her body for the fight. Like I'd told the dame to begin with, there was no way this guy would ever take the chance of killing her.

Ness hesitated. It was only a second, but hey, my instincts were as good as they were back in the day. I saw my advantage and I took it, going on the attack.

I landed a right to his jaw. I sent him staggering with a left to his gut. He slammed against the far wall and got tangled up in his own feet, and when he went down, I was ready. I threw myself on top of him and wrapped my hands around his neck.

He was strong. But I had anger on my side. I had all those years of being stuck in the grave.

My fingers closed over his windpipe.

And squeezed.

'You can't do this!' I had to give the dame credit, she tried to sound tough. But her words were nothing more than the buzz of a gnat in my head. 'I won't let you kill him,' she said.

'There's nothing you can do to stop me!' I told her and, hey, she should have known it. I was looking out of her eyes, and she saw what I saw.

Ness's face, red and sweaty.

Ness's eyes, bulging.

Ness's mouth, open, gasping.

The sound that came out of him was a pathetic gurgle.

The ones I heard from her, not so much.

'There is no way in hell you're going to do this, Capone!' Her words were louder this time and, in them, I recognized anger, just like the anger that had been my companion throughout my life. Only this anger . . .

A feeling like electricity zipped through the woman. It tingled through my fingers, surprising me, and for a second, I loosened my hold and sat back.

But I wasn't going to be stopped, and even as Ness pulled in a desperate gasp of air, I tightened my hold again.

That was when I realized that her anger came from a different place. Because she wouldn't have been angry at all. Not if she didn't care for this guy.

'I won't let you do it, Capone,' she told me. 'It's my body. My hands. And my hands won't hurt the man I love.'

Like the explosion of a charge of TNT, that last word – love – erupted inside my head along with Pepper's voice. 'I won't let you do this. I don't care who you are. You're not going to hurt Quinn!'

How the hell she shoved me out of her body, I don't know. I only know that the next second, I was standing outside her, staring into that pretty little face of hers, amazed at her determination and her mettle.

'You think you can shove me around!' I might not have been able to see Al Capone before, but I could see him now. Just as tall as me, a little pudgy, and looking more than a little surprised that I'd managed to kick him out of my body. I put both my hands to his chest and shoved. Hard. Yeah, he was a ghost. Sure, my hand turned to ice at first contact.

I was way too pissed to care and, just to prove it, I gave him another shove.

'You're not going to do it,' I told him, backing him against the half-wall of the gallery. 'And you know why?' I looked into the eyes of evil and, if I was smart, I would have backed down. But what was it I'd say about love and being smart? 'Because love is stronger than hate, Capone. And you . . .' I gave the spirit one last push that sent him over the edge.

'You're the mortadell!' I said. His arms windmilled and he kicked his legs and swooped through the air above Caleb's head.

'Love? Stronger than?'

Poor Al Capone. He never did have a chance to figure it out. It wasn't falling over the wall of the gallery that did him in. He was a ghost, after all, and he should have been able to recover and come right back at me – and into me – in an instant.

It was what was inside me that cast him out and kept him out. It was trying to fathom it that made his spirit explode into a million little pieces

A clear, pure wind blew through the room, a gust of something glittery hit what was left of him and, on the tail of that wind, all those bits and pieces of anger and hatred and evil whooshed through the nearest windowpane and out into the night. And the only thing that remained of him was the high keening of his amazed voice as Al Capone's ghost disappeared over Cleveland. 'No! No! No!'

TWENTY-ONE

The rest of that night is pretty fuzzy. Caleb took both of us back to Quinn's loft, and if he was surprised by the elephants, he kept his opinion to himself. He made us coffee and soup, too, got us settled and left us, and Quinn and I fell into bed together and slept the sleep of the dead.

The next day was Friday and I called in sick because, really, how was I supposed to explain the cuts and the bruises and the black eye? For the first time ever in his brilliant career, Quinn called off, too, and we spent that day and the rest of the weekend tossing out elephants, holding each other, and climbing into bed more than a few times and making love in spite of all our aches and pains.

As for bringing McClure's murderer to justice . . . well, there were plenty of ethical questions involved and we talked about them and came up with the only solution that seemed right. The murder weapon Al Capone had Quinn steal to hamper the investigation and buy time so he could find the ashes? We wiped it clean of fingerprints – Wally's and Quinn's – and deep-sixed it in the lake. Yeah, yeah, I know, not exactly the way a cop should handle evidence, but let's face it, there was no way either one of us wanted to see Wally take the rap for a crime committed by Al Capone. It wasn't Wally's fault he'd killed McClure – he'd been possessed at the time – and it sure wasn't Quinn's fault that he snatched up that pen holder and stashed it where no one could find it.

And that old beer bottle that started all the trouble in the first place?

Funny, but as soon as Al Capone swooped inside me (which wasn't all that funny, and I'm not going to think about it because when I do I get queasy), I understood that piece of the puzzle perfectly.

See, thanks to that spell Ness had cast at Capone's grave, the gangster's spirit couldn't just come and go like so many ghosts do. That's where Dean McClure came in. Weak mind, weak will, and the only way Capone could ever escape was with the help of a living person. McClure was the perfect patsy, and it had cost him his life.

Capone convinced McClure to cork up his spirit in the bottle and bring it to Cleveland because, remember, I'm the talk of the Other Side, and Capone knew if anyone was going to be in touch with Eliot Ness, it would be me. Capone was the one who made that bottle jump in Quinn's hand so it would fall and break and he could be free, and he was the one (the bastard!) who possessed Quinn and had him take the pieces of the bottle from the Garden View trash. He thought the less I knew about the bottle, the longer it would take me to figure things out.

That ought to teach him!

Or at least it would have if I hadn't consigned him to the deepest reaches of nowhere.

Nothing can keep a good PI to the dead down. Not when the hearts and souls of the people she loves (well, except for Wally, but hey, even a curmudgeon doesn't deserve what happened to Wally) are at stake.

I guess that means in the great scheme of things, Justice was served in its own, weird way. As I was learning each day I dealt with my Gift, the world isn't as black-and-white as it is gray. At least Wally, crabby but innocent, didn't go to jail and, just for the record, neither did Cindy McClure. The guy she was messing around with provided her an alibi that Quinn was only too happy to accept.

Not a perfect solution, but then, what is? In spite of it all, we both came to realize what really mattered – Quinn was grateful I'd saved his life. I was grateful he was part of mine.

And glad when the last elephant was in a big, black trash bag and down in the dumpster.

By Monday morning, I was able to cover up most of the damage with makeup, but I wasn't taking any chances. I told Ella I had a mild case of pink eye, and I wore sunglasses in the office and kept the lights turned off, and when Ella was busy in some bigshot board meeting and I knew she wouldn't corner me and ask where I was going, I slipped outside. It was a beautiful afternoon and, even though I hadn't planned it, I wasn't surprised when I realized I was headed to the Ness monument. I parked my car and found the G-man near his granite marker.

'I'm heading out,' he said, glancing around to drink in the scenery. The cherry trees were in flower and, all around us, daffodils bloomed and dipped their heads in a gentle breeze. 'It's time.'

'Who would have guessed that Al Capone was going to be the one who made it all possible!' Yeah, it was warm and the sun was shining and the clouds were so white and puffy, they reminded me of a kid's drawing. I still shivered. I knew it would take me a long time before I could think about Ness and Capone without reliving the horror of their final confrontation.

'I appreciate your help, kid,' Ness said.

'Hey, no problem.' Of course, that wasn't true, but it sounded good and softened the hard edges of our goodbyes. Sure, ghosts are a pain in the tushy, but when they leave . . . well, when they leave, I always feel all warm and fuzzy.

'He's a good man.' Ness looked past me and down the road and I recognized the car coming our way as Quinn's. 'I could have used him back in the day. It's important to hang on to a good cop.'

The words hit a spot that still ached from a punch thrown by Ness, and I turned away for a second and watched Quinn slow down and park the car.

'So—' I turned to Eliot Ness.

But he was gone.

'Thought I'd find you out here.' Quinn brushed a gentle kiss against my cheek right below a spot that was cut and scraped from when his fist had connected.

'Hiding out from Ella,' I admitted. 'And saying goodbye to Ness.'

Quinn glanced around. 'He's gone?'

'For good, I think. He's finally getting the rest he deserves.'

'And I'm finally getting . . .' How many times have I said how cool and collected Quinn is? I guess that's why seeing a splash of color in his cheeks made a little kerthump start up inside my aching ribs.

He stuck a hand into his pocket and pulled out a small blue box. 'I wanted to do this over the weekend,' he said. 'But we both just needed a little quiet time, and I didn't want you to feel as if you had to do anything you don't want to do.'

I thought back to how it felt to have Al Capone's spirit snaking through my insides.

I looked at the little box Quinn bobbled in one hand.

'You know me better than that,' I told him. 'I don't do things I don't want to do.'

'That's for sure.' His smile was tender. 'And I've been putting off something I've been wanting to do for too long. Pepper . . .' I actually thought he was going to get down on one knee, but one look at the ground that had been churned up when Al Capone had departed his body and left him crumpled against the Ness marker and Quinn changed his mind. Instead, he took my hand. 'Pepper Martin, will you marry me?'

Ignoring the bruises on his hands and my scraped knuckles, I wound my fingers through his and held on tight. But then, I pretty much had no choice when my world was about to tip and the universe was about to change forever.

I sucked in a breath and looked into Quinn's eyes. 'No.'

He thought I was kidding. Which would explain the dumbfounded half-smile. 'That's not what you're supposed to say.'

'I know what I'm supposed to say.' If I kept looking into those amazing green eyes of his, I couldn't do what I knew I had to do, so I dropped his hand and turned away. From this angle, I could see the lake where I'd first met Eliot Ness, and the marker where I'd found Quinn on that foggy night that I thought I'd lost him forever.

I took a deep breath and turned back around. 'I wasn't bullshitting Al Capone. I love you, Quinn. More than anybody. Ever. That's why I can't marry you.'

He hadn't looked that surprised even back at the Van Sweringen apartment when I gave him a right cross to the jaw. 'This is some kind of crazy joke, right?'

'It's not. It's . . .' I refused to cry. 'What happened the other night,' I said instead, 'that was because of me. Because of my

Gift. I can't . . . I won't let it happen again. I can't let the people I love be put in danger because of me.'

'Danger?' His face twisted like he'd been sucker punched. 'You're forgetting what I do for a living.'

'That's different,' I told him. 'It's what you're trained to do. What you're paid to do. And you're really, really good at it. But there's no training that's ever going to prepare either one of us for the kind of trouble I have to deal with. When Capone took over your body, I was scared to death. But not nearly as scared as I was when I almost killed you. I can't let that happen. I won't.' I lifted my chin because I either had to act like my heart wasn't breaking into a million pieces or I was going to collapse right then and there. 'I'm glad we had the weekend together,' I told him. 'We needed the healing. And you . . .' I laughed and sniffled at the same time. 'You needed help tossing all those elephants.' I kissed his cheek. Quick. So I couldn't change my mind.

'Goodbye, Quinn.'

The next few weeks went by in a fog. Mom came with me when I returned all the pre-engagement pre-shower shower gifts, and though I told her that Quinn and I were through, I never did reveal that he'd actually bought a ring and that I'd never even taken a look at it.

There is only so much a woman itching to be the mother of the bride can take.

I slogged through my duties at Garden View, and the good news is that except for Chet and Jean and Albert, the dead-but-not-gone left me alone. By the time June rolled around and the weather heated up, I was to the point of hoping my Gift was just as dead and gone as my clients had always been and I could settle down to a nice, normal life.

Maybe my mother was right (and don't tell her I said that or I'll never hear the end of it!). Maybe Mom and Dad and I should go into the private eye business together. Maybe then I'd be so busy tailing unfaithful spouses and checking out peoples' backgrounds, I wouldn't have time to get involved with things that go bump in the night.

White collar crime.

Vandalism.

Lost pets.

It all sounded wonderfully boring, and boring was exactly what I was thinking about when I dragged into my apartment after another long day at the cemetery, tossed my purse down, and flopped onto the couch.

That's when my TV flickered on.

Strange, because I hadn't touched the remote.

And stranger still when the first thing I saw on the screen was Caleb.

I sat up like a shot. The show was *Jeopardy* and he was a contestant! Not only that, but the lighted board in front of him showed that he had a grand total of nearly eighty thousand dollars of winnings, far more than either of the other two contestants.

It was late, and the show was almost over and the contestants were just giving their final answers. The category: the periodic table, and the clue was 'The chemical element that has the shortest name.'

Some time while I was staring at the screen, in wonder, the other contestants answered. Since Caleb was winning (by a lot), he had the final turn.

The camera zoomed in on him and on the question he'd written in bold, heavy letters:

'Did I tell you my parents were vampires?'

I was as stunned as the show's host. Which is why I didn't even think not to answer my phone when it rang. I didn't need to look at the caller ID, either.

'You said you were always right,' I told Caleb.

'Yeah, well . . .' His laughter was soft and low. 'Figured you wouldn't pay it no mind if I answered like I was supposed to answer. You haven't been picking up your phone or answering any of the messages I left you. How else was I supposed to get your attention?'

'By telling me your parents are vampires on national television? Weren't you afraid of looking stupid and losing all that money?'

'Anything for you!' His laughter settled. 'So now that you're finally listening—'

I really wasn't. Because I blurted out, 'And when did you go on *Jeopardy*, anyway? And how can you be calling me when . . .' I watched him on the TV screen and wondered why he was smiling.

'It don' madda, cher! The show is taped. But what really matters is that my momma and daddy, they're in boo-coo trouble and they need our help.'

'Your parents, the vampires.'

Of course I couldn't see Caleb. So why did I picture him giving me a wink? 'I'll pick you up at eight. Pack light. It's hot in N'Orleans this time of year.'

'I'm not going to New Orleans.'

'No worries, sugar, I'll take care of all the expenses. I won a bundle, and I might as well spend some of it.'

'But your answer was wrong!'

'You don't think I bet the whole wad and lost it all, do you? I wanted to get your attention, cher, but I didn't want to get it that bad.'

'But—' I wasn't sure why I even tried to protest, he'd already ended the call.

And me?

I thought about the boredom of unfaithful spouses and lost pets, and a life free of woo-woo.

And I went to pack my bags.

ACKNOWLEDGEMENTS

We writers live inside our heads. It's where we create characters, give them their voices and concoct their adventures. But there are outside influences too, for every book and with this book, like with all the others, there are people I need to thank.

My brainstorming group – Shelley Costa, Serena Miller and Emilie Richards – is always there for me, answering questions, coming up with ideas and helping me find my way out of the corners where every writer finds herself trapped once in a while. I appreciate their enthusiasm and their support.

My family, especially my husband David, who indulge me when I want to explore old cemeteries and tag along on ghost hunts. He may not buy into it, but he knows it's all valuable research.

My agent, Gail Fortune, who helped find Pepper a new home.

For this book, I want to offer a very special thank you to Drew Rolik, Forest City Enterprises and Tower City archivist, for giving me a tour of the incredible Greenbrier Suite, once the home of the Van Sweringen brothers. Oh, and for a peek at the Tower City ghost, too!